Gasping, Ro

Entering the ante

He looked at the   glance travelled to her face. What he saw there threw a shaft into his chest. Revulsion! He had known she must feel it. She had tried to gainsay it yesterday. Tried to make him think that she did not regard it. But here was proof, if he had needed it.

Rosina could not fail to notice his flawed features. But anything she might have felt at the sight of it was overborne by an absurd sensation of guilt, as if she had been caught out in wrongdoing. Without thinking, she put her hands behind her back, as if she would hide the key. His bitter look of cynicism became more pronounced.

'Don't trouble yourself to make a secret of your feelings. You are welcome to lock the door and pocket the key, if it will make you sleep safer at night. I am unlikely to break down the door, no matter how strong my desire!'

Elizabeth Bailey grew up in Malawi, returning to England to plunge into the theatre. After many happy years 'tatting around the reps', she finally turned from 'dabbling' to serious writing. She finds it more satisfying for she is in control of everything: scripts, design, direction, and the portrayal of every character! Elizabeth lives in Surrey.

Recent titles by the same author:

AN ARDENT FRIENDSHIP
MISFIT MAID

THE VEILED BRIDE

Elizabeth Bailey

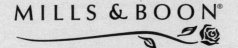

First published in Great Britain 2000
Harlequin Mills & Boon Limited,
Eton House, 18-24 Paradise Road, Richmond, Surrey TW9 1SR

© Elizabeth Bailey 2000

ISBN 0 263 82338 5

Set in Times Roman 10½ on 11½ pt.
04-0201-81823

Printed and bound in Spain
by Litografia Rosés S.A., Barcelona

Chapter One

An air of must and gloom shrouded the dimly lit interior of the narrow church. High walls entombed the line of wooden pews, and the sound of Rosina's footsteps on the cold stone flags seemed to echo round the vaulted arches above. At the sight of the dark figure awaiting her before the altar, the flutter in her stomach intensified.

He was half in shadow, a shaft from the simple rose window casting light in a diagonal across his back, so that only one stiff shoulder and a partial outline of his head were visible. There was a glimpse of waving brown hair tied back, a coat of sombre hue, and that was all.

Rosina felt sick. Her throat dried. Without intent, her fingers closed tightly on the arm of the man who walked beside her. He looked down, and she caught a kindly look of reassurance on the lawyer's face as he laid his hand briefly over hers, and pressed her gloved fingers. It was meant, Rosina thought, for comfort, but it had the effect of bringing a lump to her throat to add to her fervent apprehension.

Biting her lip, Rosina fastened her eyes once more upon the faded silhouette of the unknown gentleman into whose keeping she was about to pledge her life. He had not turned, though he must have heard her approach. It was all of a piece. Had he not rejected any desire to meet her before the wedding? She must suppose that he would not look at his bride one moment before he was obliged.

The aisle appeared endless, giving rise to a flurry of panic. She was making the most dreadful mistake! What was she about, to marry a man of whom she knew little more than his title? Probe how she might, there had been nothing of any significance given away. The lawyer who led her so stolidly to her fate had been uncommonly discreet. Anton, Lord Raith, remained an enigma.

Yet here she was, throwing herself headlong into intimacy with this stranger. Had any other course offered to afford her equivalent protection, she would have taken it. Indeed, as she neared the end of the aisle, she began to wish she had done so. If only she had not been tempted away from that other—so much less appealing!—solution to her hideous dilemma. It was too late. She was almost at the altar, where the pastor stood ready to bind her in wedlock to an obscurity.

Rosina was aware that she was shaking as she took her place at the gentleman's side. The most dreadful palpitations warred with an upsurge of nausea, threatening to choke her. It was all she could do to remain standing upon her two legs as the support of the lawyer's arm was removed. She drew raggedly on her breath, trying both to still the tumult of her bosom and to conceal its effects from the silent creature at her side.

Yet she could not resist a flying glance cast up at him. She was rewarded only with his stern profile. As well might she be marrying a statue, for all his interest. Curiously, this lack of attention had a slight calming effect, and a little of her panic subsided. She dared a second look.

At close quarters, the profile was personable enough.

As much at least as she had believed when she'd had the only glimpse of Lord Raith that he had permitted—through the glass of a coffee-room window. Mr Ottery, with whom all her dealings had been done, had arranged it at her insistence, for in this she had been adamant. Willing though she was to compound for a man she had never met, she would not marry one she had never seen. Not that she had got much good by it. Her prospective bridegroom had been as still then as now, she remembered, where he sat at the large table within the inn, only one side of his face turned in her direction—and that partly concealed by the sweep of loosely tied hair that looped upon his cheek, and the broad-brimmed hat that cut off any sight of his eyes.

Rosina could not see much more of him now, for he was taller than she had expected and her head reached only to just above his shoulder. It was enough to note the tight set of a firm jawline and the dip below a high cheekbone.

All at once her attention was recalled to the priest, as he began the marriage rites. 'Dearly beloved, we are gathered here today in the sight…'

She stared blindly at the pastor. Dear Lord, it was happening! The heart rattled in Rosina's chest. She wanted to cry out to him to stop. She wanted to flee from the church. She could not do this! Was she mad to have consented? Dear Lord, let him not continue. She had no notion what the clergyman was saying, although snatches of the ceremony reached her ears.

Wild thoughts of denial chased one another through her head. She could wait for the impediment bit. Only there was no impediment beyond her own dread: she was of age, and free to marry. Why should she not refuse him? She had only to answer, when the vital question was asked if she would take him, that she would not. No, that was unthinkable. She must speak immediately—interrupt. But her tongue cleaved to the roof of her mouth, and she had no words.

Beside her, Lord Raith listened to the drone of the cleric's voice with even less attention than his betrothed. But, contrary to appearances, he was far from disinterested in his bride, though he did not look at her. When he had heard Ottery's murmuring voice, and the priest had said that he rather thought the bride was arriving, Raith had trained his gaze upon the statuary behind the altar, and fixed it there.

The light footfall that accompanied his lawyer's heavier tread had thrown him into his habitual tight control. Of all things, he must withhold himself until the last. Whatever the outcome, he could not endure the mortification of a last-minute withdrawal. More than that, he would not afford her any opportunity for regret. At least, not until the knot was tied. After—let it be as it might. He would know how to act. But he would not go through this ignominious process a second time. He would have this girl to wife, or none!

He pictured her as he heard her approach, the image strong in his mind. Fine-boned and delicate, with coal-black eyes in a face ashen with fear—or want? He had been unable to decide. A riffle of unease at his deception disturbed him. The advantage was all on his side. But then, Rosina Charlton need not have agreed to the bargain. She had chosen to sell herself. There had been no coercion. Her need, he must suppose, was as much a goad as his own.

Not that her story had been any more particular than that of others. It was common enough. An orphan without means, and no better future to which to look forward, he imagined, than the dreary prospect of tutoring other people's children for a pittance, or a drudgery of companionship hardly less appealing. Marriage, even to a man with whom she was utterly unacquainted, must be preferable.

Only Raith had seen something in her eyes that was out of the ordinary. Something indefinable, but a sense of mystery had struck him. It might have been attributed to that air of fragility, but he had thought there had been ·more to her story than she was willing to tell. On the second meeting, Ottery had probed on his instruction, but had got nothing by it. His fascination had intensified.

Yet Raith could not gainsay a trifle of self-disgust at his subterfuge, necessary though it had been. No matter how cogent her reason, he could not but feel that there was more than a touch of the sacrificial lamb in the waif that arrived at his side.

It was with difficulty that he refrained from risking a glance. He felt her eyes upon him, and was barely conscious of stiffening. His thoughts were swallowed up by a wholly unlooked-for surge of sensation in his chest. Like the rush of power at the onset of battle! It was a moment or two before he was able to command himself again. By the time he did so, the cleric was fully embarked upon his litany.

'Wilt thou, Anton, take this woman...'

For a moment of hideous suspense, Raith could not think what he was being asked. There was a breathless pause before the answer came to him.

'I will.'

He heard a tiny sigh beside him, and bit down hard against the flooding intensity of feeling. As the pastor asked the same question of the bride, he held his breath, half-afraid of her answer.

It came, a bare whisper on the air. 'I will.'

Tightly controlled, the breath slid out of Raith as the cleric's voice droned on. The ceremony seemed to drag.

'Who giveth this woman to be married to this man?'

From the corner of his eye, Raith saw his lawyer step forward and take the bride's left hand. He watched the slender fingers disappear into Ottery's large grasp, and reached out at the command of the priest. A weird sense of unreality took him as the girl's gloved hand was put into his.

The fingers shook perceptibly, and Raith was swept with a wave of compassion. He placed his thumb upon the fingers, exerting a slight pressure. They jerked once, as if she would free herself, and then stilled. Even through the silk, he could feel their chill.

'Repeat after me…'

Rosina winced a little as the fingers tightened. She watched the bare browned hand imprisoning her own, listening with only half an ear to the low-pitched murmuring beside her, conscious of the warmth emanating from the firm grip. Without warning, the shadowy figure had become real, and only one phrase penetrated her consciousness: *for better or for worse.*

It echoed in her head, tauntingly, as the parson turned to her. She was about to take that final, fatal step.

'I, Rosina, take thee, Anton…'

As she repeated aloud the words she was given, she had only one conscious thought. There was no going back.

Raith could not resist the impulse to turn slightly, that he might keep her under surreptitious observation. He heard only vaguely the words of her promises, listening rather to the hushed tone of her delivery, almost in question, as though she was not aware of the meaning of what she said.

She was as intriguing as he remembered. That elfin face, its pallor heightened by the mere wisps of black curl escaping from the confinement of a close cap. He had thought, that first day when he had watched her, himself unobserved, from his post behind Ottery's judas painting, that she looked younger than her given years. Of all the candidates, she had been the only one who had caught his interest. Something in her look had touched him. She had it now as she repeated the phrases that were giving her into his keeping. She seemed lost. There was a wistfulness, a vulnerability, which had struck with him an instant chord of sympathy. He could feel her plight, with the memory of his own.

'Have you the ring?'

Raith turned quickly back to the priest, looking to the man at his side. The plain gold band Ottery had purchased winked in the light. Raith watched the cleric take it, beset by an abrupt thrill of possession. She was his, come what may.

Rosina felt her fingers released, and emerged from the hushed daze that had enfolded her as she spoke the fatal words. She took in that the pastor was addressing her. The ring? Yes, she must take off her glove! She tugged at it, frantic as the silken folds resisted. Her fingers were all thumbs, feeble and unresponsive. A tiny sound of frustration left her lips.

Then she felt Lord Raith's hand once again close over her own. Removing her trembling and hopeless fingers, he turned the hand palm up with gentleness and undid the buttons she had forgotten at her wrist. The glove slid off, and was gone. Covered in confusion, Rosina kept her gaze lowered.

'With this ring…'

Only now did she see that her bridegroom was supported by a person on his other side, for her whole attention on coming up the aisle had been taken up by this man, who was sliding his ring carefully down her finger as he spoke the words of its significance. Riveted, Rosina gazed at the encircling gold as if in a waking dream, a fog wreathing her brain. All thought suspended, she heard herself pronounced a wife.

'Those whom God hath joined together, let no man put asunder.'

It was done. Trance-like, she turned to the man to whom she was vowed, and found his eyes upon her.

They were grey, and in their depths was a mix of apprehension and defiance. But Rosina did not see it. Her heart felt as if it had stopped. Time did not exist. The dream had turned to nightmare.

The only reality was the shock of the countenance that was at last turned full-face towards her. A countenance destroyed, hideously marred, by a disfiguring scar that ran from eyebrow to chin, cutting across Lord Raith's right cheek. Ridged and ugly, its harsh ragged line stood out white against the tanned roughness of his skin.

Rosina was still in a state of dumb stupor as she was led into the vestry to append her signature under that of her spouse. It lasted while she waited, standing to one side in the little room, through a low-voiced conversation between His Lordship and the lawyer. The cleric offered her a chair, which she took with a murmured word of thanks, sinking down upon its wooden seat, and staring directly before her. When Raith came to her at length, she did not even look up at him.

'Are you ready to go?'

Rosina got up, allowing him to take her arm without protest or acknowledgement and walking where he urged, her gaze blank and unchanging.

Raith felt acutely her withdrawal. He had been afraid of this. She could not bear to look at him! No doubt she was distressed by his trickery. She knew now why he had made an issue of their not meeting before this time. He was sure it must rankle with her for some time to come. It was a question whether she would ever forgive it.

Sighing a touch, he turned his attention to his groom as they reached the portals of the church. Parton had acted as his groomsman, for want of any other trustworthy person he might have introduced as a second witness. Ottery having been otherwise engaged, there was no one else. Raith remembered that, having signed the register, Parton had slipped away.

'Catterline has the chaise ready at The Dog over yonder, me lord. Would you wish to leave directly, or will Her Ladyship require refreshment before we set out?'

Rosina started out of her deep abstraction. *Her Ladyship?* It was a moment or two before she realised that the man was referring to herself.

'Ottery has arranged for coffee and cakes, I believe,' Raith answered.

'We'd best not leave it too late, me lord,' advised the groom, with a worried glance at the greyness outside. 'It don't look to me as if the rain'll hold off. Roads are bad enough as it is, and the nights drawing in an' all.'

It was indeed drab, even for late October, Raith reflected. They had only ten miles to reach Marton where they were to spend one night, but there was only a pair harnessed to the chaise—he could afford no more with his present means, though that was a situation shortly to be remedied—and it was already close on two. Parton was right. They must not dally.

He turned to Rosina and offered his arm again. 'Will you walk, ma'am?'

He was dismayed to find that, although she took his arm, she kept her gaze firmly turned away from any possibility of encountering his unsightly features. It was a relief when Ottery caught them up as they passed through the high gateway.

Raith glanced back at the austere outlines of the church. It was an ancient edifice dedicated to St Nicholas. Not large, with pretensions to the Gothic in its tall spired tower and arching interior. From Raith's point of view, its chief attraction lay in its situation, towards the outskirts of Coventry in a little-frequented area that had almost the atmosphere of a village. On a Tuesday, with the world busy about its concerns, the place was all but deserted.

'You chose well, Ottery,' he said, and turned to cross the road towards the small public inn so conveniently placed.

'I thank you, my lord,' said the lawyer, and moved to keep pace beside Rosina. 'I trust Her Ladyship will approve the light collation I have bespoken.'

Becoming aware that she was addressed, Rosina looked quickly up. The lawyer was smiling kindly at her, and a little of the deep abstraction in which she had been enwrapped began to leave her. Once more she realised how she had been styled, and the strangeness of it sent a shiver through her.

'You must be cold,' Ottery observed, and glanced over her head at his employer. 'Her Ladyship had a cloak. We left it in the church, I must suppose. I'll fetch it.'

Before Rosina could say anything, he had turned back. Her cloak? She remembered now. She had been wearing it when she arrived with the lawyer. Mr Ottery had taken it from her and draped it over a pew. Such was her state of mind that she had forgotten all about it.

'Lady Raith?'

She jumped. He was calling her by his own name! She had not turned before she saw that he was holding something before her. Her glove! He had taken it off for her when she could not. The memory of his gentle action returned.

She took the glove, glancing fleetingly up at him. He

was on her right and she could not see the scar. 'Thank you.'

She had barely drawn it on when Lord Raith ushered her into the inn. In a moment, the landlady was curtsying before her and offering the services of the house. Rosina allowed herself to be led away, hearing behind her the voice of the man to whom she had entrusted control of her life bidding someone bring to a private chamber the refreshments that had been bespoken.

It was with a rapidly growing feeling of heaviness that Raith awaited her in a cosy parlour. The nonsense about her forgotten cloak had depressed him, serving to remind him not only of her missing glove, but of the acute shock into which she had been thrown by his appearance, or else she would have recalled its existence for herself. Had he made a mistake not to allow her to see him before? Should he perhaps have met her several times so that she had grown accustomed? Only he could not have endured it! To be obliged to spend time fidgeting in the company of a girl whom he hoped might find it in her to stomach his disfigurement. Small hope of that—as was all too obvious. But it was a pointless exercise to engage in such thoughts. It was no use to cavil. He had taken what measures he had taken, and must live with the consequence.

He stiffened as the door opened. But it was only Ottery. He let his breath go. He need not dissemble for the moment. The man was more than his lawyer, he was a long-time friend.

'It all went off reasonably well, I thought, my lord,' said Ottery, laying the dark cloak across the back of a straight chair set in a corner of the room.

Raith laughed harshly. 'Is that what you thought? I wish I might say the same, by thunder! Did you see the way she looked at me?'

The image of her shocked countenance came back to him, the coal-black eyes enormous in her white face.

'My dear sir, a touch of astonishment was to be expected,' the lawyer pointed out gently.

'A touch!'

'I believe the young lady was somewhat overwhelmed by the whole business, my lord. I cannot think it was merely a reaction to—'

'Don't try to spare me, Ottery,' Raith said wearily. 'I have seen quite enough of a like reaction in females to be sure of the cause.'

He moved to the table where the landlord had set the light repast which had been ordered. He picked up the coffee pot in slightly unsteady fingers, and felt Ottery's hand upon his shoulder.

'Don't refine too much upon it, my lord. Even if you are not over-sensitive, as I believe, I am sure you will find that custom will ease the difficulty.'

It appeared, when Rosina presently entered the room, that there might be truth in this. Raith braced himself as she glanced at him, but it seemed to him that her gaze did not flinch. Rather it travelled from his face to the table. He was glad, however, when Ottery took it upon himself to supply her with a cup of coffee, which was all she would take.

'Will you not eat something as well, ma'am?' said the lawyer persuasively. 'It will be several hours before you are able to do so again.'

'Thank you, but I am not hungry.'

In fact, Rosina was feeling a trifle sick. When the land-lady had left her in a bedchamber, she had sat down abruptly on the bed, overcome by faintness. A little water splashed on her face had eased the sensation after a short rest, and she had not troubled herself to do much more than cleanse her hands after making use of the house facilities.

She had straightened the set of the dove-grey chemise gown, which was the only one she possessed with any suitability to the occasion. It was of damask, close-fitting at the bodice with a low round neck sloping to a V-shape in front, where the edged lacing of her underdress afforded modesty. The skirt was full and long, with a plain hem, the sleeves tight to the wrist. She wore no sash, and had added one of her habitual enclosing caps, of silk and lace.

The rest of her meagre wardrobe had arrived in a small trunk, along with herself and Mr Ottery, in the hired carriage in which he had fetched her from The Crown at Brinklow, for she had not wished to advertise her departure from Gatty's cottage in the little village of Withibrooke. The trunk was now, she must suppose, bestowed in Lord Raith's chaise.

Lord Raith! And she was now his lady, for better or for worse. She was recovering from her stupefaction, and could even sympathise with His Lordship's reluctance to show himself prior to the wedding. If this was his secret, so also had she hers—and one susceptible of a more acute reaction than her own had been to his.

Once refreshments had been consumed, Raith was inclined to hurry, bearing his groom's pessimistic forecast in mind. In short order, he was handing his bride into his chaise, and turning to speak brief words of farewell to his lawyer.

'I will come to Raith Manor as soon as the legalities have been formalised, my lord. Your signature will undoubtedly be required on several papers, but I do not anticipate any difficulty with the procedure.'

Rosina had noticed the coat of arms on the door of the chaise, and remembered how fortunate she had thought

herself to have secured a haven with a peer of the realm.
It must assure her safety, so Gatty had said. But would
her old nurse, to whom she owed so much, have let her
go so readily into this had she known of Lord Raith's
unfortunate affliction?

He had told her during their brief sojourn at the inn
that, his estates being about twenty miles distant, they
would make the journey over two days. His own horses,
it appeared, were stabled at Marton, where he had made
a change this morning when he was driven up for the
wedding. He did not wish to put them through a second
such journey on the same day.

'Besides, it will be growing dark by the time we arrive
there, and it will not be comfortable for you to travel by
night. I have secured accommodation at the Bell Inn. It is
not the posting-house,' he had added quickly, 'so we need
not risk running the gauntlet of curious eyes.'

Rosina had immediately had a vision of a bedchamber
such as the one she had left upstairs, with a bed easily
able to accommodate two persons. She had felt herself
grow hot, and had quickly looked away, forgetting in her
agitation to wonder at his not wishing to meet acquaintances.

She thought of it again now, for she had leisure enough
to think. Having stepped up into the coach—electing to
sit upon her right hand for a reason which was not hard
to seek—the companion of her future life had loosened
his bulky drab greatcoat, enquired civilly of his wife
whether she was comfortable, and thereafter turned his
gaze upon the restricted view from his window.

He was sticking closely to the letter of the agreement,
Rosina reflected, for no further word had been spoken
inside the carriage. She was glad that he did not expect
her to engage in polite conversation. She would have been
hard put to it to think of anything untoward to say. Their

brief acquaintance had already crammed her mind with questions which she would shrink from asking—not least concerning the fearful gash, the unexpectedness of which had thrown her into shock.

To her shame, she felt herself burning with curiosity. She had forced herself to look at him casually, afraid of betraying herself, but she had wanted so badly to stare! How had he come by it? It was so vicious a blemish. She could not blame him for concealing it. Nor for not wishing, as he put it, to endure the gaze of the curious. Or was it because he was bent upon keeping the manner of their marriage secret?

Rosina supposed that a man might not wish the world to know that he had felt himself obliged to advertise for a wife. She had been considerably taken aback upon first seeing the advertisement. Before, that was, she'd had any thought of applying for the position herself.

It had become a ritual for the apothecary's boy at Hopsford to trudge the half-mile from his employer's shop to the cottage at Withibrooke where Gatty had taken her in, to bring the *Gazette* for her. Toly Aughton had befriended poor Gertrude Hoswick some years ago, Gatty had told her.

'It was when I could still see a little, my dove,' had said her old nurse. 'I'd sent to the shop to get something for my rheumatics, I think it was, and Toly brought it over. Well, when he saw what a sad and sorry state I'd got myself into, not being able to manage quite with the fire and what not, he took pity on me, bless the boy.'

Rosina had been poring over the newspaper, looking for a post that might suit a female with few accomplishments and no references, while her old nurse slowly felt her way about the kitchen making a meal of sorts, when her eye had been caught by the oddity of the advertisement.

'Dear Lord, Gatty, here is a gentleman advertising for a wife!'

At first she had been inclined to be dismissive when her nurse, once the extraordinary announcement had been read out to her, had suggested that perhaps Rosina should write in reply.

'Gatty, are you mad? I have not escaped one tyranny to put myself into another! Why, who knows what sort of a man this person is?'

'You won't find out, my dove, if you don't write,' had urged her nurse prosaically. 'It may be as he's perfectly amiable and respectable.'

'A man who is obliged to advertise, Gatty? He cannot be respectable!'

'Could be all kinds of reasons. No harm finding out. It ain't needful to do more. He won't know where you are— no more than that other—if you only give the Receiving Office at Brinklow for your direction. If you don't wish to take it no further after, that'll be the end of it.'

'But, Gatty—'

'I know it ain't what your poor mother would have wished for you, my dove, but things ain't turned out no-wise the way she hoped. And it might be the saving of you.'

Rosina had been sceptical. But the slim chance that Gatty could be right persuaded her to do as she suggested. She wondered now whether they had made a horrible mistake that day. She glanced across at her lord, and discovered that he had, to all appearances, fallen asleep. How could she know if she had been wrong? If she had, it was in that first moment of putting pen to paper. Because once she had set events in train, she had found it hard indeed to halt them, for the opportunity had rapidly become too advantageous to pass up.

To her surprise, she had received, in response to her letter, a request to come for an appointment, her credentials—such as they were—apparently meeting the requirements. She could not, she thought, have withdrawn at that stage, for curiosity had got the better of her. Within a matter of days, she had found herself travelling the relatively short journey on the stage—for which, to her surprise and gratitude, a ticket had been sent—to Banbury, where a clerk had met her, and conducted her to the offices of Mr Ottery, situated in the business quarter of the town.

The exterior of the building had been pleasant enough. But after climbing two sets of narrow stairs within, she had entered an outer office of chilling formality. Two further clerks sat writing at desks, which were piled with beribboned parchments and folded documents. Open bookcases of dark wood, fairly stuffed with voluminous and hefty volumes, groaned against every wall, rendering the atmosphere so dull and gloomy that Rosina felt immediately intimidated.

She was shown directly through into a slightly less austere apartment, where two large windows at least let in light, and a couple of paintings adorned the walls between similarly overburdened bookcases. One was of the hunt, the other a particularly dark portrait with a pair of eerie eyes.

Mr Ottery, with whom she had been corresponding, proved to be a pleasantly avuncular man of middle years, besuited in plain black, with a grey tie-wig atop a friendly face. He had a kindly smile, and a manner that put Rosina as much at ease as the awkwardness of the situation would allow. He had done what he might to allay Rosina's quivering anxiety.

'There is no cause for alarm, ma'am,' he said calmly. 'My client—the gentleman in the case—is merely desirous of gaining access to his fortune.'

Was that all? She had ventured a question. 'Must he marry to do so?'

'The inheritance has been so arranged, ma'am, yes.'

'But, why?' It slipped out, but she retracted the question at once. 'I beg your pardon. It is none of my affair—only, it seems so odd.'

'Such clauses are not uncommon, ma'am,' Mr Ottery offered reassuringly. He gave a slight smile, his voice dry. 'Marriage is thought to have a sobering effect.'

Rosina was betrayed into a laugh. 'I hope you would not wish me to understand that the gentleman in question is wild?'

'Quite otherwise.'

This was so cryptic that Rosina felt herself tense up again. What sort of man was he, then, that he must needs advertise for a wife? She eyed the lawyer. He was not very forthcoming. He waited rather to see what she might have to say. She bit her lip, and took a determined breath. If he would not tell her, then she must ask.

'Forgive me, sir, but I do not quite understand. If his only motive is to gain his inheritance, why should the gentlemen use this means of finding a wife? There must be eligible females enough to suit his purpose.'

'There are reasons,' the lawyer answered, 'why my client would not wish to make his choice among the females of his acquaintance.'

So she had supposed! But what were they? Were all her questions to be treated to evasion? A hollow opened up inside her, as the enormity of the whole proceeding came home to her. Had she taken leave of her senses, to be considering this course of action? She should not have listened to Gatty. For all she knew, the man in question was a monster!

'What is wrong with him?' she blurted out suddenly.

The lawyer looked blank. 'I beg your pardon?'

Rosina glanced away, feeling suddenly acutely uncomfortable. Exposed—as if she were being closely scrutinised. She brought a hand unconsciously to rub the back of her neck under the chignon that held her black curls in place below the confining cap. Her gaze darted about the room, and she slid her hand down, clasping it with the other and entwining her fingers. Mr Ottery's face came back into view, and she stared at him, hardly aware of what she said, or that her voice was shaking.

'It s-seems logical to s-suppose, sir, that if your client does not wish to marry from his acquaintance, that they must find him in some way…unacceptable.'

She thought the lawyer's eyes narrowed a trifle, and her discomfort increased. Illogically, she felt guilty—as if she had said something hurtful. More than ever the conviction crept over her that someone—he, it must be, for there was none other in the room!—was watching her, seeing into her very thoughts. Mr Ottery was speaking again, and she tried desperately to focus her mind again.

'My client wishes for nothing more than a marriage certificate. He is not willing to offer other than that. It is to be an arrangement purely for convenience. That, he believes, is *unacceptable* to the ladies of his own circle.'

The underlying antagonism below the flat tones penetrated Rosina's anxiety. It had, strangely, the effect of calming her a little. There was more than loyalty here. She had felt from the first that Mr Ottery was to be trusted. If he was the gentleman's champion, then neither his person nor his character could be quite devilish.

She gave a tiny smile. 'He is fortunate in your friendship, I think.'

The lawyer looked taken aback. He said nothing for a moment, looking her over in frowning silence. 'Miss Charlton,' he said at last, 'you are a shrewd observer. Is there anything else you have seen that I have not been at pains to tell you?'

A little of Rosina's tension eased, and she gave a self-conscious laugh. 'I might guess at some things.'

'Pray enlighten me.'

She bit her lip again, but the temptation to unburden her mind of its puzzles was too strong. 'I think your client is a man of means—or this fortune will make him so. Not rich, perhaps, but comfortable enough.'

The lawyer smiled. 'Well reasoned, ma'am. Anything else?'

'I imagine he has property, for a wife would only burden him if there was nowhere for her to live.'

'You are correct,' said Ottery. 'There is an estate in Warwickshire, your own county.'

Rosina's spirits rose. Come, this was more encouraging. At least she was eliciting some detail. Her own desperate need urged her to probe further. If she could only know enough of the gentlemen, perhaps she might be emboldened to think of—or hope for?—such a solution. She gave him a speculative look.

'You have not mentioned the circumstances of his birth beyond the fact of his gentility.' She paused, but Mr Ottery had nothing to say. Rosina's fingers travelled unknowingly to her upper chest, as if to quiet the uneven flutters there.

'I would guess that your client is titled,' she suggested, 'or there would be no need for this—charade. Nor, if his degree was very high, would he marry by this means, risking his name with the Lord only knows what obscure family connection.'

The lawyer, Rosina saw, was beginning to look amused. She could not help smiling. 'You are surprised?'

'That fairly describes it, ma'am,' he returned, with a laugh. 'I have not met with this level of deduction in any other candidate.'

Rosina's eyes clouded. 'Perhaps they had none of them as insistent a need to glean the truth.' The reminder of her purpose here threw her into acute consciousness. Dear Lord, she was falling into it so easily! Abruptly, she rose. 'I think I have wasted enough of your time, Mr Ottery.'

The lawyer had stood, coming quickly around the desk. 'Pray don't go, Miss Charlton. I assure you, there is no cause either for alarm or distress. You are young, and perhaps you do not know that circumstances now and again so arrange themselves that a gentleman feels himself forced into taking a course of action that might be considered unusual, to say the least. But as to my client's reasons, they are intensely personal. I beg you to believe, however, that his proposition is both simple and honest. May I beg you to sit down again?'

So much understanding sounded in his voice that Rosina allowed herself to be persuaded. But as she re-seated herself, she was once again struck by that unaccountable feeling of being observed. Almost involuntarily, she cast another searching glance about the room. No, they were alone. It must be the lawyer's own regard that was making her nervous.

Or perhaps, she thought, catching sight over Mr Ottery's shoulder of the portrait, it was a trick of those charismatic painted eyes. She shivered and dragged her attention back to the matter at hand.

The lawyer was outlining the details of the gentleman's stipulations. 'My client proposes, upon my advice, that his wife should be passed off as a female to whom he has been betrothed by a long-standing arrangement made between the parents or guardians of both parties. The lady in the case will be supposed to have lived retired in the expectation of his addresses being paid in due course. It will therefore not be considered particularly odd, my client believes, should his wife continue to live in a quiet way upon his estates.'

Rosina frowned in painful concentration, trying to follow the thread of his discourse. It did not quite ring true. And it was a matter of acute importance in her own case.

'Forgive me, but why should his wife do so, if she is marrying the man of her expectations, whose social standing cannot be in question? Would she not rather suppose that the marriage would bring her into contact with the circle of his friends?'

'A just observation,' agreed the lawyer. 'But the case is that my client has been abroad for many years, and his acquaintance with such a circle is but slight. He has no desire to increase it, and will himself therefore be content to live in a similarly restricted manner.'

This was so exactly what Rosina herself wanted that anxiety rose up once more. She did not wish to become so deeply enmeshed in this affair that its attraction became great enough to tempt her. Only—a marriage of convenience, which would ensure a lifetime's security at the trifling cost of marrying a stranger, with the added advantage that she might live in the obscurity she craved—it would be difficult indeed to find anything to equal it. What in all conscience was there to be said against it, beyond her own deep-rooted dislike of selling herself for profit?

Oh, but there was one thing. Her heart sank. How could she have overlooked the one aspect of the matter that would, at a blow, render it impossible? An uneven beat started up in her pulses. She looked at Mr Ottery, and was obliged to swallow on a dry throat. Could she bring herself to speak of it? She must. It was unthinkable to continue ignorant of the answer.

'There is one thing…' Her voice died. She drew another painful breath and tried again. 'The gentleman must wish, I suppose, to be provided with—'

Dear Lord, she could not even say it! Even less could she look at the man across the desk. His eyes—worse, the hateful eyes of that horrid portrait!—must see clearly her confusion, for she felt heat rising in her cheeks.

The lawyer's voice came, devoid of all expression. 'Naturally, my client will wish to be provided with an heir.'

Rosina's breath sighed out. He had guessed it! Relieved of the necessity of speaking of the matter, she almost forgot her reason for asking it. Until Mr Ottery spoke again.

He coughed delicately. 'Such a matter will be arranged at the convenience of my client. There is to be no aspect of the marriage vow excluded in the agreement.'

What did that mean? Her eyes flew up, meeting the blandness of Mr Ottery's gaze. No doubt that she would be expected to obey—in all things! At the convenience of a stranger who was obliged to advertise for a wife? Oh, she could not! It was to escape one vile trap only to fall into another. She said nothing, forming mentally the resolve to leave this place at the termination of this horrid interview, and apply immediately instead for a post as housekeeper, which was all the occupation she felt fit to obtain.

'There is one further proviso,' said Mr Ottery, as coolly as ever. But his eyes watched her narrowly, Rosina thought. 'It will be impossible for my client's prospective wife to meet him prior to the wedding.'

On her return to Withibrooke, it had been this last that had formed the chief topic of discussion between Gatty and herself.

'Can it be that the gentleman's age is against him?' had wondered her nurse.

'It cannot be that, for Mr Ottery gave me to understand that he has a year or so yet to reach thirty. No, he must be deformed, or crippled,' Rosina had insisted. 'Perhaps he is a dwarf.'

'It does seem so, my dove, I must say. Mayhap the man has a horror of women. One of these fellows they call a molly.'

'Or he is merely ugly, or extremely fat.'

Whatever it was, they had been agreed that this reluctance to meet a female with whom he expected to spend his life must betoken some deficiency of person. Which meant, as Rosina had pointed out with a shudder, that the conjugal duties involved constituted a fate more undesirable than the one for which she had been intended.

'Nor,' had said Gatty worriedly, 'since I can't settle it in my mind that this housekeeper business will perfectly answer the purpose, can we yet be certain you have escaped it.'

A fact of which Rosina was only too well aware. But if this was the alternative—! Dear Lord, let her not be recommended to this unknown gentleman's attention.

'I have only to hope, Gatty, that Mr Ottery found me so probing that he will cross me off the list without a second's delay.'

Rosina had so convinced herself that her application must be unsuccessful, that an invitation to a second interview had thrown her into acute indecision. A vehicle was to be sent for her conveyance, which indicated to her old nurse's mind—if not to Rosina's—that her candidature had been approved.

A lurch in the road brought her out of her reverie. Startled to find herself in the coach, for the memories had been all too vivid, she glanced at the man beside her. Dear Lord! She really had gone through with it. Despite all her misgivings, she had thrown herself upon the mercy of this unknown man whom she must now call 'husband'.

The thought caused a tiny sound of distress to escape her lips, and Raith looked round. It was dim now in the chaise, but even in the half-light, he could see that the elfin face was pinched and strained, the dark eyes luminous. Concerned, he said the first thing that came into his head.

'I thought you were asleep.'

He heard her indrawn breath, and noted that her voice shook a trifle. 'No. I—I thought you were.'

There was silence for a space. Raith could not think what to say to ease her evident discomfort. Perhaps there was nothing to say. He fell back upon convention.

'We will be at Marton very soon.' He glanced out of the window again. 'Dusk will be upon us in a trice. It must be well past four.' His gaze came back to the piquant features. His voice dropped. 'Are you tired?'

The gentle note drew Rosina's tears at last. 'I believe I am still in shock,' she blurted out, and put her fingers to her eyes, pressing them there.

His voice came again, rougher, a species of pain within it. 'I should not have sprung the thing upon you. I know how repellent are my features.'

Chapter Two

Rosina was struck by the bitterness of his utterance. She had not been referring to his scar; the remembrance of it had not penetrated her roving thoughts. But it was in her mind now, all too vividly. How deeply he must feel it, to imagine that it was the one thing he must conceal at all costs. Equally, to suppose that it was the focal point of her distress. It loomed, evidently, all too large in his mind.

The desire to weep was receding, and she was conscious of sympathy. Her hand fell, and with deliberation she turned her head to look at him. Lord Raith was facing the window. She could see the outline of his hat, the queue of his brown hair, and the edge only of his chin, dark and indistinct in the gathering gloom.

Rosina realised that this was the first time she had given a thought to his feelings. Was it as hard a thing for him to be saddled with an unknown female for his wife? He had chosen it. But so had she—necessity having forced the decision upon her. It had not made it any easier. Why should Lord Raith feel it less acutely? Her words came without intent.

'How did you come by it?'

She heard the echo of her own voice with dismay. She

should not have asked so tactless a question. She thought
he stiffened, but he did not look at her. His head straightened and his profile stood out strong against the light from
the window. Rosina thought he was not going to answer.
When he did, she found that she had been holding her
breath.

'I have been soldiering these many years.'

Then he had been wounded in action. She did not like
to ask how he had received such a blow as this must have
been. But why such bitterness?

'My father was a soldier,' she said impulsively.

He turned to look at her, and Rosina kept her eyes on
his face. She could barely see the blemish now, in any
event. Without allowing him an opportunity to respond,
she quickly resumed what she wanted to say.

'Had he come home thus tarnished, neither Mama nor
I would have thought less of him, nor loved him the less.
We should not have cared how he looked—only that he
had come back.'

Her voice cracked on the last words, and she turned
from the intentness of his gaze. She had meant to offer
comfort. Not to remind herself of that difficult loss. She
strove for control.

'I did not know that you had lost your father to war,'
came from the man at her side. The tone was gentle, all
trace of bitterness vanished. 'I am sorry.'

'It was some years ago,' Rosina managed to say.
'Mama took it badly. She did not long survive him.'

'Which is why you find yourself in this unenviable situation,' he said drily. 'Life deals harsh blows.'

The bitter note was back, and Rosina turned again to
look at him. She found herself moved by an unaccountable desire to ease him, if she might. Too eager to question it, she broke instantly into speech.

'Lord Raith, forgive me, but you do yourself too much

injury! This is your battle scar. It is an honourable wound. You should wear it with pride.'

A harsh laugh escaped him. 'Indeed?'

Even in the dim interior of the carriage, Rosina saw his eyes glitter strangely. Danger emanated from him, and she drew back into her corner of the chaise.

'And if the wound is dishonourable? Should I not then wear it with shame?' His tone was low but rancorous. 'You know not of what you speak, therefore don't speak of it at all!'

It was a moment or two before Raith regained control. When he did, he was equally distressed by his own outburst, and the effect of it on the blameless girl beside him. She had not spoken again. He dared to look at her, and his spirits dropped the more to find her not sunk into her corner, as he had half-expected, but sitting bolt upright on the edge of the seat, one hand grasping tightly the looped handle at the side of the chaise. Her head was firmly turned away, but the stiff outrage of her shoulders was sufficient reproach.

'That was unforgivable,' he uttered raggedly. 'I beg your pardon.'

The silhouette of her features were turned towards him, but he could not see her expression. He was unprepared for what she said.

'For better or for worse, my lord.'

Then she sank back against the cushions, and did not look at him again.

Raith cursed inwardly. He had made a mull of it. He would have to school himself to better control, if he was not to alienate her altogether. What had she done, after all? Tried to mitigate the virulence of his own response to the welt across his face. He had drawn it on himself, leading her to suppose that he had received the wound in battle. Better that than the humiliating truth! Only the deception rankled. Why quibble, Anton Raith? It was as much a lie as leading her to believe that he had no interest in seeing her, when he had done so from the first. His choice had been almost instantaneous!

Since he must adopt this method, even Ottery had believed that he had chosen well. Despite the fact that his lawyer—his truest friend!—had disapproved of the entire proceeding.

'God only knows, my lord, what sort of dreadful female you may attract by such an advertisement!'

'Which is why I am relying on you, my friend, to weed out the graspers and whores,' he had replied frankly. 'She must be genteel, I grant you that.'

'Genteel!' Ottery had scoffed. 'I dare say we may count ourselves fortunate not to be besieged by an army of maiden aunts and governesses.'

His guess had not been far off, Raith reflected. The majority of some fifty replies had been from ladies old enough to have mothered him, a number of whom were already engaged in employment. Others were poor dependents, eager for release. Of all the applicants, there had been only six or seven whom Ottery had deemed worthy of interview. They had all been sad women, Raith thought, and more than one might have done for his purposes—if Rosina Charlton had not applied.

Even her letter had been different from the others. Without exception, all the rest had dwelled upon what they conceived to be their own attractions. Catalogues of beauty had battered at his eyes as he had sifted through the sheaf of applications handed to him by Ottery.

'"Item: two lips, indifferent red,"' Raith had quoted, laughing, as he came upon yet another effusion.

Ottery had smiled, but had then picked up one letter set aside from the rest. 'This one, my lord, has nothing to say of her own appearance.'

Raith had run his eyes down the sheet. It was obviously penned with care, the characters looping gracefully. There was no embellishment, no embroidery to a simply stated list of facts. She was an orphan, obliged to earn her living, and had been seeking for some few weeks a position suitable to a female of gentility. She gave her age as two and twenty, and added the names of her parents to her own. The only indication to her character came in the final sentences. She had no wish, she said, to intrude upon society, and would be content to be earning her board by the bargain.

She had offered no references, unlike most of the others, who listed in the main names of title or repute. In a word, she had given nothing away—a reticence that had its own attraction. Which was why Ottery had been surprised that he wished to see her.

'My dear sir, there is no recommendation whatsoever, beyond her age.'

'That is precisely my reason,' Raith had insisted. 'She is a mystery, and therefore the more tempting.'

Ottery had been sceptical, but he had admitted, after that first interview, that he was drawn to Miss Charlton. Raith had been lured by his first sight of her, despite the intervening gauze screen of the central portion of Ottery's convenient portrait. It was cleverly designed, for one saw as if through a veil, yet from the other side the deception was undetectable. Ottery believed it had been used for darker purposes in former times during the years of the Civil War, for it had come down in his family through generations. Raith had been glad of its provision of his anonymous presence—else he would not have chanced upon Rosina Charlton!

He had instructed Ottery to check her credentials after that first occasion. The lawyer had located records of the Charlton family, of which one member's name tallied with that of Rosina's father. There were living members, and he supposed there must be reasons why Miss Charlton did not sue to them for help. He was the last man to question that. But her mother's family proved for the moment untraceable.

Rosina had been evasive on the subject at her second interview, saying that her mother had been an only child of genteel, but insignificant, parentage.

'And when she died?' Ottery had asked.

There had been hesitation. That vulnerable look had come into the black eyes. Raith had seen, with a lurch at his chest, the quiver of her lips.

'I was fifteen. I had…guardians.' Again she had looked away, moistened her lips. Then she had brought her gaze directly to bear on his lawyer. 'They—died.'

Raith had been convinced that she had fabricated that last. But he had refused to let himself be troubled by it, for he had already instructed Ottery to make the offer.

'Let us see how she reacts. We can always reject her.'

Not that he'd had any intention of doing so! It would have taken much to push him to it. He had thought the better of her for not jumping at the opportunity.

She had fidgeted in some degree of nervousness, he recalled, looking about rather wildly. Almost as if she sensed his presence! Ottery had been patient—more so than he would have been himself, had he been sitting at the desk.

'Take your time, Miss Charlton.'

The black eyes had darted to his face. She had seemed to gather herself. 'I cannot agree to it—until I have at least had a sight of him.'

Ottery had hesitated. Raith had shrunk away from the portrait, moving into the little room behind his lawyer's office. He heard Ottery excuse himself, and was not surprised to see him come through the intervening door.

'What do you wish, my lord?'

Raith had striven within himself. His ingrained instinct of hermitage battled with a dawning respect. In her place, would he not have held out for the same? How could he blame her, when he had himself made certain that he did not wed where he had not examined the wares? Yet if it would make her retract! He had faced the lawyer squarely.

'I cannot afford to let her go, Ottery. I must agree.'

But not the whole! That had been far too risky. He had been aware of his own urgency, delivered in a low tone so as not to reach through into the next room.

'Let her see me from a distance. Go. Ask if that will content her. If she is in agreement, we will arrange it at Brinklow. After—I rely on you to secure her consent.'

He had posted himself once more behind the portrait, deeply anxious. It had been evident that Rosina Charlton resented the recognition that Raith had been in the next room all along. She had said little, but her manner was enough.

'Can one hear through that wall?' she had asked, a flash of something like defiance in the black eyes.

Raith could only be thankful that she had not known how closely she had been both heard and observed. Ottery had ignored the question, instead putting the proposition Raith had outlined. To his relief, she had agreed. But not without further reference to his proximity.

'It would be simpler, would it not, if the gentleman would only walk through that door?'

Ottery had smiled, he remembered, but had not answered. The girl had become agitated.

'Does he not wish at least to see me, Mr Ottery?'

'It is immaterial to my client what you look like, Miss Charlton.'

A response which now made him writhe at the memory. He had deceived her at every turn! Even more, because of his conviction that a mystery attended the female who had today become his wife. Had he selected any other of the candidates, he might have revealed himself, for he would have taken an oath that his disfigurement would not have deterred them. Their intention had been plain: to better themselves and their position in life, at any cost. But Rosina? No, she was far too intelligent, too shrewd. She had taken this step to secure some other goal. But what?

She had given nothing away. And Raith had not dared to risk her disgust. He had ensured that she could not see him full-face, for fear that she would refuse the contract, which would have been unendurable! He was forced at last to realise the truth. Once Rosina Charlton had entered the lists, he had wanted no other wife.

The private parlour Lord Raith had hired at the Bell was comfortably ill-lit. A glow fell from two wall-sconces either side of the room, but neither reached the table where the new-married pair were dining. By the light of the single candle placed in its centre, Rosina saw only the gleam of her spouse's face rather than its features. The stresses of the day had so exhausted her, that she welcomed the relief from a too intimate tête-à-tête.

She had been relieved, on arrival at the inn, to discover that His Lordship had arranged for her accommodation in a separate bedchamber to his own. The intimation that he did not intend to insist upon his rights this first night did much to ease the strain of being obliged to dine with him. She had been a trifle apprehensive—after the acerbic exchange in the chaise!—but Lord Raith had thus far behaved impeccably.

At his suggestion, neither of them had changed. Rosina was grateful, wondering if he had done it out of deference to her undoubtedly meagre wardrobe. She had noted his own fresh cravat, and being at last sufficiently composed to be able to take in his appearance, had been relieved to find him not at all fashionable in his dress. His coat and breeches were of a blue so dark as to be almost black, the sobriety relieved only by a cream waistcoat of brocaded silk. Were it not for the facial defect, he must be counted not ill-favoured.

Once the covers were removed, and dishes both of fruit and sweetmeats placed upon the table, Raith had, to his bride's consternation, told the landlord that he did not wish to be disturbed again until he rang the bell.

Rosina's breath caught in her throat as he looked across at her. But his first words were not at all alarming.

'Have you eaten sufficient?'

'I thank you, sir, yes.'

Rosina had in fact made a good meal, for she had found herself to be hungry. She had begun with a little difficulty upon a steaming bowl of pease pottage. But at the first remove, her appetite had quickened, and she had managed to consume a portion of pigeon pie, together with stewed mushrooms and pickled French beans. A white fricassee of chicken had followed, of which Rosina had taken but a mouthful, only to obviate the need for persuasion from across the table. But she had rejected a Bath pudding, opting instead to partake of a little fruit.

Lord Raith, she noticed, had been almost as sparing, instead refreshing himself liberally from a bottle of claret that was provided along with the food. Rosina had taken only water, but now her husband reached out to the wine-glass that stood to one side of her place, and filled it half-full of the red liquid.

He laid it down in front of her. 'It is appropriate, do you not think, to drink to our nuptials?'

Rosina did not think so at all, but she was chary of saying so. Lifting the glass, she sipped a little of the wine.

Raith followed suit, watching her. She looked, he thought, a trifle more relaxed, if a little wary. He was glad, for he felt impelled to make amends for his earlier lapse.

'It is early days, I know,' he said carefully, 'but we may as well go over our expectations for the future.'

Rosina gazed at him blankly. *Our* expectations? Dear Lord, was she supposed to have any? He must be referring to his own. To show willing must be her first concern.

'I will be glad to know what you require of me.'

'Let me rather ask first what you expect,' he countered.

She was goaded into instant response. 'Why, nothing, sir.'

For the first time, Lord Raith smiled. Oddly, the scar changed with the smile. He looked far less sinister, Rosina thought. Unless it was due to the poor light?

'Come,' he said gently, 'that is quite unreasonable. You must have some thoughts of what you would wish your life to be. More now than ever, I would suppose.'

But Rosina was not fully attending. The word she had thought of echoed in her head. Sinister. Was it appropriate? Yes, it had been so, the first moment that she saw him. But not now. Not when he was gentle, when he smiled.

He was eyeing her, and she suddenly realised that he had been speaking. What had he said?

'I beg your pardon, sir. I was distracted for the moment. What did you ask me?'

The smile faded, as did the cordiality of his voice. 'You must have expectations, ma'am. I would be glad to hear them.'

Rosina sighed. If he was going to be this difficult, any expectations she might have had were vain! It was as well that she had none.

'I gave up all thought of deciding my own future a long

time ago. I would rather you tell me what you wish, so that I might school my conduct accordingly.'

'How dutiful!'

'Is that not what you wanted?'

'I don't know what I wanted!'

Raith controlled himself with difficulty. This would not do. He was only driving her further away. But before he could say anything less abrasive, she forestalled him.

'My lord, I am grateful for your protection.'

Raith caught at the word. 'Protection?'

He thought the dark eyes flickered, but he could not be sure in the uncertain light.

'I—I meant only to s-say,' Rosina faltered hastily, 'that—that I am happy to be given this much improvement in my life. I only wish to keep my side of our agreement.'

Raith had not missed the flurried cover-up. Protection was exactly what she had meant. His suspicions were aroused again. Protection from what? Or was it, from whom? Better to pretend not to have noticed it. At least she was talking!

'Pray tell me what I must do,' she said. 'I know you have made precise plans for this marriage. It is, after all, for your convenience.'

She was right. He'd had very precise ideas about how he was to live with the mythical wife of his imagination. She would, he had supposed, keep the household running smoothly, be at his call when nature so demanded, and in due time bear his children. He had seen them lead all-but-separate lives while existing side by side. But that was before this girl entered his ken. The prospect appeared to him bleak beyond words, now that he was married to Rosina Charlton.

Impossible to state anything of what was in his mind!

She was waiting for a response. He smiled again, unconsciously.

'We will have to work it out as we go along, Rosina.'

Rosina's attention caught on his use of her name, coupled with the smile. Her breath tightened. He really did look quite different. Only what had he said? Was she to have no guidelines? Must she tread blindly? And with a man so prickly that every utterance could make him withdraw into his shell.

'What are you thinking?' Raith asked softly.

She looked quickly away from him. 'I had hoped that I might have an indication—some hint of how I should go on. I do not want to draw your fire…' She faded out. What had possessed her to say that? Now he would grow cold again.

But Raith was shamed. She was right. He had shown himself disgracefully apt to snap—and on her wedding day. He looked her over while her gaze was averted. She had removed the cap, leaving her head so dark in the dim glow of the room that the white elfin countenance looked still more vulnerable. He had noted the old-fashioned gown. It had made her look the more delicate, drawn in to her small waist. Something would have to be done about her wardrobe. She must be possessed of little suited to her new station. Not that she needed anything to enhance her allure, he reflected.

Becoming aware of his regard, Rosina glanced back at him, and met his eyes. There was that in them which she barely understood. But the message spoke to her depths, and the image of her bedchamber came to her, shortening her breath. He had ordered separate rooms. But what if he chose to enter hers tonight? She would have to receive him! Only she had rather they had been better acquainted first. The notion of being bedded by a total stranger was almost as nightmarish as the fate she had previously faced.

Curiously, she did not feel him so much a stranger still, though she had known him less than a day. But she could hardly feel sufficiently acquainted with him to be indulging in that particular intimacy.

Raith noted the changes of expression that flitted across her face, and wondered at what caused them. She was afraid of him, he thought. Small wonder!

'You have no reason to fear me,' he said quickly.

'I don't!' she returned, but much too pat.

'You need not dissemble. I can see it in your face.'

Rosina looked down, and then away, as if she would hide her features from his too-penetrating gaze. 'If—if I am a trifle apprehensive, it is not to be wondered at.'

'I agree with you,' he returned unexpectedly. 'It is a situation any young woman would find intimidating. The more so—under the circumstances.'

What circumstances? Was he again referring to the blemish of his looks? She was tempted to mention it, to say that it was not that which held any terror for her.

'You are doing it again,' he accused.

Rosina frowned. 'Doing what?'

'You look as if you will ask me something, and then— through apprehension, I must suppose—you withhold it. Be plain with me, Rosina. I am not a monster!'

'Then why,' she asked, goaded, 'did you think so badly of yourself to wish to become riveted only to a stranger?'

'Because I could rather bear the cringing revulsion of a stranger, than that of some society damsel!' he flashed back before he could stop himself.

Rosina threw her hands over her face, her breath unsteady. Her eyes closed, and she shook her head against the hurt. He was impossible!

'Forgive me!' he uttered hoarsely. 'I did not mean to throw that at you.'

Her hands dropped, and she regarded him hopelessly. 'I did not cringe, Raith. I was only shocked to see it.'

It warmed him that she had dropped the title, if only because he had driven her too far. 'I know. I beg your pardon.' He gave an unconvincing laugh. 'Ottery will have it that I am over-sensitive. Perhaps he is right.'

Rosina bit her lip, and gave him a direct look. 'No, you were right earlier. It is better if we do not speak of it.'

She meant that his sensitivity made him too difficult to discourse with on the subject, but she was unsurprised— even after this little acquaintance—to see him retire again behind his wall of bitterness. She felt too tired to deal with it.

But Raith had been aware of his own stiffening. He made a deliberate effort to pull back. She had meant nothing untoward. He must not take needless offence. He recalled her question, and amended his answer.

'The truth is, I think, that most society damsels would be affronted if I were to offer for the reasons I have given. And what is worse, they would expect me to alter my whole way of life to suit them.'

'I am hardly in a position to do that,' Rosina conceded, adding darkly, 'and the last thing I wish for is to flaunt myself in society.' To encounter that man? No, Lord help her!

Raith was again struck by a queer intensity in her response. She had a particular reason for that remark, he was sure of it. Dared he probe?

'Why so?'

Rosina shifted in her seat, and took up her wineglass, not looking at him. 'I am not equipped for it, my lord.'

'In what way?'

She sipped at the wine to gain time. What could she say? How she wished now that he might have remained withdrawn! She dreaded such questions almost as much as he dreaded any mention of his lacerated cheek.

'I have been out of the expectation of anything of the kind for many years,' she said, prevaricating. 'I should not know how to go on.'

To her relief, he did not pursue the subject. A silence fell. To Rosina, it was more difficult than conversation with him had proved. She glanced at the timepiece on the mantelshelf, its dial lit by the glow from candles in the near wall-sconce. It was growing late. She could not avoid the dread question of the coming night for much longer. She sought for a neutral subject, anything bar what was in her mind.

'Is—is your home a large place?'

It was, she thought, innocuous enough. But it appeared that the sensitivity of Lord Raith extended even to this.

'It is vast,' he said flatly, and there was an edge of bitterness in his tone, 'but I dare say you may find the situation there less attractive than you anticipate. I think I will let it speak for itself.'

Which left Rosina in greater mystery than before. She had not had any particular desire to know about his home. To her it had signified nothing more than a haven up to this moment. But his attitude, together with the faintly derisive note in his voice, gave rise to the liveliest apprehensions.

It was all too much for one day. She wanted very much to leave him, but the consciousness of his right to enter her bedchamber at any time he chose kept her glued to her seat. She toyed with the wineglass, fidgeting.

Raith saw it with a growing sense of disappointment. Yes, she might disclaim her fears, but he was no fool. What had he expected? Let him at least try to keep his unamiable tongue in check. He tried for a soft approach.

'You must be tired. Why do you not retire?'

He noted the faint colour that rose to her cheek. Hell and damnation! What in thunder did she suppose he was going to do? Did she truly believe him such a monster? Hurt rose up, and he could not help himself. A mocking laugh escaped him.

'Don't look so dismayed! I will not inflict myself on you tonight. You may go to bed with a quiet mind.'

Rosina got hastily to her feet, tears stinging her eyelids. He rose also, but she barely noticed.

'Good night,' she said huskily, and made rapidly for the door. She had almost reached it when his voice checked her.

'Rosina!'

She halted, biting her lip, but she did not look round. She heard rapid footsteps behind her. Then his hand was on her shoulder, and she had perforce to turn.

The candlelight was stronger near the door, and Raith could see the wetness under the coal-black eyes. His chest caved in. He groped for her hand, and brought it to his lips, kissing it lightly.

'I've made you weep. A bride should not weep on her wedding day.' A slight smile curved his mouth. 'Save it for tomorrow. I have no doubt I'll give you cause.'

The rueful tone warmed her. She thought he was for once unconscious of his disfigurement, for she could see the scar clearly in the brighter light, and it did not dismay her. It struck her that with the smile some might even think it attractive. So strange a thought! She smiled back at him.

'Sleep well, my lord.'

'And you,' he answered, and released her.

For a moment or two he looked despondently at the closed door. Then he returned to the table, and once more took up the bottle of claret.

* * *

It had rained again in the night, and the roads were soggy. The journey was necessarily slow. It seemed slower to Rosina, for the heavy fact of her husband's relapse into taciturnity. She was not much refreshed, for she had slept little, her mind full of unquiet prospects of the future and beset also by a tiny fear that Lord Raith would change his mind, after all, and visit her bedchamber.

She had heard, she thought, his footsteps on the stairs, for they had passed her door. Rosina knew his chamber was adjacent, and a latch had clicked somewhere behind her head. She did not know what time that had been, except that it must have been very late. That her lord was asleep now in the coach seemed to bear out the conjecture.

At breakfast, he had been civil, but reserved. Rosina, in whom the night's cogitations had engendered no small degree of curiosity about her spouse, was conscious of disappointment. Small hope of getting to know him if he was bent upon retiring into his shell in this disagreeable fashion. The prospect of long years of increased loneliness stretched ahead of her.

Not that she had ever known anything else. These few short weeks with Gatty had been all the heaven that she had known since her mama's demise—and even these had been clouded by the ever-present fear of discovery. She must suppose that her hateful guardian could not imagine that she had taken refuge relatively near at hand. Or else he was never sober enough to work the matter out!

If only Cousin Louise had not died. She had been a faded and sickly creature—and no wonder, married to a drunken sot whose gambling must have fairly ruined her life!—but her presence had afforded protection. And her advice had been sound, if singularly undutiful.

'Keep out of his way, my dear. Say nothing to draw attention to yourself. Take your cue from my example, Rosy. I see him as little as possible, and if I am obliged to be near him, I never give him cause to notice my presence. It answers very well.'

Since Louise Cambois spent most of her days in her bed, Rosina was not much surprised that she was able to evade her husband's attention. She had herself chosen to avoid him by taking on the duties of housekeeper, which her mother's cousin was happy to relinquish. Her efforts had met with success for close on seven years. She had been one and twenty when Louise had faded away completely one day. Astonishingly, Herbert Cambois had been distraught at the death of his wife. Rosina had been moved to attempt to console him. A fatal mistake. For it had brought to his notice that he had in his charge a young girl of—in his own words, Rosina remembered, wincing—'no mean worth in the marketplace.'

She had not understood at first what he meant. For a short time, she had supposed that he was referring to finding her a husband. An unexpected and not unwelcome prospect—anything was better than to continue in his house! By the time she had realised her error, her guardian had already enmeshed her in his foully cruel design.

Shuddering, Rosina came out of her thoughts as the chaise halted. She started up, and looked from the window. An inn sign swayed in the wind.

'Ladbroke,' said Lord Raith's voice beside her.

Rosina turned quickly. He was lying back against the squabs, but his eyes were open.

'Are we stopping here?'

'Briefly. We turn off the Banbury Road beyond this village. I imagine Parton is checking whether the horses are in need of rest. You may get down if you wish.'

'I thank you, my lord, but I am comfortable enough.'

He said nothing more, and Rosina sank back into her seat, consciousness returning, for she was aware that his eyes were upon her. It was hard indeed to behave normally in any respect in his presence, now that she knew he was awake. Recalling her late remembrance of what she had left behind, she wondered if indeed she was any better off with Anton, Lord Raith.

A tap came at Raith's window. He turned his head and saw Parton signalling. He let down the glass.

'They'll do for a few miles yet, me lord. Catterline and me reckon to go on to Itchington Bishops and bait them there before we tackle the Heath.'

'Very well, Parton. Do as you see fit.'

'Likely Her Ladyship will be in need of a bite by then, an' all, me lord.'

Raith agreed to this and shut the window. In a moment, the chaise was on the move. He turned his head to look at his bride again. What thoughts had they been that so disturbed her? She had been lost in abstraction, staring at the bobbing backs of the horses through the window in front—though he could swear she did not see them!— seemingly unaware of the fidgety movements of her gloved hands, flicking incessantly at her fingers' ends.

They were quiescent now, tightly clasped in her lap, her head downcast. But that was because she knew that he was observing her. The thought caused a wave of unrest that was already becoming familiar. Such an unsettling effect as she had upon him! He eyed the neat profile, with its wisps of black escaping from the close cap. Did she always wear that thing? Raith saw, with satisfaction, that she had left her hair loose beneath it, so that one long waving tress hung down the centre of her back. So black against the grey of her gown where her cloak had slipped away behind. He was tempted to reach out and touch it, stroke it, curling it about his hand.

A shaft of heat shot through him, and he shifted abruptly, turning away. Enough! He must crush all such thoughts. It was too soon to be pressing her to that duty.

She had expected him to be demanding it of her last night, by thunder! He trusted he was enough of a gentleman to curb himself until she'd had a little time to adjust. He closed his eyes, intending once more to feign slumber. He had proved his hasty temper too unpredictable in conversation with her to risk indulging his fervent wish to engage her attention.

But Rosina had other ideas. She had not bargained for it, but she found herself yearning for companionship. To be travelling with a man to whom she was now tied for the rest of her life, and to behave as if they were each alone in the chaise, seemed to her absurd. If Lord Raith would not make an effort to establish cordial relations, then she must. It would not be easy, for he was so very unapproachable—not to say touchy! But the prospect of the years stretching ahead of her, in genteel isolation, were too lonely to be contemplated.

She cast about in her mind for a safe topic that she might introduce. Rejecting as dangerous the notion of asking him whether he had seen much action—or indeed anything about his soldiering life—Rosina settled for a question about Mr Ottery as being the least potentially harmful.

'My lord?' she began.

He opened his eyes. 'My lady?'

'Oh, that sounds so odd!' Rosina said impulsively, on a breathless laugh. She turned and found his eyes upon her, in mute question. 'Of all wild possibilities, I never dreamt of hearing myself thus styled.'

Raith's features relaxed a little. 'That I can appreciate. It is still new to me also.'

'You have only recently inherited?' asked Rosina, her curiosity aroused.

'It was wholly unexpected.'

She waited, but he volunteered no more, looking away

from her again. Dear Lord, but it was uphill work with him! She would have to use the ploy she had already thought of.

'You have known Mr Ottery for some while, I gather? He seems a very good sort of a man.'

Raith knew not how to reply. What sort of a question was that? Did she wish to know, or was she merely trying to engage him in conversation? He glanced round at her, and found the dark eyes trained upon him. Was there a trifle of wistfulness in their depths? Whatever it might be, its effect was to cause him to answer automatically, though little conscious of what he said, for her countenance took up all his attention.

'He is an excellent fellow. I hold him in very high esteem. Indeed, I know not what I should have done without him—on occasion.'

The memory his words evoked jerked him into consciousness. He looked quickly away. No—he must not. Anything but that. He did not want to provoke himself into again losing control in her presence. Hell and damnation! She was trying. The least he could do was to follow suit.

'How have you been living?' he asked at random. And then thought it might be taken wrong. 'Ottery said you were with your—nurse, was it?'

'She had been my nurse,' Rosina confirmed. 'Only when—when Mama died, and I was obliged to…' She faded out, realising where her words were tending. That would not do. She would be bound to evoke questions about just that part of her life that she wanted to keep secret.

'Obliged to?'

Dear Lord, must he hold her to it? Necessity brought inspiration. 'Obliged to leave Gatty—my nurse. She was going blind, you see.'

There could be no harm in revealing that much. No need to state how Herbert Cambois had refused to have the elderly dame in his household, believing poor Gatty to be useless at her work. Which she was, poor lamb, but through no fault of her own. Rosina had begged in vain, appealing to her cousin. She had not known at that time how little influence had Louise.

'Fortunately, Mama had provided her with some little means. Not a pension, but small savings that she had acquired over many years of service. She was Mama's nurse before me, and she came with her as maid upon her marriage. I believe it was Papa who insisted upon it, for he knew that Mama would be often alone.'

'She did not follow the drum, then?' Raith asked, finding himself eager even for this scrap of her history.

'She could not, for she had a weak chest, and Papa would not permit her to endure the rigours of campaigning.' Rosina had become lost in her own tale, almost forgetting to whom she spoke. 'Mama knew her own frailty, and with the dangers attendant upon my father's profession, she saw to it that my guardianship was assured.'

'Who was your guardian?'

Rosina started, gazing wildly round at him. She might have known she would make a slip! Her breath caught, and she wished fervently that she had not so foolishly begun on this course. Why could she not have left him to his close-tongued reserve? But she was giving herself away every second that she refrained from answering.

'My—my mother's cousin. At least—not her, but her husband.' She did not dare look at him for fear that her disgust and hatred would show in her face. 'When I went to him, Gatty bought a little cottage. I took refuge—' stopping with a gasp, and hastily correcting herself '—I mean, I went to her there…after his death.'

She fell silent, and Raith eyed her profile with a good

deal of misgiving. Had he not suspected all along the apparent commonplace of her story? What in thunder had occurred? The guardian must be the key. That he was dead, Raith highly doubted. *Refuge,* she had said. One did not take refuge from a dead man! The suspicion filtered into his mind that he had taken to wife a runaway.

Rosina could have cursed herself for inadvertently letting out so much. That was what came of making conversation! She resolved not to do so in future. But it appeared that she had aroused the curiosity of her husband.

'Why did you not go to your father's family?'

A shadow crossed her face. 'The Charltons did not approve the marriage, for they considered Mama to be beneath them.'

'Surely they would not visit his mistake upon you?' objected Raith.

'My mother's cousin did not think so either,' Rosina said drily. 'I did write, at her instigation, when I was eighteen. I received no reply.'

'It would seem that you have been unfortunate in your relatives. Was your guardian at least good to you?'

Rosina's pulses jangled. Dear Lord, how could she answer him? To say anything at all would be to invite further question, yet more probing. How could she extract herself? One thing she decided: if Lord Raith chose to be inaccessible in future, she would not attempt to lure him out.

She avoided the question. 'His wife was a friend to me.' Then she yawned ostentatiously. 'I beg your pardon, my lord, but I am still a trifle tired. You will not mind if I sleep?'

'Not at all,' Raith returned politely.

As little as he believed in his own pretence did he believe in this. She had betrayed too much, and now she was withdrawing. If he had hoped to catch her out, he had been cleverly deflected. She was determined to be secretive. He foresaw a string of stilted interchanges between them.

When they stopped at Itchington Bishops a short while later—he was as little fooled by Rosina's artless awakening as he had been by her pretence of sleep!—he was disheartened to discover that he had been right. The consciousness of distance gnawed at him all through the simple luncheon at the Hart and Hounds. His wife made play with a selection of patties and fruit, which conveniently prevented her from engaging in anything but the most desultory remarks.

The weather was inclement enough to provide food for some of them, the state of the roads and the distance still to be covered offered the rest. Raith found himself irritated beyond words, although he initiated no subject himself.

On the whole, he was glad that his lady chose to pretend sleep for much of the remainder of the journey. Had they attempted to talk, he knew he must have been provoked into ill-temper. He could see nothing for it but to keep well out of her way.

Rosina had reached much the same conclusion. It had not been easy to remain aloof. Were it not for her dread of giving anything more away, she might have burst out a number of times. It seemed to her that, under the calm exterior, Lord Raith smouldered. She could feel it emanating from him, like a black fog. It was almost as if the bitterness exposed in him last night was now directed at her.

She was nettled the most by the deliberate manner of his choosing always to place himself to her right, that she might see as little as possible of his rent face. He did so when he escorted her into the inn, and again when he took a seat at the table. Had he not gone to elaborate lengths to hide the thing from her, Rosina was convinced that she would not have given it a thought. The initial shock over, she was growing as readily used to it as one did to any new countenance. Several times she was obliged to bite her tongue on a protest. It would be better, she decided, if they were not too often together. She could only hope that her new abode would prove large enough to allow her to avoid him.

It was dusk by the time her husband told her that they were turning into the gates of his home. But there was still light enough for Rosina to see that her hope was not misplaced.

Raith Manor was a huge grey mansion, standing four-square to the long, open approach. It had an air of total isolation. Shuttered windows, bare grainy walls, discoloured in places. A huge arched frontage stood out from the central section that was slightly inset to the square bays at either side. Black wooden double doors opened directly on to a stone-flagged porch almost level with the ground. To either side was a mass of lumped trees, like a hungry forest, bushy even in their sparse winter garments, stretching away into distant acres.

Bleakest of all, where green lawns should have been, lay a sodden sea of black that gave off an acrid stench. Gazing in growing dismay from the chaise window, Rosina perceived that the whole area was covered in ash.

Chapter Three

'I must apologise for the state of the place,' said Raith, as the chaise came to a stop before the entrance doors. 'I hope soon to remedy some, at least, of its ills, now that you have enabled me to obtain control of my fortune.'

Rosina could find nothing to say in answer to this. The chaise door was opened and the steps let down. An elderly male servant was waiting to hand her out.

'M'lady,' he said, bowing.

The oddity of being thus addressed upon her arrival was swallowed up by the realisation that the servants had gathered on the porch. She climbed down from the chaise, staring in perturbation at the little knot of persons in uniform. What was she supposed to say to them all?

'I am Kirkham, the butler, m'lady.'

'How do you do?' she murmured, glancing back almost instinctively to Lord Raith, as if seeking guidance. He had jumped down, and came forward to offer his arm.

'This will not take long,' he said quietly, and to the butler, 'Good evening, Kirkham. Be so good as to make the introductions, if you please.'

Rosina felt like a fraud as she was drawn to the porch and presented to a gaunt, harassed-looking female in black, who turned out to be the housekeeper. There were two footmen, three maids and a cook, besides a few others of evidently too menial a station to be given more than a wave of the hand, together with the cryptic addendum that they were from 'below stairs'. Rosina's mind became fully taken up with the impossible idea that this gallant little band comprised the entire domestic staff. How could so few possibly manage to care for a house this size? She knew enough of housekeeping to be appalled at the amount of work they must each accomplish.

Within minutes, she had entered a draughty hall, and the domestics had dispersed, with the exception of Mrs Fawley, who was detailed to show her to her personal quarters, while Lord Raith went off with the butler.

Rosina did not know whether to be glad or sorry to have been deprived of his support. But as she followed the housekeeper through the hall into a central lobby, and began to mount the stairs there to the upper floors, she could only be thankful that her husband was not there. She doubted whether she could have disguised the crushing despair that gripped her.

The place was so empty! It was clean enough, but austere. She caught glimpses through doors of draped huddles—of furniture? The walls were painted rather than papered, in muted tones. And from the few framed pictures hanging from them stared disapproving ancients from classical myth.

In the bedchamber to which she was led, however, an effort had been made to create a homely atmosphere. There was a fire in the grate; a vase of greenery dotted with a tiny collection of flowers had been placed upon a wide bulky table set in the window embrasure which fronted the dead lawns; and a painting depicting a lady on horseback in a charming landscape had been placed upon one of the walls.

'The master chose this one to be put in here, m'lady,' offered Mrs Fawley, coming to stand behind her as she examined the painting. 'It's His Lordship's mother on the horse.'

Rosina looked at the female with new interest. But the features were too indistinct in the gathering darkness for her to be able to make out any resemblance. She was intrigued by the thought of Lord Raith having made this choice, however, and resolved to look at it more closely in daylight.

She turned back into the room, and felt her spirits drop. No amount of prettifying could serve to alter its depressing solidity. The walls were drab, the bed hefty and old-fashioned, with a high ornate tester and thick turned posts, its blue velvet curtains heavy and dark, matching the drapes at the windows.

The housekeeper moved to an inner door by the outer wall. 'Your Ladyship's dressing-room is through here.'

Dressing-room? She went through the door indicated and found a room only a little smaller in size to the bed-chamber. Here was a dressing-table and stool, a long pier-glass, and a washstand. Two large presses stood at one side, along with a chest of drawers, a small armoire and a chest.

Rosina stared about her, fascinated. What would she do with such a place? Who could have sufficient clothes to fill all these receptacles? Not she, certainly. Her entire stock would fit into less than half the armoire and a single drawer!

'And through here,' the housekeeper said, crossing this room to a further door on the other side, 'is the antechamber adjoining His Lordship's similar apartments.'

A sick feeling settled in Rosina's stomach. Why had she not anticipated as much? With unwilling feet, she moved slowly to follow Mrs Fawley. The antechamber was a small no man's land, placed directly over the front door of the mansion, where a large window let in light. It contained a fireplace, with two plain chairs either side, a little table against the wall.

Rosina stared at the door that opposed her own. It was mercifully closed, but she could readily picture the rooms beyond. Rooms that at night contained her husband.

She moved to the fireplace and stared down into the empty grate. For what purpose was this used? To make assignations, perhaps? The cynical thought was pushed away. Lord Raith needed no assignation. Four doors only separated him from taking up his marital rights at any time he chose. Of what use to think of it? She had agreed to this of her own free will, and there was nothing she could do about it.

'Will there be anything further, m'lady?'

She turned quickly, and forced a smile. 'No, I thank you, Mrs Fawley.'

The housekeeper curtsied, and withdrew through Rosina's own apartments. She stared after the woman, feeling acutely assailable and unprotected. Not that she could imagine how Mrs Fawley might save her from nightly raids!

Rosina fought down her discomfort. She must not think like this! Only…how else was she to think of it? The whole dread notion had loomed hideously into view again—the worse for the situation of these carefully convenient arrangements. Rosina felt more distanced than if she had been presented with the *fait accompli* of having to share her spouse's bed from the outset. It had been the way Mama and Papa had lived. And Cousin Louise had only taken a different bedchamber to her husband's out of choice.

But she was no longer Rosina Charlton, of no account. She was Lady Raith, a baroness, and she must learn to accommodate herself to the different circumstances attending that life.

The only difficulty was, she thought dismally, as she moved towards the door to her apartments, that she did not feel remotely like Lady Raith. That female was some fabricated individual, with whom Rosina had nothing to do. She felt like an intruder. It was inconceivable that this was her home, and that the man who occupied the suite of rooms across the way was indeed her lord.

Arrived in her dressing-room, she discovered that her trunk had been brought up and placed upon the chest. It was already opened, and one of the maids was engaged in removing her garments from it and bestowing them in the various receptacles about the chamber.

'Oh!' she uttered, startled. 'I can do that myself.'

The girl looked astonished, but she bobbed a curtsy. 'Begging your pardon, m'lady, but Mrs Fawley instructed as I should do it for you.'

Dear Lord, she was become a lady indeed! No one but Gatty had ever waited upon her before. She felt excessively uncomfortable. Particularly to have a servant go through the unprepossessing collection of her clothing. For the first time she wondered with what fabricated tale Lord Raith had fobbed off the domestics. The story Mr Ottery had outlined? Unlikely that any of them had believed a word of it! And if they had, they certainly would do so no longer once this girl gave out the details of her belongings, as she undoubtedly would.

Unable to endure the humiliation, Rosina went through into the bedchamber, only to find a second maid preparing the bed for her occupation. A lit candelabrum was set upon the table in the window, which had the odd effect of darkening the room. Another curtsy was offered. She would have to become accustomed to that. She, who had been upon cordial terms with Toly Aughton, the apothecary's boy, and innumerable persons of all conditions these seven years, servants and traders alike.

'I'll bring the warming-pan, m'lady, if you'll ring when you wish to go to bed,' said the girl, turning down the sheets. She curtsied again, and made for the door. Then halted with a gasp, and turned. 'Begging your pardon, m'lady, I forgot. His Lordship's compliments, and he'll do himself the honour of dining with Your Ladyship in an hour, if that is convenient.'

It was as much as Rosina could do to assent. Before she could recover herself, the other black-clad maid came in from the dressing-room, bobbing again.

'Will Your Ladyship select which gown you choose to wear this evening?'

It was too much. Rosina sank down upon the bed, and clasped her hands tightly together in her lap, her eyes fixed upon the maid.

'Pray…what is your name?'

'Joan, m'lady.'

'Joan—' She took a steadying breath. 'Pray don't ask me what I am going to wear. You must see for yourself that I have few gowns. Indeed, this is my best, and I have worn it since yesterday. I am sure His Lordship will not expect me to make any change this evening.'

Joan looked nonplussed. She was small, plump, and apple-cheeked. Likeable rather than pretty. Not much older than Rosina herself. She curtsied again.

'As Your Ladyship pleases.'

Rosina sighed. 'That is all, thank you. You may go.'

Joan curtsied again, and left the room. Rosina got up and went into the dressing-room. The trunk was tucked in a corner. It was empty. Rather wildly, Rosina opened drawers and closet doors, looking where her things had been stowed. She felt as if nothing belonged to her any more. Her life was at the beck of others. Even her clothes

were no longer hers to use as she chose. And as for that—
that despicable little room next door! She wished she
might lock it and shut herself off from invasion.

Pausing, Rosina straightened as a daring thought struck.
Was there a key? She darted to the bedchamber door—
and found none. Neither within nor without. Fairly running back across the dressing-room, she looked in the lock
of the door to the antechamber. Nothing.

Fiercely, she grasped the handle and dragged open the
door. An intense feeling of relief swamped her. There was
a key on the other side. Not pausing to consider her action, she moved into the little room and triumphantly extracted the key from the lock.

A latch clicked behind her. Gasping, Rosina turned.
Entering the antechamber from his own dressing-room
door was Lord Raith.

Raith looked at the key in her hand, all thought suspended. His glance travelled to her face. What he saw
there threw a shaft into his chest. Revulsion! He had
known she must feel it. She had tried to gainsay it yesterday. Tried to make him think that she did not regard
it. But here was proof, if he had needed it. One had only
to look at her!

In fact, Rosina was consumed with consciousness. She
could not fail to notice his flawed features, for light from
the window fell directly upon that side. But anything she
might have felt at the sight of it was overborne by an
absurd sensation of guilt, as if she had been caught out in
wrongdoing. Without thinking, she put her hands behind
her back, as if she would hide the key. To her consternation, her spouse's eyes followed the movement, and the
bitter look of cynicism became pronounced.

'Don't trouble yourself to make a secret of your feelings. You are welcome to lock the door and pocket the

key, if it will make you sleep safer at night. I am unlikely to break down the door, no matter how strong my desire to molest you!'

Rosina heard the words with resentment, despite an increasing sense of guilt. Need he be sarcastic? Was it surprising that she should be apprehensive? Last night he had acknowledged that she had reason. She eyed him. He stood stiff and tight-lipped in the doorway, grey eyes glinting. There was no trace of melting—as there had been last night.

She straightened, bringing the key from behind her. Fitting it into the lock again from the side where she had taken it, she looked back at him.

'I married you for better or for worse, my lord. I will abide by the terms of the contract.'

He leaned against the door jamb and folded his arms. 'Am I expected to thank you? You set inordinate store by that part of the marriage vow, I take it. Let us hope that my gentlemanly instincts may prevent me from forcing the worse upon you before we have had time to become better acquainted.'

Irritation flared. 'Oh, Raith, must you be so—so naggy?' she uttered in a fretful tone.

She moved into the antechamber and crossed to the fireplace, tweaking at her fingers. Raith watched her, the fire dying out of his eyes. She was right to reproach him. What in thunder ailed him, to be picking on her in this brutal way? He had driven her into disquiet again, and it was the last thing he had intended. But what he had said, he reflected soberly, was not so far from the truth. He had been married to her for little more than four and twenty hours, and already he was chafing at the necessity for patience. If he did not take care, he chided himself savagely, he would lose her utterly.

There was little point in excusing himself yet again.

She would grow weary of his apologies, even if she believed—as he did not!—that it excused his offences. He moved into the room. She must have heard him, for she turned.

'If you wish to speak to me at any time, you have only to send your maid to consult with my valet.'

Rosina was wary of the change of tone. He was so apt to alter at a second's notice. He looked no less dangerous, despite the relaxation in his voice. The light was at his back, and his face was shadowed. But the white gleam of his scar could be clearly discerned. Like a tiny streak of lightning in the dark! Now he did indeed look sinister.

What had he said? Her maid? 'I have no maid,' she said on the thought.

'I was forgetting that.'

His words rose to her consciousness, and she suddenly took in what he had meant. Send her maid to consult with his valet? A flash of anger sparked. She was not yet so great a lady!

'If I should wish to speak with you, my lord,' she said in a tight voice, 'I shall use no go-between! Such a course could do nothing but increase the distance between us.'

She passed him quickly and, with an ostentatious gesture, removed the key from the lock and replaced it on the inside of her own door. He had turned, and she looked at him with some degree of defiance, but he did not speak. Rosina waited a moment. Then she went into her dressing-room, and shut the door behind her.

Rosina woke to strong daylight. She lay blinking in the huge bed, unable for a few moments to recall where she was or what she was doing there. When it came back to her, she started up on one elbow, glancing about the bed-chamber in quick alarm.

The place was much less disturbing with the velvet

drapery drawn back. Rosina remembered that she had come in last night to find that the chambermaid, whom she had met coming out of the room armed with a warming-pan, had closed the curtains about the bed. It would have been like sleeping in a tomb! In a frenzy, Rosina had flung them all back, and, regardless of the cold, done the same at the windows, opening the chamber to the night.

She had been warm enough, snuggled in well-dried sheets, several blankets and a down coverlet. Her sleep had been fitful, however, and she had woken several times, and found herself listening out, straining her ears for some sound from the interconnecting rooms. Her husband had shown himself so changeable that she had found herself unable to rely upon his assurances—flung at her with such abrasion! Particularly in the light of his attitude at the dinner table last night.

The thought drove her out of the bed. A fire had been lit in the grate, and in the dressing-room next door the ewer was already full. The water in it was tepid, and Rosina guessed that she had woken late. Forgetting that she had only to ring the bell to acquire freshly hot water, she made use of what was there, and began to ready herself for the day.

Not that she had any idea what she would do. Her spouse, she recalled, had told her that she was unlikely to see much of him. Judging by last night's encounter at the dinner table, Rosina felt it to be unlikely that she would have much chance to talk to him either.

Having washed off the stains of the journey and tidied herself, Rosina had left the room to find the butler waiting at the top of the stairs to show her the way. If she'd had any apprehensions about dining once again tête-à-tête with Lord Raith, they had been put to flight the moment she had entered the dining-room below. A table of inordinate length had been set with places at either end. She could not have conversed with His Lordship if she had tried!

Her husband had already been at the table, but he had risen civilly and bowed as she took her place. Rosina had looked down the long gleaming wood surface, and then at his face. Was this how he intended they should live? They might as well be on separate islands!

She had glanced about the room. Two chandeliers hung from the ceiling, but they were unlit, illumination being provided only by candelabra set upon the sideboards, and single candles in ornate sticks placed at intervals down the table. This was the main item of furniture in the long room, apart from a couple of sideboards where the food was waiting. All the other chairs were set against the walls. It was the most absurd arrangement. But if that was what her spouse wished for, she had supposed it was not for her to cavil.

At least she had anticipated him aright. He was dressed, as she was, in his wedding gear, with a less formal waistcoat of plain blue silk that he had been wearing from that morning. His hair had been combed and retied, looping casually.

The meal had been well prepared, if a trifle heavy. A ragout of veal, served with artichoke hearts, mushrooms and forcemeat balls, and a gravy of meat broth. It had been removed with a rabbit pastry, a dish of scallops and stewed cucumbers, followed by a blancmange and red-currant tarts.

Rosina had eaten a little from each dish, not wishing on her first day to cause offence to the cook. She knew well the amount of work that went into the preparation of dishes of this calibre, and had often been called upon to console the Cambois cook for the frequent waste of her efforts. Neither her guardian nor his wife had been healthful enough to display hearty appetites.

But the food before her had taken up less and less of her attention, as she had become aware of her spouse's fixed regard. He had hardly taken his eyes off her. He had eaten and drunk steadily, barely glancing either at his plate or his glass, apparently bent upon watching every move she made. She had felt exposed. As time wore on, her consciousness had increased, giving rise to an irregularity both in her breathing and her heartbeat. She had been drawn and repelled at one and the same time, and her fingers had stolen up more than once to touch her neck briefly, or rest lightly upon her bosom.

But Rosina's consciousness had at length given way to indignation. What did Lord Raith mean by glowering at her from his end of the table? There had been a kind of hunger in his gaze. A well of emotion that she had barely understood had accompanied that sense of danger she had felt in him before.

She had been glad at last to be able leave him to his port, and had half a mind to go straight upstairs to bed. Only Kirkham had ushered her into a large saloon at the front of the house, where a cheerful fire and a quantity of candelabra about that end of the room had given off a comforting feel.

'Tea will be served in half an hour, m'lady,' he had said, and left her there.

Rosina had taken a chair by the fire, and looked about her, unimpressed. The furnishing was sparse, the walls dull, and the dark wood overmantel of a piece with the austerity of the whole house. The place was denuded of frills, and there was no touch of elegance. All was heavy and old-fashioned. Rosina had wondered what in the world she was going to find to do in a place like this with the endless empty days that stretched ahead of her.

It had been less than a quarter of an hour later when her spouse had joined her. She had dreaded his coming, unable to determine how she was to respond to the moody intensity that he had displayed throughout dinner. But when he entered, there had been no trace of it in his countenance.

He had greeted her with a calm air of courtesy, asking whether she had enjoyed the meal. Rosina had been tempted to inform him that his behaviour had ruined any possible enjoyment, but she had been so relieved that she had chosen prudence, cautiously following his lead.

'It was very good, I thank you.'

He had taken up a place before the fire, choosing, Rosina had noted with scant surprise, a stance that kept his right side turned away from her. Looking about the saloon, he had said in a disparaging way, 'I am sorry to say that there are only one or two rooms suitable for use at this present. This is one of them. I will hope to remedy that in due course.'

Rosina had tried to think of something inoffensive to say. 'Most of the rooms seem to be very large.'

'Yes,' he had agreed, 'and draughty. They can be made habitable. I have known this house when it was a sight more pleasant to live in.'

Surprised, Rosina had gazed at him. 'I thought you had only just inherited.'

For a moment, his features had drawn in tight, and forbidding, and Rosina had felt her heart sinking. Not again!

'I grew up in this house,' he said shortly.

It was his harsh voice. She was intrigued, but she made no reply, fearing one of his lightning changes of mood. But he had made, Rosina thought, an effort to relax. When he spoke again, it had been in a more natural tone.

'It will be some days before Ottery has freed my trust fund, and in the meanwhile there is little that can be done within the house. I am presently engaged, however, in a great deal of inspection about the estate. My agent calls every day.' He had looked at her, an air of apology in his face. 'I regret, ma'am, that I must leave you very much to your own devices for the moment. I dare say we shall meet, for the most part, only at meals.'

Rosina had been secretly dismayed by the formality of his manner. Almost she had preferred him to be jibing at her. There had been too much coldness in it—at one with the alien nature of the living conditions demanded by the social standing of this house. She had answered him, however, with equal formality.

'What would you wish me to do, sir?'

She had thought he had looked a trifle impatient. If so, he had curbed whatever natural response he might have made, returning to the cool withdrawal of his earlier utterance.

'I recommend that you get upon terms with Mrs Fawley, ma'am. She will, I don't doubt, assist you to know your way about the place. You may, of course, give her any instructions that you choose.'

'Oh, I shan't do that!' she had protested involuntarily.

Her husband had glanced briefly at her. 'You are mistress here now, ma'am.'

Rosina had been betrayed into an unwise response. 'In name only!'

Lord Raith's unamiable temper had flared. He had turned, and the livid laceration matched the fierceness of his grey eyes. 'Yes, you have made your preference abundantly clear! Don't imagine I will sue to you to change it. Good night!'

With the curtest of bows, he had strode from the room, leaving Rosina to bury her face in her hands with a groan of frustration. The tea, which came shortly thereafter, had done a little to revive her. But she had gone to bed in a deeply pessimistic frame of mind, troubled for the future.

But Thursday morning found her a trifle less down-hearted. Perhaps it was the fact that the drizzling rain, which had thus far accompanied her venture into matrimony, had ceased, so that a weak October sun peeped through disintegrating clouds when she looked from the window.

She was about to leave the bedchamber when her eye was caught by the painting of Lord Raith's mother. She moved to examine it. The female on the horse was younger than Rosina had expected. There was not a great degree of beauty, though she had a sweet smile. Rosina could discern no resemblance to her husband. But it was not a large painting, and the features were small. Why had Lord Raith caused it to be placed here?

The door opened, and Rosina looked round to find on the threshold the maid Joan, who had unpacked her belongings. The girl curtsied, looking with surprise at Rosina's habited state. She had dressed herself in an old gown of blue kerseymere, made high to the throat, feeling the big house was likely to be chill despite the change in the weather.

'Good morning, m'lady. I was waiting for you to ring.'

'Thank you, but I was quite able to manage.'

Joan looked hesitant, fidgeting with her apron. 'Yes, m'lady.'

Rosina frowned. 'What is the matter?'

The girl bobbed again. 'Mrs Fawley said I was to wait upon you, m'lady, according to His Lordship's orders. Until, that is, Your Ladyship should hire a real abigail.'

She had been somewhat out of charity with her spouse, but this mark of thoughtfulness touched her. She remembered that scrap of conversation they'd had in the antechamber. Rosina smiled at the maid.

'That will be helpful, Joan. For the moment, however, I don't think there is anything—' She broke off. 'Stay! Do you know how to iron?'

'Oh, yes, m'lady,' said Joan eagerly.

'Then—perhaps you might do what you can with my gown? It is of damask, and sadly crushed from the journey, I fear.'

It was clear that Joan was delighted to be given even this minor task. Rosina, familiar as she was with the hierarchy of the servants' hall, guessed that her promotion to lady's maid, if only temporary, was a giant leap up the domestic social ladder. She resolved to curb her own instincts to look after herself and allow the girl to enjoy the just employment of her new status.

'Perhaps you would first show me where I may be served with breakfast, Joan?'

With alacrity, the maid led her downstairs to the same vast dining-room, where the butler supplied her needs. She learned that it was after eleven o'clock. She discovered, upon enquiry, that her husband usually breakfasted at ten. Rosina was tempted to use this information to make certain of *not* encountering him in the mornings. Only she knew it would cause inconvenience to the servants—especially the cook, obliged to keep food warm—who must wait upon the pleasure of the gentry, when they might have been better employed elsewhere.

By the time she had eaten in solitary state in her single chair, with only the sight of Lord Raith's empty place at the other end, Rosina was further tempted to make herself mistress of the house as her spouse had suggested. She would give much to institute changes that might lessen the dreadful formality of Raith Manor.

Raith had recommended her to talk to Mrs Fawley, but Rosina chose rather to wander about the house by herself, forming her own impressions. They were not favourable.

The house was enormous, and as she wandered through interconnected rooms, the drab silence of the empty spaces depressed her. There was everywhere dullness, an air of neglect and isolation.

Holland covers were laid over furnishings which had been pushed together in the centre of rooms. Those few paintings that remained upon the dun-coloured walls were inferior in execution. The wood mantels were clean, but unpolished—she supposed no one had time to make them gleam—and utterly free of ornaments. Chandeliers hung dully, their glass droplets long unwashed. There were perhaps two timepieces in the whole house. And as for silver—bar that in the dining-room and the various candelabra—there appeared to be none.

Walking around the first floor on the back face of the mansion, Rosina arrived in a long gallery populated by a number of ancestral portraits, obviously of former Raiths.

Her interest quickened, and she wandered slowly down the line, becoming wholly absorbed. A gentleman in an Elizabethan ruff stared back at her. The first Raith, perhaps? She had not seen any earlier style, though there were a number of later date, becoming indeed so recent that this last must be within a decade or two. Then she came upon one so startling that she almost jumped. It was of a gentleman who bore an uncommon likeness to her husband.

His hair was of a similar brown hue, worn in a ragged cut that rested upon the shoulders. He was older, she thought, but there was the same set jawline, the high cheekbone. Here, in the dip below it, was a deeper cleft perhaps, and the lips more thinly carved. Most striking of all, the grey eyes looked out upon the world with the exact air of cynicism that so characterised Lord Raith. Only there was no scar.

'Is it like, do you think?'

Rosina jumped violently. Turning, she beheld her spouse standing behind her, near a window. Her heart jerked into life, and she was unable to speak for a moment for the turbulence in her chest.

For all he was booted, Rosina had not heard him approach. He was in riding dress, a long frock of dark green over buckskin breeches, but he had discarded his gloves and hat. His hair, though tied back, was dishevelled, accentuating the resemblance. He was looking particularly bitter, glancing from her to the portrait, and back again.

Rosina found her tongue. 'It—it is like, but it is not you,' she managed, as calmly as she could.

Raith turned his gaze to the portrait. 'You are observant.' He strolled past her, and went to stand beside it, turning. 'Pray continue your investigation.'

He spoke quite coolly, but Rosina felt the bile welling within him. It caught at her curiosity, and she found herself less affected than usual. Had this significance in his virulent self-hatred? She looked from his face to the portrait, and saw at once that the resemblance was not nearly as strong as she had thought.

The unknown man on the wall had, she now saw, a look of—yes, dissipation—that had been drawn by the artist, perhaps without intent, in a swarthy shadow that edged the jaw and ran down in strong lines from nose to mouth and below the eyes. It was only, she realised, looking back at Lord Raith—whose far less mocking eyes were regarding her with concentrated attention—the addition of the ridged and ragged white lesion which gave him that sinister air. It was that which increased the similarity. The other, she decided, looked sinister without any adorning cut.

'Who is he?' she asked.

Raith came away from the portrait, and turned to look at it with her. 'My brother.' His jaw tightened. 'My half-brother, to be exact. My predecessor, the tenth Baron Raith. And to whose untimely demise you may count yourself indebted, for I would never otherwise have thought of marriage.'

Indebted! Was she not rather cursed? But to say so would be to provoke precisely the sort of contretemps that she wished to avoid. Besides, he had faced her without hiding the scar, and she guessed it had taken an effort for him to do so. Moreover, when he had moved back he was standing on her left, leaving it exposed. From this side, and so close, it was indeed cruelly ugly. A shaft of emotion seemed to crush her chest, and she wanted to weep for him.

'I am sorry if you were distressed by his death,' she ventured, faintly husky.

He glanced at her briefly, but his gaze returned to the portrait. 'Only because it meant that I must inherit this doubtful windfall.'

'When did he die?'

'In the summer.'

Rosina felt suddenly desperate to ask more, but she was already too strongly aware of the dangers of probing too far with her touchy spouse. His nearness was having an unsettling effect. Was it the sight of that graven cut?

To her surprise, Lord Raith appeared disposed to talk of the matter, though he continued to study the portrait.

'Ottery had written to me, warning me that Piers was travelling all too swiftly on the road to perdition. But I was in the midst of a campaign against the French, and paid no heed. Besides, I had no wish to watch him breathe his last. He would not have thanked me for it.'

His voice was even, but Rosina could read beneath it a wealth of unspoken emotion. Again she was swept with the oddest flood of feeling. It must be pity! And here must be the reason for his bitterness. She forgot caution.

'I am of the opinion that you did not care for your half-brother.'

Raith looked at her. 'Astute of you!'

She eyed him, unaware of the emotion that showed in her black orbs. Raith took it for reproach, and gave himself a mental kick. How could he have spoken to her so? After all his good intentions!

'Pay no heed to me,' he said quickly. 'It is not your fault that I was at enmity with Piers.'

Her eyes became questioning, and he avoided them, moving to the window. Easier not to look at her. The effect upon him of her expressive countenance was his undoing. Last night's petty bungling had ruined his sleep. He had tossed and turned, fighting the desire to go through to her chamber and beg her forgiveness for his ill-mannered departure. Had he not feared that she would think he had the intention of taking his pleasure of her, he would have done it. She could not possibly trust him. Nor, for that matter, did he trust himself!

He had spent the entirety of that interminable dinner in a state of anguish, so badly did he want her. On her departure from the table, he had gone across to the window and flung open the shutters, letting in the freeze of the night to cool his ardour. He had tossed off his port, resolved to give her no cause for distress, and broken the resolve within minutes of being in the same room with her.

This morning, her non-appearance at breakfast had been to him a relief, and he had set out with his agent on horseback, determined to remain out of doors until sunset. But memory—that intrusive betrayer!—had fed him images of his conduct, and he was riven with remorse. He had come back expressly to find her, and make amends. He drew a breath, and spoke without turning round.

'Rosina.'

'Yes, my lord.'

There was a quality in her voice—of sympathy? That was the last thing he wished for! Never mind it. This was not about what he wanted, but about what she deserved. He did not turn around, but kept his eyes on the view from the window: a deserted formal garden, the stables and outhouses just visible beyond, behind a belt of trees.

'I have behaved abominably since our marriage. More so since we arrived here. I do not know what to say to you. If I were to make you a promise to mend in future, I know I should break it. I am not fit company.'

Her voice came from behind him, a trifle diffident, he thought. 'It has, I think, to do with your half-brother. Your bitterness, I mean.'

'Bitterness,' he repeated dully. 'It was his own disease. I had it not, until he gave it to me.'

'But he is dead,' she pointed out. 'Can you not forget it?'

Would that he could! But how, when the very core of it had brought him to this pass? Else he would not have put himself on to the market—and purchased an impossible dream. But that could not be said. Easy enough to find another reason. They were all of them valid.

'It is a trifle difficult,' he said, turning so that she received his good side. 'His legacy surrounds me.' His hand threw an arc that encompassed the house and grounds. 'You've seen the place. It was never thus when my father was alive. Piers has brought it to this pass in the space of seven years.'

Rosina came to join him at the window, puzzling over his words. 'Was it then done to thwart you?'

He gave one of his harsh laughs. 'Not until he knew at the last that I must succeed him. He had only to marry and beget an heir to keep me out. Only his reputation was so besmirched that no female of any standing would have him. And Piers would never have stooped to the sort of bargain in which I have indulged.'

He saw her wince, and quickly put out a hand. 'That was not meant to insult you, Rosina.'

'I take no offence,' she replied, that wistful expression creeping into her elfin face.

It wrought havoc within him. 'You should!' he replied forcefully. He moved to her, and grasped her hands, holding them hard. 'Rosina, I meant to make a marriage of convenience, but I find myself with something quite different. I don't yet know what it is.'

A smile wavered on her lips, and the black eyes softened. 'It must be what we make it.'

He drew her closer, and Rosina found herself looking directly up into his disfigured countenance. There was a vibrancy in his tone, a throb of something she did not understand.

'Can you truly stomach this?'

Her voice shook, for her pulse had begun a slow thump that made it difficult to utter. 'If I am permitted to become accustomed, why should I not?'

He met the coal-black of her eyes, and almost gave in to the temptation to kiss her. But then he saw that her lip quivered, and felt the trembling in her fingers. She would let him do it, but she was intensely afraid!

Releasing her fingers, Raith stepped back. For a fleeting moment, he had forgotten. He turned aside, giving her again the one acceptable profile. He fought to remain where he was, though he wanted to walk away. It had cost him an effort to mention it, to ask. She had shown willing. Hell and damnation, was that to be all?

Rosina watched him, oddly bereft. For one wild instant, she had thought he was going to kiss her. A rush of heat had enveloped her, and her knees were still shaking. For the first time, she found herself wondering what it might be like to give herself to her husband's caresses.

There was a lengthy silence. Rosina cast about for something to say. Her mind was all chaos, but she wanted more than anything to hold him here. Let him not leave her flat—as he was wont to do—after rousing in her so tempestuous a reaction! All at once, she remembered.

'Speaking of paintings,' she said quickly.

He started, frowning as he looked round. 'Yes?'

'The one you caused to be put in my bedchamber,' she pursued. 'It is of your mother, I understand?'

Raith stared at her, hardly aware of what she meant, so intensely had he been involved with the too-close step towards disaster. Too close, by thunder, for comfort! He had made the highly inconvenient discovery that he could not satisfy his desire at the expense of her dignity. To know that she was forcing herself to accept his caresses? No, a thousand times.

'My mother?' he repeated vaguely.

'She seemed not to resemble you, but then I could not properly see her face. Is there no larger portrait?'

Rosina felt as if she was babbling. His abstraction had not escaped her. He was retiring into his shell again. She became aware that she could not bear it.

But Raith had caught up with her train of thought. 'There was no portrait done of her. I have a miniature.'

The vulnerable look was back in her face, and he had to turn away. Her voice came again, hushed.

'Why did you have it put in my room?'

'I thought it suitable. It is the most attractive painting in the house. Besides, it was her room once, and I re- member her with—affection.'

The word drifted between them, poignant and wistful. Rosina had no words.

Raith glanced at her. 'I must go. I came only to...say

what I did.' Reaching for her hand, he lifted it; keeping his gaze on her slim fingers, he caressed them lightly with his thumb. 'If I give you further cause to hate me, Rosina, remember that it is the last thing I desire.'

Then he dropped a light kiss on her fingers, released her and walked quickly away down the gallery. Rosina gazed after him, aware of a tingle at her fingers where his lips had pressed. She stayed thus for a long moment, thinking. Then she gave a determined nod, and went in search of Mrs Fawley.

Raith spent the day battling with his memories. His agent, Longridge, led him to Ratley, one of the villages on his estate a couple of miles away, where he lunched in the local inn, in a deliberate move to show himself. He then visited each of the farms and cottages in turn, as he was doing in all areas, day by day, meeting every tenant and listening to their grievances. They were many, increasing as word spread of his activities, and more took courage to come out with the list of wrongs.

His brother Piers had been the worst of landlords, squeezing from the estate every penny that he could, and putting nothing back. Raith made no attempt to defend him, and accepted instead the words he heard time and time again.

'T'weren't like this in your father's time, me lord.'

'I am aware of it, my friend,' he told them. 'I hope to mend matters in time, but you must have patience. It cannot be done all in a minute. Now, what is it you need? Longridge will take down a list, and we will do our best to accommodate you by and by.'

The time he had to spend with each one was lengthening, the more so today, for the news of his marriage had got about. He was obliged to accept felicitations, and answer questions about his lady. An exercise which added a new dimension to the drift of thoughts at the back of his mind as he listened with spurious attention to what were more or less the self-same complaints from end to end of his domain.

Hearing of the deprivations that had attended the tenure of his half-brother served to increase the bitterness. If Piers had deliberately chosen this way of revenge, by thunder, he could not have done it more thoroughly! Their father must be turning in his grave.

But the remembrances evoked by thinking of Piers led him instantly to visions of Rosina's delicate face. He had inflicted that bitterness on one who least deserved it. Yet she had generosity enough to forgive him, to understand. And he, ungrateful dog that he was, did not want her understanding. What he wanted, she was unable to give him, small blame to her. What female could? Which led him directly back to Piers.

It was a churning, useless circle that well-nigh exhausted him. It must have shown. They were not finished at Ratley, but his agent called a halt.

'My lord, you look fagged to death! Besides, it will be growing dark soon. There is no point in attempting to complete the task here today. We can return tomorrow, if you will.'

Raith had nodded wearily, glad enough to fall in with this scheme. They rode back to Ratley Grange together, where he parted from his agent and then cantered back to the Manor grounds. By the time he had left his horse at the stables, it made sense to change for dinner. He was early enough to call for a bath that he might wash the accumulated dirt from his person.

He dressed casually in deference to his wife's meagre wardrobe, in a coat of snuff-coloured cloth, with matching breeches, and a bronze satin waistcoat. By the time he started down to the saloon, he found himself to be in a fever of impatience to see Rosina again. She was before him, waiting.

'Good evening, my lord,' she said, with a smile.

Raith was taken aback. He replied in kind, watching her warily. Was this submissive friendliness her notion of disporting herself as a dutiful wife? Her countenance was as enchanting as ever, but his suspicion increased when he saw that she had made an alteration in her dress.

She had put off the gown of blue stuff that she was wearing earlier in the day, and had instead donned a gown of chintz. It was of a pale pink which little suited her, and from the way it fitted looked as if it had been made for a larger lady and altered down. It was, moreover, as old-fashioned as the rest, Raith realised with a rise of annoyance. He knew little of female costume, but he could tell that much. Where in thunder was Ottery with his funds so that he might alter that? That she had worn it at all, however, was a gesture that betokened a change in her attitude towards him.

He watched her rise from the chair and come to his side—the left side. She had noticed, then. Why would she not, she was intelligent enough?

'Shall we go in, my lord?'

'As you wish.' He offered his arm, and led her through into the dining-room.

Kirkham was holding the door, his face wooden. Raith took this in vaguely, ushered Rosina before him and walked in after her. He stopped short, staring.

The table had been reduced by at least half. A single candelabrum was placed to one end, lighting where two places had been set. One was his usual position, at the head of the table. The second place, obviously for Rosina, was set directly to its right. She would be seated so that she must spend the meal looking at the mutilation on the right side of his face.

Chapter Four

For a few breathless moments, Rosina thought Lord Raith was going to explode. His eyes blazed, and he shot a look at her that spoke volumes. Inwardly quaking, she turned from him and moved to the table.

'If you please, Kirkham,' she said quietly.

The butler made haste to pull out her chair for her. Rosina seated herself, as nonchalantly as her fast-beating heart would allow. Then she looked at Kirkham and nodded towards her husband's chair.

He drew it out, and coughed. 'My lord?'

Raith was within an ace of marching straight out of the place. How could she trick him so cruelly? Now he saw why she had been conducting herself in that deceptively wifely manner! He heard Kirkham cough again, and saw that a maid and both the footmen were entering the room, laden with dishes. To make a scene before the servants would hardly accord with his desire to create an impression of marital harmony.

He moved across to the table, noting that the sideboards, where the staff were busily employed, had been shifted also, so that they were closer to the table. The light was all concentrated in one area, making the room cosier.

The relief Rosina felt on seeing him approach was short-lived. He had no sooner seated himself than he leaned towards her, taking advantage of Kirkham's moving out of earshot. The grey eyes flashed, and she jumped.

'If we were alone, madam wife, I should be strongly tempted to use you in a manner that you would scarce find to your taste!'

Rosina's hands were shaking with fright, but she gripped them together in her lap, and answered him with low-voiced defiance.

'You have f-forgotten, sir,' she said, barely able to control the tremors in her voice, 'that you t-told me to m-make myself mistress here.'

'I did *not* tell you,' he returned savagely, 'to make of your husband a mockery!'

'Will you take wine, my lord?'

'What?' He turned quickly to the butler, saw that he was proffering a bottle, and snapped, 'Yes!'

The butler poured, and moved round the table.

'I will take water, if you p-please, Kirkham.'

Raith looked at her with narrowed eyes. 'You had better have wine. You may find that you need fortifying.'

She eyed him. Dear Lord, but he was angry! She looked at the elderly butler, who was still waiting. 'A l-little wine, if you please.'

Kirkham poured the wine, managing at the same time to convey to her a look of avuncular reassurance. Rosina smiled at him gratefully. He had been aghast when she had put forward her request to him and Mrs Fawley. Neither retainer had anything to say against her desire to reduce the table but, severally and together, both had advised her most earnestly to place herself upon Raith's left side. Rosina had been adamant.

'It is a risk, I know, but one I am willing to take. You

need neither of you fear His Lordship. He will have no hesitation in laying blame at the right door!'

An apprehension which had now been proven. For the moment Rosina was protected by the presence of the servants. She could only hope that by the time they withdrew, her spouse's temper would have calmed a little. Knowing already how lightning were his changes of mood, Rosina averted her gaze from his face in the hope that this might ease his consciousness. It availed her nothing.

'You need not try to mitigate the offence,' came at her in a derisive undertone.

Rosina looked to find the grey eyes smouldering. She steeled herself to meet them squarely. Her jumping nerves were steadying a trifle, and she was glad to find that she was once again able to command her voice.

'This morning, sir, you asked me if I could stomach—'

'I remember,' he uttered harshly. 'And you chose this method of forcing yourself to become accustomed. That much I had deduced.'

'Then how can you accuse me of mocking you?'

Raith stared at the soup bowl that had appeared in front of him as if he did not know what it was. 'Could you not have found a less public expression of duty?'

Rosina was hurt by the implication that she had done it from a sense of obligation to her married state. Her tongue sharpened. 'I fail to see how I might do so else, since you are shy of my regarding it even when we are alone.'

She received a look that made her quake. But since Lord Raith chose to retire into a silence choked with tension, she was not obliged to attempt to speak again. Let him fester all he wished! As long as he refrained from throwing his tongue at her, she could endure it well enough.

But her spouse became increasingly ill at ease as the meal progressed, drawing at length her reluctant admission that her wild scheme might have been misplaced. While he ate, partaking more and more sparingly of the viands that were put before him, he was subject to shifts of discomfort from moment to moment. He could not be still, and now and then his hand stole up—unknowingly, Rosina thought—and hovered, as if it sought to conceal that misshapen side. Recollection made him reach out swiftly for his glass, tossing back the wine. He drank a good deal more than he ate, and Rosina became more distressed for him each time he signed to Kirkham to pour.

His vulnerability was pitiful. By the time the last course had been set upon the table and the covers removed, she was deeply regretting having put him through this enforced exposure. It was for him, she now saw, a purgatory.

'Pray leave us, Kirkham,' she said, the moment the butler had set down the final dish, unable to help a note of urgency.

The elderly butler bowed correctly, and Rosina watched him leave, driving his minions before him. The door closed behind him and she turned in dismay as, beside her, her husband let out a groan of utter despair.

Raith's breath came thick and fast as he leaned his right elbow on the table, pressing his hand tight against the offensive wreck of his features, and closing his eyes. Blood and thunder! He had never been so near to disgracing himself with unmanly tears. Curse the wench, and her well-meaning interference! She little knew what she had put him through. He felt wrung out. Every instance of insult and ignominy that his mutilation had made him heir to had come crashing in upon him.

A whisper reached him. 'Raith...'

He shook his head with violence, unable to respond. Let her not attempt to condole with him—or plead, whatever she intended. Not yet awhile. He could not answer for his own responses.

But Rosina was too affected to be wise. His aspect was heart-rending, and she could not endure it. Her own eyes were moist, her voice husky with emotion.

'Raith, I know how you must be feeling…'

He reared up. 'No, you *don't* know! God send you never will!'

She flinched. 'I b-beg your p-pardon, I never meant—'

'Spare me, I beg of you!' he uttered raggedly. 'I know well enough what you meant.' He passed a hand roughly across his brow, and jerked out, 'It is not your fault. In your innocence, how could you know—'

'But I want to know, Raith,' she broke in desperately, driven by she knew not what need. 'I am your *wife*. You say we have a marriage other than you intended. Help me to be the wife you would wish for. Give me something of yourself.'

Raith dragged his fingers down his cheek, and his eyes, haggard in the candlelight, turned upon her face. 'This? You want to know of this?' He drew a breath loaded with anguish. 'Then for a beginning, picture to yourself a whore, for whose services I had paid, running screaming from the room upon first catching sight of it.'

Rosina put a hand to her mouth as tears sprang to her eyes, but she did not speak. He had turned his tormented gaze upon the candles, and did not see her reaction.

'And she was not alone. I took to wearing a mask—for such occasions.' His tone had roughened, though his voice was pitched lower now. 'I had reason to wish that I might do so at other times. There was a ball once, in Spain, where a bevy of ladies were obliged to use their fans for protection. But I saw them while they shunned me—whispering and pointing.'

Silent, the tears that trickled down her cheeks evoked

more by the evidence of his pain than by the words he said, Rosina listened with her eyes fixed upon the wicked injury that had made of him something of an outcast.

Raith spoke on, as if his tongue, once loosened, must run with the narrative. 'Once I thought I had found the inconceivable. A female—not respectable—with whom I became involved, who seemed indifferent. Until I found out that her particular penchant was to seek out those with deformities for an obscure fancy of her own. My disgust then equalled that which I evoke myself in women.'

He was spent. Leaning his elbow on the table again, Raith dropped his chin in his hand, only half-aware of concealment. His eyes moved to his wife, and he saw the tears on her cheeks.

'What, do you weep for me, Rosina?'

'Yes,' she said simply. She sniffed, and wiped away the stains with her fingers. 'It is cruel.'

Raith grimaced. 'It is human nature.'

There was a silence. He watched her, feeling a swelling in his chest for the recognition of her tender heart. A considerable lessening of his suffering had been afforded in the telling. He had said it all without intent, driven by her mad action. But now he could not be sorry for it. He felt instinctively that Rosina's compassion was not born of pity for his wound, but rather for his anguish. Was there that in her past which enabled her to comprehend his humiliation?

'You should weep rather for yourself,' he said unthinkingly. 'You must now live with it as well as I.'

Rosina turned her luminous black orbs upon him, and the wistfulness was pronounced. 'If you will let me.'

His chin was still resting in his hand. As of instinct, he shifted his fingers, to cover the whole scored side. 'So that you may pity me? Allow me some small measure of pride.'

She bit her lip, and a hint of mulishness crept into her face. 'I agree that you have pride—and a good deal of it false.'

'I have false pride?' Raith sat up, dropping his hand, and shifting to face her, hardly aware as he did so that he effectively removed the maimed side from her view. 'I will be glad if you will tell me how you know so much, when we have been but three days married.'

Rosina sighed with impatience. 'What has time to do with it? Today you came to me with a mouthful of gentle sentiment. Yet when I ask you for this one thing, you will not oblige me.'

Was she still at that? Had she not seen enough? 'You did not ask. You took it! And to my cost.'

'Yes, and for that I am deeply regretful,' Rosina said earnestly, twining her unquiet fingers together. 'But I am asking you now, Raith. And it can only be pride that will not let you give in to me.'

Raith drove his fingers into his hair, and groaned. This was so unfair. How she played upon his feelings. 'Rosina, I beg of you, change your seat tomorrow to the other side!'

The coal-black eyes registered acute disappointment, and her lip quivered. 'If you so command me, my lord, I must obey.'

'Hell and damnation!' Raith swore. He reached out and grasped her twined fingers, holding them hard. But his voice was soft, its menace a caress. 'How dare you put me at so vile a disadvantage, you unprincipled wretch?'

A tiny smile curved her lips. 'Well, but you are there, sir, and by your own effort.'

He had to smile. 'You are in the gravest danger, my lady. You should learn to mistrust my temper!'

Rosina's eyes softened, and his heart lurched. 'My lord,

it is my pleasure to obey you in all things—before you order me. I have already learned it.'

Raith laughed out, releasing her, and Rosina warmed to the natural sound of it. What joy to see him in humour at last! The danger had been averted. She dared not press him further. She would like to have stayed talking with him, but she knew too little to risk inviting a relapse over some chance misstep. Better to leave him now, inducing a wish for reunion.

She got up, smiling with unconscious allure. 'I will go to bed, sir. My sleep these last nights has given me little of rest, and I am sorely in need of it.'

Raith had risen when she did. He saw her smile with a rise of expectation, though her words belied it. Was it an invitation? He spoke at random, the most obvious thing.

'You must be tired.'

'Somewhat,' Rosina agreed. 'I am unused to be in so vast a chamber quite alone.'

What in thunder did that mean? Nothing, in all proba-bility—bar what his fervid desire wished to make it. Raith offered his arm.

'Allow me to escort you to the stairs.'

She took his arm, but with a laugh. 'I dare say I could find my way. Or is that another of the formalities obtain-ing in my new status?'

Raith led her to the door. 'Do you find it so formal?'

'Excessively.'

'Enlighten me. What is the difficulty?'

'For one thing,' Rosina told him confidingly, 'the busi-ness of having a maid. And my previous situation has made me apt to consider more the convenience of the servants than my own. Then, too,' she added, as they en-tered the lobby, 'there is the elaborate arrangement of a bedchamber, a dressing-room and that antechamber that must be crossed before—'

She broke off abruptly, suddenly conscious of what she was saying—and to whom! Where had her wits gone begging? To be speaking in such a way to Raith, of all things. She felt herself grow hot, and taking her hand from his arm, made a swift dash to the stairs. She turned there, and found her spouse regarding her with question in his face. Oh, dear Lord, what had she done?

A smile, a quick 'good night,' and, picking up her skirts, Rosina fled up the stairs.

Raith watched her with an increased tempo in the pattering of his pulses. Was it possible? Could she truly have been indicating a wish for his attentions? It might have been a slip. He had noticed several times that Rosina was apt to let her tongue run away with her, and stop in haste when she realised that she was giving away what she had rather not.

But his own yearning was so strong that his instinct of caution wavered. Prudence dictated that he hold aloof a while longer. For all her protestations of willingness to endure his grotesque countenance, it must take a high degree of courage to undergo the intimacies of the marriage bed. A difficult enough experience for any young wife. In their situation, it must be an ordeal Rosina dreaded.

Hell and damnation! Swinging away from the stairs, he went quickly towards the one habitable saloon, with the intention of ringing for Kirkham to bring him brandy. On arrival, he found the butler already there, placing a tray upon the table by one of the chairs near the fire.

'Your port, my lord,' he said. 'I thought perhaps you would be more comfortable in here.'

Raith thanked him, deciding that port was quite as effective—and less obnoxious. It would hardly ease the difficulty if he were to go to Rosina reeking of brandy! He cursed himself, and seized the bottle and a glass.

'I will serve myself, Kirkham. Go to bed!'

The butler bowed and withdrew, leaving Raith to pace the length and breadth of the saloon, absently sipping at the glass which he was nursing between his hands.

In the heat of his imagination, he had taken infinite enjoyment in the image of Rosina's face, watching her responses—which must undoubtedly be as unlike reality as one could well imagine! He might forgo that pleasure. Do the thing in the dark? It would spare her blushes. He need not see the efforts she would make to conceal her aversion. And she would have the advantage of not seeing him.

A ripple of distaste went through him. She would not see, but she would feel! If he kissed her, she could not avoid the abrasion of his ridged cheek. The thought of kissing her threw spasms of want into his loins. Raith crossed to the tray and refilled his glass, tossing off the wine. Enough! He could not do it, and there was an end.

But the argument persisted in his head, and he remained downstairs for a further half-hour, with a vague thought at the back of his mind that if he left it late enough, Rosina would be asleep—and only a monster would disturb her then.

When his valet had completed preparing him for bed, however, he dismissed the man before climbing between the sheets.

'That will do, Paulersbury. Good night.'

The valet bowed. 'Very good, m'lord. May I suggest a bed gown, if Your Lordship intends to remain out of bed? The night is chill.'

When the man produced a silken morning gown with a handsome blue print, Raith felt his cheeks darken. Paulersbury had guessed his intent. Of course he must present himself before his bride decently clad! It took all his resolution not to snatch it from his valet and throw it aside. He allowed the fellow to assist him to don the thing, and then paced impatiently about his bedchamber as he waited for the man to finish dealing with his clothing in the dressing-room.

At last he heard Paulersbury's discreet cough, and the click of the outer dressing-room door that let onto the corridor. Yet now that the way was free to Rosina's bedchamber, Raith still hesitated. She would be asleep by this time. What was he doing, pursuing this course tonight? Only if he did not, perhaps he might disappoint her expectation—if she had indeed meant to issue a guarded invitation.

Bracing himself, Raith took up the single candle from the bedside table, and went through to the antechamber. Stealthily he opened the door to Rosina's dressing-room. He listened within, but could hear no sound. The door opposite was shut, but a gleam under it indicated that there was light within the bedchamber. By thunder, she was expecting him!

Touching an unconscious hand to his cheek, he softly opened the door. To his dismay, its hinges protested with a mild shriek, and he quickly entered the room, shutting the door again with unprecedented haste.

He turned. The bed-curtains were drawn back, and by the candlelight that came from one side, he could see Rosina sitting up in bed, an open book in her hands, staring across at him. She was without a nightcap, her dark hair falling about her shoulders. Her bosom rose and fell rapidly, and Raith broke quickly into speech.

'Am I disturbing you?' No, that was stupid. Of course he was disturbing her. And with intent! 'Don't be alarmed!'

Rosina was more than alarmed. She was frozen with terror. He had come! In an instant, she forgot how she had worried that he might, after her incautious words. Forgot, too, how she had persuaded herself into believing he would not.

An image sprang into her mind. That dread image that had haunted her these many weeks. Her guardian, stumbling through her bedchamber door, the candelabrum in his hand lighting up the coarse, drink-sodden features.

For a hideous moment, she did not see Raith. She was back in her drab little room, in the house where she ought to have been inviolate, with Herbert Cambois—come, he said, sputtering the words, to teach her what awaited her in the future he planned for her—with that hateful man.

Her breath pumped as she stared at him, and a measure of sense returned. This was not her guardian, she reminded herself, over the frantic eruptions at her pulse. This was Raith. He would not fall sobbing on to her bed, and crawl his loathsome way towards her. That was past. This—this was her legitimate husband. He had a right.

Raith had not moved from the door. She looked away from him, snapped shut the book, and laid it quickly aside, sitting up. But her jangling nerves would not settle, and her fingers travelled unknowingly over her bosom to the back of her neck.

'F-forgive me…you s-startled me,' she managed to say.

His own discomforts forgotten, Raith came quickly to the bed, laying his candle down. Next moment, he was seated beside her, taking her trembling hand into his warm clasp.

'Don't, Rosina! Don't be afraid. I will do nothing to frighten you, I promise. You have only to say the word, and I will retire again this instant.'

'N-no,' she quavered. 'It—it is not you, Raith. Pray—pray don't l-leave me.'

Deeply concerned, he watched the tremors of her white face, his mind thronging with questions. What did this betoken? There was something here that could not be explained by all the careful arguments that he had made with himself. This reaction had no reference to his arrival. If that were all, she would have greeted him with wary uncertainty—not this stark fright. The black eyes were dilated, a nightmare in their depths. Even his disfigurement did not warrant this, considering her attempts to adjust to it.

Her fingers shook pitiably within his own, and her whole frame shivered. Raith saw the tears on her lashes, and without thought, he shifted forward and drew her gently into his arms, holding her close.

'Hush now, sweetheart, hush,' he murmured, wholly unaware of the endearment he used, intent only upon easing her. 'All is well. There is nothing to harm you. Hush!'

Insensibly comforted, Rosina felt her jumping pulse begin to subside. She sagged against him, letting her head fall upon his shoulder. His hold was warm, and completely unamorous, one hand stroking down her back in a rhythmic movement that readily increased her relaxation.

But her proximity started at length to disturb Raith, coupled with the feel of her nestling thus within his arms and the warmth and scent of her skin under the thin stuff of her nightgown. His senses swam. The quality of his embrace began to alter. The motions of one hand took on a sensuality that delineated her contours, while the other shifted upwards, allowing his fingers to run and writhe within her hair. He laid his lips to the wispy curls and kissed across her forehead, travelling downwards as he brought her face up.

For a moment or two, Rosina felt the subtle adjustment of his ministrations as natural, and accepted them. Warmth pervaded her, but it was a pleasant sensation, unalarming.

Then his lips reached hers. The warmth intensified with

a rapidity that mirrored the sudden increased pressure of his mouth. She heard his indrawn breath, and fire streaked down her belly. Panic took her. Her hands came up, struggling, and she thrust away from him, pulling back into her pillows.

'N-no,' she uttered breathily. 'I cannot, I cannot.'

But the taste of her had overwhelmed Raith, and he forgot everything but his own need. His hands reached for her, pulled her back into him. He brought his mouth down on hers again, drawing hungrily at her lips, forcing them open.

Sensation flooded Rosina, melting her bones, burning her deep with a febrile throbbing that was too intensely vivid to be borne. She fought him, striving for release, her hands flailing at him, her fingers reaching frantically to drive his face from hers. They came, all unknowing, into contact with the scar. Its rough edging brushed Rosina's fingertips, and a vision of it burst into her head. Shock made her whimper.

An instant later, she was released, half-flung upon her pillows. Raith threw himself to his feet, a weal of agony in his breast. He felt her revulsion as acutely as if she had spoken of it. The fluttering touch against his mutilated skin, followed by a muted squeal of protest, had been enough to jerk him into awareness. He knew it to be his own doing, even as he extricated himself from the intensity of his passionate demand upon her. He had lost control—and come by his deserts.

'I beg your pardon,' he jerked out hoarsely. 'I forgot myself. It will not occur again.'

He thought, as he turned from her, that she reached out to him. Her voice followed him as he got to the door.

'Raith, wait!'

He halted there, but he did not turn. 'It is of no use, Rosina. I cannot do it!' Then he was gone.

* * *

The day being a degree finer than any that had gone before, Rosina took herself outside for a breath of fresh air. She told herself that she must do so while she might, for November was almost upon them. She did not truly expect that Raith would come riding in. And if he did, and she caught him thus unawares, it was unlikely that she would be treated to anything other than the distant civility to which she had been subject for the last several days.

It struck her that it was Monday, and she had been married for a week. If those first three days had been tempestuous, at least that had been better than this dull emptiness which made the time pass slowly. She could not even enliven her existence with an attempt to render Raith Manor more homelike. Her one effort had been crushingly rejected.

Upon the morning after her husband's abortive entry at her bedchamber—for which she had railed in turn at her own irrational fears and at his absurd sensitivity!—Rosina had come down to breakfast to find that her place had been changed so that she must sit upon Raith's left hand.

'His Lordship's orders, m'lady,' Kirkham had said apologetically. 'He instructed me on no account to allow it again to be altered.'

Pride had driven her back to the original terms of the contract. She was here on sufferance, merely to provide a means to an end. That Raith could countermand her request to the servants proved that he did not consider her to be mistress of his home. Her interference was not wanted.

As for that other matter, she must assume that His Lordship's requirement for an heir was to be put aside indefinitely. That one attempt—which she had bungled disastrously!—was to be the end of it. If only he had warned her of his coming. She would not have been shocked into remembering. She would have prepared herself to receive his caresses. So different from the foulbreathed fumblings of her guardian. Lord, the fever of Raith's kiss! How could she know that it would flame thus in her most secret depths?

The loss when he left her had been unbearable. The intensity of the sensations he had aroused had alarmed her, but the instant he had let her go, a tempest of longing had erupted within her. If only he had kissed her once more! She knew she would have responded quite differently. But he had instead taken hurt, and his withdrawal was complete.

They met only at dinner, and once at breakfast. Rosina had tried to reach him, but his barrier was of ice. He was polite, treating each overture with courteous attention—which did not extend to looking at her beyond an occasional glance of cool detachment. Rosina wanted often to hit him! Anything to break through that aloof isolation. She missed his violent outbursts, even his cynically bitter remarks.

Rosina had abandoned her efforts to thaw him out. She had hoped that Sunday would keep him at home, thinking that a whole day together must break down his reserve. But he had instead driven out, and Kirkham had told her that he had gone to spend the day with his maternal relations. Disheartened, Rosina had feigned sickness, refusing to appear at dinner last night, and requesting a tray to her bedchamber. Joan had attended her, and she had indeed felt so low that her poor appetite had lent colour to the fabrication.

A half-formed hope that her absence might rouse her husband to enquiry was found to be vain. He neither sent to her, nor ventured—as Rosina had secretly dared to envisage—to enter her bedchamber to find out how she did.

This morning, driven by loneliness, Rosina had written

to Gatty. Her old nurse would be anxious, and she had promised to let her know as soon as she could that all was well. She could hardly do that. But since Toly Aughton would be reading the letter, Rosina was obliged to write in coded phrasing, trusting that Gatty would read between the lines. She mentioned cagily that her lord had an unfortunate scar on his cheek about which he was a trifle sensitive, knowing that her nurse would instantly realise that this was the deficiency over which they'd had such earnest cogitation. She said that a degree of understanding might have been set up but for this circumstance, and that she wished it might not prove a barrier to an achievement one day of that sort of happiness that had attended the marriage of her dear mama and papa. Gatty would know from this that her feelings had become involved, and that her path was strewn with difficulties.

Rosina was glad that it was outside of her power to explain the extent to which she had allowed herself to warm towards her lord, for she did not know the answer to that herself. She knew only that she had started out with the intention of living a separated existence in a cold marriage meant only for her protection. Instead, she was beset by yearnings that she barely understood, and remembered glimpses of a ravaged creature whose distresses had played upon her heartstrings. She could not conceal from herself that Raith had engaged her sympathies.

She had ended her letter with an oblique reference to the state of the house and grounds, adding that she was glad at least to be the means of enabling His Lordship to make much-needed improvements.

The reminder of the ills that Raith had intimated were due to the activities of his half-brother had caused her to wonder again about the ash-strewn lawns at the front. Rosina had sealed her letter, written the direction to the

Brinklow Receiving Office and laid it aside, intending to ask her husband for a frank. She had sent Joan to fetch her a shawl, and, donning it over her blue kerseymere gown, had come outside.

She had been strolling for about fifteen minutes, puzzling over the state of the grounds, when the sound of horses reached her from behind. Turning, she perceived a phaeton turning in at the main gates. It contained one gentleman, heavily coated against the cold, and a liveried groom. A trifle of apprehension stirred in her breast. It was the first visitor she had seen since she had arrived. How was she to greet him? She watched the approach of the vehicle down the long central drive, and realised as it came closer that the gentleman driving was none other than Raith's lawyer.

She moved back towards the house, experiencing a rise of delighted anticipation at the prospect of seeing a friendly face—and one she knew at that.

'Lady Raith!' uttered Mr Ottery in a tone that gladdened her heart.

In a moment, he had handed the reins to his groom, and jumped down, doffing his hat. Rosina felt her proffered hand taken in a strong clasp, and found the well-remembered kindness in his face as he smiled down at her.

'How do you do, ma'am?' he asked, with real interest. 'I am very glad to see you again. How do you go on?'

'Mr Ottery! Oh, you cannot imagine how nice this is! I am safe enough, I thank you.'

'Safe!' He eyed her in frowning question. 'I hope so indeed.'

Rosina blushed, stammering out, 'I d-did not m-mean to say that. I am v-very well, I assure you.'

'I am glad to hear it, ma'am. You are settling in, I hope?'

'Settling? In some sort, yes.' What was she saying? In an attempt to gloss over this ticklish subject, she hurried into speech again. 'You have come to see my husband, I dare say. He is out riding. He does so every day. Indeed, I never see him but at meals.'

She thought she detected concern in his face, but he said nothing untoward. 'Ah, yes. I know His Lordship to be extremely occupied about the estates. It is often the case, when first a gentleman takes possession of an inheritance.'

Rosina smiled waveringly. 'I know nothing about it, Mr Ottery. The bargain is being carried out—in most respects.'

He looked as if he might probe the matter, but just then the sound of hoofbeats, travelling fast, interrupted them. From between the trees on the other side of the house, a horseman came cantering through on to the drive. It was Raith.

He saw the lawyer and reined in to a trot, riding up to where Ottery and Rosina stood. He touched his hat to his wife.

'Ma'am, your very obedient.' Then he turned to the lawyer, and smiled, holding down his hand. 'A thousand welcomes, my friend! Do you bring glad tidings? Do not tell me that your cursed legal complexities are any longer to keep me from my purposes.'

'By no means, my lord,' responded the other, laughing. 'I am come with papers a-plenty for your signature, but no quibbles, I assure you.'

'Excellent!'

The marked difference in his greeting of his lawyer, to that which he had extended to herself, had worked powerfully upon Rosina's feelings. He was insufferable! How dared he treat her so? After all his protestations, his tender mouthings, thus cruelly to shut her out. She could not think how she had accepted it for so many days. What, was she to be thus slighted by the man who had shown her so violent a passion? He was not indifferent to her, as it would seem he would have her believe. Why should she endure it?

Vaguely she heard Raith advising his lawyer to send his equipage round to the stables. 'I will meet you in the library, Ottery.'

He rode off towards the rear of the house, and she waited in a state of quivering indignation while Mr Ottery instructed his groom. She had no intention of betraying herself, but only to say that she expected to see him later in the day. But the lawyer most unfortunately said quite the wrong thing.

'My dear Lady Raith, forgive my interference, but I know His Lordship of old. His mask is a shield. He will lower it in time.'

Tears stung her eyelids. 'Oh, it was not always up so stiffly, Mr Ottery. Only I am lumped among those evil crones with whom he had past dealings, with no opportunity to redeem myself.' She caught herself up. 'I should not have said as much. Forget it, pray!'

He took her hand. 'Don't mind me, ma'am.' She thought he was going to say more, but he evidently checked himself. He pressed her hand instead. 'Take courage!'

Releasing her, he went off, heading for the front door. Rosina bit her lip, blinking away the threat of weeping.

The library at Raith Manor was, unlike the rest of the house, a room almost fully furnished, with cases wall-to-wall filled with books, and a sturdy oak table that served for a desk. Two long windows let in plenty of light, and a cheerful fire burned in the grate, flanked by two large chairs, with seats and cushioned patches of leather at both head and arms.

In these, Raith and his lawyer had settled, once a quantity of papers had been read over and signed. Raith was conscious of an easing of his inner tension—not entirely due to the happy nature of the business that had brought Ottery.

He poured them both Madeira and handed one of the glasses across. Then he stretched his booted legs out and crossed them at the ankles, sighing deeply.

'You must be relieved to have the business settled, my lord,' remarked Ottery, with the smile that always warmed his employer.

'It is so very much needed, Ottery, that I must say I am.'

'Do you really mean to use the substance of your means to bring the place about?'

'You are afraid that it may swallow the whole, I dare say,' guessed Raith, catching his concern. 'No, Ottery, I hope by good management to restore the estates into decent repair so that they may pay for themselves again. But I have warned everyone that this will take time. We will only put the most urgent of requirements into immediate effect.'

'I am relieved to hear it, sir. What of Longridge? Do you wish me to look about for a new agent, as we discussed?'

Raith shook his head. 'I am perfectly satisfied that Longridge was not to blame for the deteriorations. Indeed, he is obviously delighted to be able to offer better prospects to my tenants. And they trust him, Ottery. I have heard over and again how he tried to halt the decline, or play off the income from those with less to lose against that missing from the poorer element.'

He was glad of Ottery's approval. 'That is good to hear, my lord.'

He was surprised then to see that his lawyer dropped his gaze to his glass, and turned it, looking at the ruby liquid within. What ailed him? This was unlike Ottery. Had he something on his mind? He was about to question it, when the lawyer forestalled him.

'What of your marriage, my lord?' he asked, looking up.

Raith felt a hollow enter his chest. 'What of it?'

'Is it satisfactory?'

Eyeing him narrowly, Raith thought he detected a trifle of consciousness in his lawyer's gaze. He recalled that Rosina had been speaking to him before he arrived. He had known that Ottery was coming today, for he'd had his letter yesterday. But she had not known! Raith sat up sharply.

'What has she said to you?' he rapped out.

Ottery's eyebrows rose. 'Lady Raith, my lord?'

'Who else? Come, Ottery, I am no fool! My wife is apt to blurt out anything that is in her head—and then be sorry for it. She is not, I know well, in good spirits, and you caught her unawares.'

To his consternation, his lawyer gave him a look of rare severity. 'Why is she not in good spirits, my lord?'

Raith set down his glass and jerked to his feet, pacing away a little, the unruly beat of his pulse overloud in his own ears. He halted, turning to face Ottery.

'Why ask me? It is my fault—you've guessed that much.'

'Then why will you not mend it, sir?'

Before this one true friend, Raith could throw off the burden of concealment that he had put upon himself in the presence of his wife.

'Would that I knew how, Ottery! Or whether indeed I

should.' He came back and re-seated himself, sighing deeply as he took up his glass again. 'My friend, have I made the most terrible mistake?'

The lawyer looked deeply concerned. 'I warned you against a too-hasty decision, my lord. You will recollect that you were adamant. If it is a mistake, you can only now rectify it by pursuing your course. As for Miss Charlton—or rather, Lady Raith—I fear her interests are not being served as perhaps they might.'

'What do you mean?' demanded Raith narrowly.

Ottery folded his lips. 'I would not wish to presume upon my position, my lord.'

'By thunder, Ottery, don't do that! You know how I value both your advice and your friendship. I do not forget what I owe you. Say what you wish to me, but be plain, I beg of you!'

The lawyer set down his glass. 'Has she deserved of you such coldness? She does not know, I presume, that you chose her—above any other, my lord.'

'Do you blame me?' Raith protested. 'Only think what the others were like!'

'My lord, you did not select Miss Charlton merely because she was a cut above the rest,' said Ottery gently.

Raith gave a bitter laugh. 'You see too much, my friend.'

'Yet—your pardon, but you bade me speak plainly— you have not, for want of a better way to say this, taken advantage of your rights.'

Impossible to answer that! He could think of nothing to say, so he remained silent. No doubt Ottery would guess from it that he was perfectly right.

'Perhaps,' went on the lawyer, 'the lady in the case may be wondering why this does not occur.'

Raith frowned in quick suspicion. 'Did she say anything? No, she cannot have spoken of that!' He rubbed his forehead in painful concentration. 'Ottery, there is some mystery. I felt it from the first and, from things she has let fall, I have become convinced that this is so.' He met the lawyer's eyes. 'She married me for a reason other than the one she gave.'

'So also did you,' Ottery pointed out.

'True, my friend. But I fear my wife's reason is less palatable than my own.'

It was the first time he had put it into words—and it was as far as he could go. He had left Rosina that night, driven by the depth of his own self-disgust as she struggled to free herself from his grasp. He had been unable to pursue his need of her, even though she had called out to him. Her revulsion, as he had then thought, was born purely of her recoil from the ugly blemish of his face.

It was only later that he had, in calmer mood, become slowly convinced of his error. She had recoiled, but there had been more to it than that. He had found himself going through the events of that night, in moment-by-moment detail. Rosina's first inexplicable terror. The shivering limbs. The anguish of her utterance: 'It is not you, Raith.'

Who, then, had it been? Whose presence in her bed-chamber had been in her mind? What vile happening had she remembered that caused her to fight against his ca-resses—*before* her fingers felt his face? He had been re-called to his senses—as how could he not be when her fingers fatally touched his cheek?—and had retreated from her presence. But what if some other man had not retired? What if he had forced his entry, and sullied the purity of the future Lady Raith?

Chapter Five

Rosina was glad to encounter Mr Ottery at the breakfast table on Tuesday morning, for she had been afraid he might leave before she had an opportunity to say farewell. She had met him at dinner, where, to her chagrin, he was seated opposite herself, and on Raith's right hand. Her husband could tolerate his lawyer's gaze without difficulty. But his wife was not permitted to look at that side of his face, for fear of her non-existent disgust of it!

No opportunity had offered for her to be private with Raith, despite the fact that he had been home all day since Mr Ottery's arrival. Perhaps it was as well, for her emotions towards him were so tangled that she felt certain she would only destroy all hope of breaking down his reserve. He had been a trifle less remote at dinner, not quite thawed, but certainly not as formal. Not, she dared swear, for any other reason than the presence of his lawyer.

Rosina had chosen to wear the damask grey gown that had served for her wedding, realising only after she came down—and by Mr Ottery's widening eyes—that it was scarcely appropriate. Her spouse had on a cloth suit of blue, while the lawyer's usual black had been augmented only by fresh linen.

She had thought, from the way Raith suddenly shifted to the fire a moment after her entrance, that she had angered him. But his slightly softened manner towards her seemed not to bear it out. But perhaps Raith had changed only because Mr Ottery took pains to secure her participation in any conversation—an effort for which she had been grateful.

Ottery had spoken of the estates as they had been in the time of Raith's father, recalling his early association with the family. He had taken over the practice from his own parent, pleased to be honoured with the continued trust of most of his father's clients.

'If he was anything like you, Ottery,' Raith had said, smiling, 'I am sure the honour was more on our side.'

Ottery had disclaimed, and talked of another of his clients, and an acquaintance with Lord Brook of Warwick Castle. This led to a discussion on the history of Warwick, which lasted until it was time for Rosina to leave them. She had not gone to the saloon, saying that no doubt they had further business to discuss and that she would only be in the way.

The fact that Raith was also at the breakfast table when she entered this morning was not entirely unexpected. He was dressed in his green riding frock and buckskins, but he would hardly go out before his lawyer had left. Rosina was instantly conscious of nervousness, for it seemed to her that he regarded her somewhat narrowly as she came to the table. It turned out that both men had finished their meal, and Mr Ottery was upon the point of departure. Recalling her letter to her nurse, and expecting that Raith would leave immediately after seeing him off, she stopped him as he made for the door.

'A moment, my lord.'

He halted, turning with a slight frown. 'Yes, ma'am?'

She was daunted, but said with a little diffidence, 'I only wished to ask if you will frank a letter for me, sir.'

'Ah.' He seemed to hesitate. 'Certainly. If you will bring it to the saloon, I shall do so as soon as I have seen Ottery to the door.'

'Thank you, but there is no hurry.'

'When you have done with breakfast, then,' he said. There was a pause, then he added quickly, 'I wished, in any event, for an interview with you.'

An interview! Dear Lord, for what purpose? The formality of his announcement chilled her, and she sank into her chair.

Mr Ottery came up to her, and took her hand. She thought there was reassurance in his smile. 'I will hope to see you very soon again, Lady Raith. Keep well.'

She was obliged to clamp down on a rise of emotion. Would that he could stay! He had brought a change to the atmosphere of Raith Manor—and that softening on her husband's part. If only it might persist! The two men went out, and she took up her fork to address a plate of baked eggs. But the consciousness of the coming interview with Raith had destroyed her appetite, and she could only manage a mouthful or two. She drank a cup of coffee, and then rose with determination. If she must face it, she had better get it over with.

She went swiftly upstairs to fetch her letter. By the time she returned to the saloon, Raith was already there. He was standing at the window, looking out over the desecrated lawns. He turned as he heard her enter.

Rosina steadied herself, and walked boldly across to him, holding out the letter. He took it from her, and looked at it. Dully, she thought.

'I have not a pen to hand,' he said. 'I will sign it later, and give it to Kirkham to send to the post office.'

He moved into the room, and laid the letter on the mantelpiece. Then he stood for a moment, silent, looking down into the fire.

Rosina could see only the loop of his tied-back hair against the tanned skin. She felt her pulse start up, and a flutter at her stomach. What did he want? The waiting began to chafe her. She crossed to a chair—careful to choose one that would admit of his being able to turn his bad side away from her—and sat down, gripping her hands together in her lap. Still he did not move. She could not endure this! She had to speak. She could not help the tremor in her voice.

'What is it you w-wanted to see me about, my l-lord?'

A groan escaped him, and he flung a hand up to his forehead. 'Oh, dear God, Rosina!'

He dropped his hand after a moment, and turned. His ravaged countenance drew from her a swift indrawn breath. He looked haunted, and she knew instantly that his barrier had been dictated by suffering.

'What is it, Raith?' she asked, anguished.

He threw up a hand. 'Don't ask. I cannot answer you.' He made an effort to pull himself together. Hell and damnation! He had known how hard it would be to be with her, and obliged to discuss more than the commonplace. His feelings threatened every moment to get the better of him. And he could not let that happen. He would not gain her trust by ranting at her. On the other hand, he was no nearer to gaining it—as Ottery had pointed out—by his persistent withdrawal.

He wished that his lawyer had not thus advised him, though he knew well that he was right. Ottery had been adamant that he must seek out the mystery, whatever it might be. And he should do it, not through his lawyer's enquiry—as he had himself suggested—but by asking his wife.

'It is your best chance of securing your own happiness,

my lord. To have me spy upon Lady Raith will serve only to alienate her affections. Try, if you can, to get upon terms that will bridge this iniquitous divide. Then you may ask her, and she will trust you enough to tell you.'

Well, let him begin with the business at hand. At least it would open the way to conversation—without entering dangerous waters. He moved to take a chair, noting with mixed emotions as he did so that Rosina's selected position gave him the advantage of sitting with his right side away from her. So much for her wish to accustom herself. Now that she had successfully driven him from her bedchamber, what need was there to put herself through that particular discomfort?

And she had succeeded in driving him off. No matter how strong his desire, he was unlikely to risk a repetition of the farce of the other night. He had discovered, to his cost, that he could not bed Rosina, if she could not accept him with more than mere duty—overcoming revulsion to do so. She must want him. Worse, she must care. What price that for a marriage of convenience?

But it afforded, he had admitted to himself, a sop to his conscience. Any of the candidates might have come to him tainted. It was unlikely that he could find, by means of advertisement, a lady of unimpeachable virtue. Ottery had warned him of it, and he had accepted the hazard. But he had not anticipated Rosina. He had not bargained for his emotions becoming involved. It was hard indeed to accept the disagreeable possibility—likelihood, even?—that another man had been before him. Even though his suspicion tended to the idea that she had been an unwilling participant in the act.

Until he had found out the truth, he could not deal with the inordinate difficulties confronting him. God knew his ardour was as strong as ever! Seeing her last night in her wedding gown had near been his undoing. But to take her—with, if he read her aright, the utmost care and gentleness—he must control his passion, and overcome both her reluctance and these misguided seedlings of jealous possession.

Enough! Futile to dwell upon it. Let him rather pursue this attempt to follow Ottery's advice, and get upon better terms with his wife. Terms—yes, there were other terms to be looked at. He was to begin with those.

'Ottery has secured the release of my fortune,' he began. 'It will shortly be in the hands of my bankers, and it is time to formalize the financial arrangements between us.'

'Formality again?' Rosina's tone was cheerless. 'Very well, sir. Pray continue.'

'It is only the matter of your allowance, Rosina,' Raith said, a trifle less stiffly. 'It cannot, I regret, be as large an amount as I could wish, for—'

'My lord, I am in need of nothing,' she said quickly. 'I did not marry you for—'

'I am quite aware of why you married me,' he interrupted, with a faint rise of hostility. Deliberately, he amended it. 'Or, at least, of why you say you married me.'

Her breath caught, and she threw a wary glance at him. She had given too much away. What had she said to make him suspicious? She did not speak, fearing what he might ask.

But Raith was already regretting his manner of introducing the subject. Her defences were up. He would not reach the truth this way. He backtracked.

'There are bound to be items that you will need, apart from the obvious—'

'The obvious?' she cut in, dark eyes flying to his face.

'For God's sake, Rosina, do not take an affront into your head!' he begged, seeing her expression. 'I am talking of clothing. You are a peeress. You need gowns suited to your station.'

Involuntarily, Rosina looked down at the faded open robe of blue floral, worn over a dimity petticoat. Another of Louise's cast-offs that she had imperfectly altered to fit her trimmer figure. The implied criticism sent heat into her cheeks, and she fidgeted with the set of the garment.

'You need not look like that,' came Raith's gentler tones. 'It is not your fault.'

The black orbs rose again to his, defiance in them. 'Only in having married you.'

There was instant hurt at his eyes. She had wanted to hurt him! The realisation smote her conscience, and she looked away, her fingers wafting to the fluttering at her bosom.

'I d-did not m-mean that,' she uttered, low-voiced.

'If you did, I must be the last to blame you,' came the leaden response. 'However, it is too late for regret.'

'You can say that?'

His glance raked her. 'What does that mean?'

Rosina's hand crept up to her neck. 'N-nothing.'

'It was not nothing.' He waited, but his wife remained steadfastly silent, refusing to look at him. Raith fought down an inward sigh. 'Never mind. Let us return to the point of this discussion. An allowance is a simple necessity. You cannot be forever applying to me.'

'I have no intention of applying to you!' she flashed. Checking herself, she bit her lip. 'I b-beg your pardon.'

'You need not,' Raith said dully. 'I am aware that I have made it difficult for you to speak to me with any degree of ease.'

Rosina looked down at her hands, hardly conscious of her repetitious pulling at her fingers' ends. 'I brought it on myself, my lord. I overstepped the boundaries of our agreement.'

'Yes, you did, by thunder!' he returned. 'But you know well that we have long thrown that agreement out the window.'

There was reproach in her eyes. 'I thought so, yes.'

Raith sighed. 'You need not look at me so. I have already admitted that the fault was mine.'

Rosina kept her gaze steady on his. 'Do you regret our marriage, Raith?'

'Not that, no!' He took a step towards her, and checked. 'It has been only a week. We must give it time.'

'Willingly, my lord. But what is the use of assigning blame, if there is to be no change?'

A slight smile creased his mouth. 'That is why we are here.'

'Oh? I thought you said it was an "interview".'

There was a silence. He eyed her with a resurgence of the emotions he had been keeping in check. Those expressive eyes, with such power to move him. She could sweep him in seconds from desire, to fury, to remorse, to tenderness. She roused him in every possible way. So readily could he become her slave, if he had not so fervid a need to be her master! And yet he would have her confide in him, that he might free himself of restraint. As if he could free himself of his own chains! It would be laughable, if it were not so tragic.

'What is it you want of me, Rosy?'

It was involuntary, said with a sigh, and he did not know that he had shortened her name to a child-like endearment. To Rosina, it was as if the barriers were coming down. She answered with no thought of preconception.

'I want you to be yourself! I hate it when you retire into your shell. I had rather you railed at me, or threw at me your bitterest acrimony. Anything—than that you should treat me with this civil *indifference*. I know it to be a lie!'

He looked away. What would she say if he told her that it was the only way he could induce himself to keep his hands off her? Recoil, belike. And if she did not, and he gave in to temptation, the very touch of her would drive him into unwise accusation. Unwise—and unfair.

'Accept my apologies,' he said as gently as he could. 'I will try to do better.'

Rosina subsided in defeat. She felt quite as much shut out, and she did not know why. For all his changed tone, there was an indefinable barrier still. A withdrawal—but one even more difficult to penetrate. Instinctively she felt that it had less to do with his self-loathing than with her. In some way, he found her wanting.

Raith saw the vulnerability creep over her features, and she was again the waif he had married. Inwardly he cursed, and rose, crossing to the window so that he need not see her. He spoke without turning round.

'You may have more need of funds than you know. We cannot forever avoid meeting with our neighbours, and you must prepare for it. They will soon be returning from London for the winter break. We will have to put up some kind of show together, for the sake of appearances.'

He turned on the words, and saw, with a sense of shock, that Rosina was looking deathly pale, the coal-black eyes regarding him with stunned surprise. Her lip was quivering, and her hands were so tightly clasped together in her lap that the knuckles jutted out white. Concern gripped him.

'What is the matter?'

'You said I should live retired,' she uttered on a gasp.

Raith frowned. 'Yes, but I did not mean without any sort of intercourse.'

'There was to be no social life,' Rosina protested.

'That is quite impossible. A man of my rank cannot live as a hermit, especially not in the country.' He came a step or two towards her. 'It will not be so very bad, Rosina. There are, unfortunately, no other peers in this immediate vicinity, which means that I cannot help but attract the interest of the gentry hereabouts. Furthermore, I have put a notice of our marriage in the *Gazette*, and—'

'Dear Lord, the *Gazette*!' she echoed, aghast.

'It is usual, you know,' he said, on a note of puzzlement. 'I regret the necessity, but it had to be done.'

'Why had it to be done? Why must anyone know of it?' She sounded frantic, a rise of panic in her voice.

'What in thunder is the matter, Rosina? What objection can you have to be seen to be my wife?'

'It is not that,' she said in a tetchy tone.

'Then why should you care?'

Why? Dear Lord, but for a very good reason! Only she could hardly tell Lord Raith.

She was up, pacing the room. Raith watched her, tweaking at her fingertips one moment, the next throwing her hands to her face in another of her unquiet gestures. In growing alarm, he wondered at her thoughts.

They were frantic. Suppose her guardian were to read of it? Dared she hope that he would not make trouble? And what—Lord help her!—what of that other dread creature? If he did not see the announcement for himself, he was bound to hear of it, for he moved in circles where gossip was ever rife. What if he spoke of it? Dear Lord, she might meet with his acquaintances! Herbert Cambois was not his only gaming crony. And he was of this county, though in the northernmost part. She had naïvely thought it a sufficient distance from here.

'They were bound to know of it sooner or later,' she muttered. 'But later, please God! I had not thought the mischief would be out this early.'

Halting, she turned on her husband, and found him regarding her with a heavy frown. Of suspicion? Well might he think her behaviour deserving of it. But that was past mending. This was a disastrous turn.

'Who will come here? Who is it you expect?'

'My immediate neighbours,' he answered cautiously. 'There may be others from further afield. The curious are bound to wish to meet you.'

'You knew this!' she accused. 'And you never warned me. I asked you what you expected of me, and you would not say.'

'I said, if you recall, that we would have to work it out as time went on,' he pointed out.

It was true, Rosina conceded, but it did not help. 'This is not what I bargained for.'

'What did you bargain for, Rosina?' he demanded sharply. 'You have spoken of protection. Who is it you fear?'

'No one.' She whisked about, pacing rapidly away from him, pulling at her fingers. 'It is only that I did not wish for such a life. Had I known of it, I should not have married you. I do not wish to be obliged to indulge in that sort of social interaction.'

Raith curbed his impatience with difficulty. Better to reassure her, than demand enlightenment. She was clearly too afraid to give him any rational answer.

'I am sorry if the necessity upsets you. I have no more wish than you to engage in social activities. But the surest way to invite excessive interest is to try to avoid such contacts. If we accept social intercourse, but do not ourselves initiate it, we will soon be classed as dullards, and people will be glad to leave us alone.'

Rosina checked, a set look in her face. By that time, the damage would have been done. She did not dare to hope that either Herbert Cambois or his odious friend would leave her alone. At the least, their knowledge of her whereabouts was bound to lead to unpleasantness.

Yes, she had entered into this marriage for protection. Once securely a wife, she knew neither could physically touch her. But that did not mean that they could not harm her. Or, which was worse, her husband.

'Lord Raith,' she said flatly, but with a giveaway tremor in her voice, 'it was ag-greed that I should live r-retired upon your estates. And that is what I intend to d-do. I shall engage in no s-social intercourse. If anyone p-presents themselves here, I shall r-refuse to see them.'

'Oh, indeed?' he said, equally flat—and dangerous beyond words, the livid welt standing out on the stern line of his cheek. 'Then, by thunder, Lady Raith, you have much to learn of me! You will do precisely what I tell you.'

Rosina's bravado collapsed. She threw her hands over her face. 'I can't, Raith, I can't!'

Caution vanished. He crossed the room, and seized her hands, pulling them down. 'Why, Rosina? Tell me why!'

'I cannot! There is no other reason.'

'No other? You have given me no reason at all.' He took her shoulders and shook her. 'Rosina, I will not be denied in this! I must know what happened to you, I tell you. What skeletons have you in that closet of yours?'

'None,' she cried frantically, pushing against his arms. 'You have more skeletons than I!'

'Don't try to fob me off! I will find you out.'

She struggled vainly in his strong grip, thrusting at his chest. 'Let me go! You will tell me nothing of yourself— yet you expect me to give up my secrets.'

Raith pounced on this. 'So there is something! I knew it.' He shook her again. 'Tell me!'

'No! You are mistaken—there is nothing to know,' she uttered desperately, trying to pull away.

He would not let her. 'Who is it who frightened you so? Believe me, I am no fool. What is the explanation for your upset in your bedchamber the other night? The man, Rosina! Who was he?'

She gave a gasp, and stilled. 'What did you say?'

'You had some sort of encounter, did you not? What man was involved?'

Rosina wrenched herself out of his slightly slackened grasp, backing away, and looking up at him with sudden fierceness in her black eyes. 'What do you mean? How— *involved*?'

Raith paused. That had been foolish. Now she would believe him suspicious of her. He wanted to pursue the subject, but the change in her dictated caution. More in that strain, and he would alienate her utterly. He drew a breath to steady his pulse, realising only now how uneven it had become.

'I meant nothing untoward,' he said raggedly. 'Not on your part.'

He was suspicious! How could he think it? But of course he could. She had known how it must be, which is why she had been careful to conceal it all. Men could not be trusted in the matter of the honour of their women. Mama had taught her that, when she was preparing her for—as she then thought—a normal married life to be looked forward to. The least hint of lightness would arouse a demon of jealousy. Men, Mama had said, might be as unchaste as they pleased—had not Raith even spoken to her of his amorous adventures when he had talked of the effect of his scar upon women?—but their wives must be beyond reproach. Nevertheless, the intimation that he thought it, even if he believed her innocent of blame, hurt her so much that, in that moment, she hated him for it.

All at once she recalled how he had put her from him. Not physically, but mentally, earlier in this dreadful discussion. The barrier was now explained. He thought her impure, and he would not touch her. There was nothing she could say. It mattered little what she said, if she were to try to explain. Without proof, he would never believe her.

She looked at him, unknowing that her eyes were sombre. 'Well, you have made up your mind, I suppose.'

About her guilt, Rosina meant. But Raith took it differently. Yes, he had made up his mind. There was no escaping the burden. No matter her fears, she would have to face the inevitable.

'I will take you to Banbury tomorrow. It is the nearest large town, and there are one or two modistes from whom you may purchase gowns a trifle closer to current fashion.'

Rosina thought that he was wilfully misunderstanding her. There was no point in arguing.

'You command me, sir,' she replied, on a distinct note of sarcasm. 'I must obey.'

Upon which, she walked out of the room, leaving Raith fuming. Whether he was more angry with Rosina or himself, he did not know. He had bungled it thoroughly. Had he not guessed how it would be? All his careful plans for nothing. He had drawn Rosina's enmity.

The chaise bowled comfortably along the road to Banbury, for the lack of rain had left the ground dry. It was a dull day, which was why Raith had elected not to drive his phaeton. He was doubly glad of it after five miles or so, for his temper worsened every moment, and in an open carriage he would have been obliged to hold his tongue against the ears of his groom behind.

'Is it your intention to hold to this attitude indefinitely?' he demanded acidly.

Rosina refused to answer, maintaining her fixed gaze out of the window. He could make her come with him, but he could not make her speak. And how dared he complain of her 'attitude'? What of those days when he had withdrawn into his ice castle, refusing to deal her more than polite civility? Let him now have a taste of his own medicine.

'It is of no use to sulk, Rosina!'

Oh, and had he not sulked? With what unmitigated injustice had he not taken himself out of her orbit for an offence he could only have imagined? Rosina could not forgive him: for the unspoken accusation, for condemning her, for his lack of faith. Most of all, for withdrawing without the slightest attempt to communicate with her.

If he had been gentle, open with her, tried to win her trust—she might have told him all. Instead, he had thrown it in her face. And now he complained of her silence! Could he not see that she was too hurt and angry to converse with him?

'Rosina, I warn you, I will not endure this. You forget yourself!'

It was too much. She turned on him, white with rage. 'Do your w-worst, sir! I care not.'

'You will care soon enough, I promise you,' he returned, 'if I have much more of this.'

The black eyes flashed. 'Are you threatening me, my lord? What will you do, b-beat me?'

'I am sorely tempted!'

'It is no more than I would expect,' she threw at him.

Raith's own eyes burned, and he seized her wrist. 'I have done nothing to deserve that from you.'

A choked sob escaped her, and she dragged herself from his hold. She stifled the onset of tears, clutching her fingers together in her lap. Husky, she spoke without looking at him.

'The rules have changed, my lord.'

He was shamed by her burst of sobs, and a little of his anger died. The last thing he had wanted was to lose his temper with her. But at least she was talking again. Not that he understood what she meant.

'How so?'

Rosina swallowed. Her fury had dulled, leaving a dead weight in her chest. She wanted to say that he had forfeited her esteem, and therefore she had no longer any desire or purpose to be the conformable wife for which he had advertised. But she could not make her tongue say such words to him. Already she had wounded him by an undeserved rebuke. Better that she refused to answer. But if she again relapsed into silence, he would only provoke her out of it.

'How much of my allowance am I permitted to spend, sir?' she asked instead, her tone stiff.

Disappointment struck at Raith. He had hoped to bring her out of this intolerable alienation. If the rules had changed, it was by her hand. She was no longer the vulnerable waif he had married. From the instant he had mentioned that accursed contretemps in her bedchamber, he had lost her to some other creature whom he did not recognize—one who regarded him with hatred. If he thought it would answer, he would attempt a soft approach. Only that, in her present mood, was impossible.

He accepted the change of subject. 'The expense will not come from your allowance. You will need whatever it takes to create the right impression. Do not stint, and tell the modiste to send the bills to me.'

Rosina instantly resolved to spend as little as possible.

Ottery regarded his client with perturbation as Raith marched about his office, the drab greatcoat swishing about his ankles. Raith saw the doubt in his lawyer's face, but refused to allow himself to be deflected. He had explained the urgency of his need, reporting Rosina's reaction to the whole matter of being publicly seen. Not omitting, though without going into detail, how that had provoked such a divisive quarrel that he was now driven to this means of enquiry.

'I care not how you do it, but find out what you can. You can start, I suppose, with this nurse of hers.'

His lawyer frowned. 'I have no direction, my lord. Lady Raith and I corresponded only through the Receiving Office at Brinklow. What is more, I don't even know the woman's name.'

Raith cursed. 'And I had that letter in my hand, by thunder! I cannot remember it, for I was too much out of my head to pay any heed.'

'Out of your head, my lord?'

'You need not look at me like that, Ottery. I know I have ruined everything, and there is no immediate resolution to be hoped for. Which is why I am asking for your help. Think, man! What can you do?'

Ottery considered. 'Do you know anything about this nurse, sir?'

'Only that she is blind and lives in a cottage somewhere.'

'Then it must be within easy reach of Brinklow. I had best begin at the Receiving Office, and check the villages roundabout.' He paused, thinking. 'Is there no other lead, my lord? Have you found out nothing at all?'

Raith's lips tightened. 'There was a guardian in the case. My wife claims that he died, but I think she is lying.'

He hesitated. He had hoped to avoid broaching this, but if Ottery was to appreciate the significance of his need—!

'Either he—or some other man, I don't know—has had at least designs on her virtue, if not...' He faded out, tugging his breath on the rise of emotion.

The lawyer got up from his chair in a good deal of consternation. 'My lord, you are not suggesting—?'

'Ottery, I do not know! Something occurred—of that nature. You are the only person I could trust with such a confidence.'

'Who was the guardian?' said his lawyer, suddenly brisk.

'I believe the husband of one of her mother's cousins.'

'Then it behoves me, I think, to try to find him, assuming he is not dead.'

There was a brief silence. Then Ottery came around the desk, and put a hand on his shoulder. 'Are you certain, my lord, that you cannot find a way through the impasse you have described? I am of the opinion that the results would be happier if you pursued the question with your wife.'

'No doubt,' Raith said dully. 'But that road is, I fear, closed to me.'

'It will not help your understanding with her if she discovers that you have set me to this task,' he warned.

'Do it! I will deal with that when it comes—if I have to.' What other choice had he? Battle was fairly joined with Rosina, and nothing would serve him but this.

The emporium outside which her husband had set Rosina down was not by any means of the first stare. It was hardly, he had pointed out, to be expected in a town like Banbury. Rosina had made no comment until she'd heard that Nadine had been recommended by Mr Ottery.

'Mrs Ottery, he tells me, has taken her custom here, for the woman has the Parisian touch.'

'Is she one of those poor creatures who has escaped from the Terror?' asked Rosina, forgetting to be stiff.

'I dare say,' agreed Raith, warmed by her more natural delivery. 'She has not been here much above two years, I gather, and I must suppose that not all French seamstresses can be accommodated in London.'

However that might be, on entering the portals of Nadine, Rosina felt herself to have been transported to paradise. Never had she seen such a collection of delightful gowns. Not that she had much experience. She had only been previously to any shop of the kind as a messenger for Louise. Not since Mama's time had she gone to a modiste to buy anything for herself—and then she had been so young that only the most demure of gowns had been permitted.

Her reception, when she announced herself to be Lady Raith, was gratifying. Taking her cue from her spouse's words, and not wishing to appear gauche, she said that she had been recommended by Mrs Ottery. *Madame* had at once been sent for by the assistant, and Rosina had the honour to be served by Nadine herself. The woman was indeed French, but she spoke good English, and there was no difficulty in understanding Rosina's needs. No hint of disapproval was given of the obviously ancient fashion of the gown she presently had on—that made-over pink chintz which had belonged to Louise.

Rosina was led about the salon, and shown a quantity of elegant gowns, almost all made with an astonishingly high waist. Rosina had not seen anything like it even in the last of Louise's copies of the *Ladies' Magazine*.

'Ah, but it is de very latest mode, milady,' Nadine assured her, when she questioned this. 'It has come from Paris. All de mesdames at London are wearing it.'

No matter the recent upheaval in their land, it seemed the French were yet the dictators of fashion. The gowns were made up in plain, sprigged or spotted muslin, mostly of white. The modiste assured her that, as a married woman, she was not obliged to wear white, and might with propriety even wear silk.

Rosina was at first overwhelmed, but the lure of new clothes—and those uncommonly à la mode—proved too great. Forgetting utterly her quarrel with Raith for a space, she tried on a variety of gowns and pirouetted about before a long mirror, in a state of delightful enchantment. The new waistline felt odd at first, set a little below the bosom, the skirt falling loosely to the ground. It had less fullness than she was used to, but a deal more movement in the petticoat.

'But de fashion, milady, it is perfect for you!' exclaimed Nadine, and Rosina was indeed gratified to see how well it suited her slim form. She looked taller, and altogether more graceful, she thought. And when Nadine produced a ribbon bandeau, threading it through her hair, the result was much more attractive than her close caps. The modiste showed how her hair could be worn otherwise in a high knot, which gave her the elegance of a long neck.

Rosina had set four gowns aside, together with accessories suggested by Nadine—a green net cloak for the white muslin and a sarcenet scarf to accompany the sprigged walking dress—and was debating between a Turkish robe with lace trimming, and an open robe with a pleated bodice, when a chance remark of Nadine's recalled her resolve to her mind.

'If milady will be advised,' she said, 'de Turkish it is nice, but de pleat it is more becoming to milady's figure. And so,' she added with an arch look, 'shall be more interesting for milord, I think.'

Milord? Raith! Oh, no. How could she have fallen into such extravagance? She was not the young newly-wed Nadine imagined, courted for her charms. She was the wife of Raith's convenience, purchased by advertisement. It was not fitting that she spend so much money. She did not ask the price of the gowns. It might not be London, but she was well aware of the exorbitant cost of female attire.

If there was an undercurrent of another purpose in her decision, Rosina refused to recognise it.

'I am sorry, *madame*,' she said, with real regret, for it was hard to give them up, 'but I fear I must decline all but the white muslin I first chose.'

Nadine looked utterly confounded, but that could not be helped. She said nothing, and Rosina realised one advantage of her status. Traders would take care not to offend her. The modiste had one of her assistants pack up the gown in a bandbox, and carry it outside to where the chaise had been left to await Rosina's pleasure.

She shook hands with Nadine, left the shop—and found Raith waiting for her outside its door. He was looking extremely irate, and the grey eyes glinted as he addressed her in a sarcastic undertone.

'Where, may I ask, are the other bandboxes?'

Unprepared, Rosina bit her lip. 'There is only the one.'

'One?' he repeated ominously. 'One bandbox? And how many gowns does it contain?'

Rosina began to feel sick, wishing that her spirits had not been so uplifted that she was now unequipped to fight back. But it had to be said.

'One.'

Raith's eyes narrowed. His voice was acid. 'Your notions are so nice, I take it, that you could find only one gown to your taste.'

She was nettled by his sarcasm. 'On the contrary, there were several, but I do not need them.'

'How many?'

'I do not know how many!' she retorted, anger rising fast.

'*How many?*'

She jumped, quivering a little. 'Five or six—I think.'

He spoke with careful restraint. 'Then be so good, madam wife, as to go back into that shop, and purchase the other five gowns.'

'No, I—'

'Rosina!'

She fell silent, glowering at him.

'I am not going to argue the matter, Rosina. But I warn you that we will remain here—all day, if necessary—until you do what I tell you.'

Rosina hesitated. He watched the black eyes waver, and kept his own directed at her face. He had been blazingly angry with her, but it was only by sheer effort of will that he maintained the appearance of it. The waif was back, and he could not endure her distress. He saw her crumble, and his heart melted. But he was not going to show it.

With one last defiant flash of the coal-black eyes, she turned from him, and went back into the shop. Raith let his breath go, and moved back towards the chaise.

Rosina went slowly through into Nadine's salon, wondering what in the world she could possibly say. Her humiliation was intense. How could Raith make her do this? Fervently did she wish that she had not let her determination to thwart her husband override her good sense. She might have known that he would react thus. To her cost, she knew him to be uncommonly dictatorial, if not always as peremptory as this. She had no choice but to obey him. How she hated her marriage vow!

She must think fast, for Nadine was coming towards her, a look of interest in her sharp French features.

'Milady?'

'I think—' Inspiration failed her. Dear Lord, what could she say? 'The other gowns, *madame*… His Lordship…' Oh, but this was hateful! She would never forgive Raith.

A look of comprehension came into the modiste's face, and her eyes registered a quick flash of amusement before she veiled them. 'Can it be that milady has changed her mind?'

Rosina was torn between relief and embarrassment, but she seized the excuse. An idea came—too late, but still of use.

'His Lordship has—has reminded me that we have a number of engagements. I—I think it would be better to take all the gowns that I liked. Can you recall them?'

'But yes, milady.' The modiste moved in the direction of the back, clapping her hands at one of her assistants. She gave Rosina an understanding smile. 'Milady would perhaps prefer dat de gowns are delivered?'

To spare her further ignominy while the gowns were packed up? With gratitude, Rosina accepted the offer, and found that there was more to Nadine's solicitude.

'If milady will permit—' She offered the added assistance of arranging the purchase of suitable accessories—bonnets, shoes and gloves—to go with the gowns, and would ask the traders to send their bills to His Lordship. 'If milady will trust to my judgement?'

Milady was only too glad to do so. She had not thought of the inevitable need for accoutrements to go with the new styles. Lord help her, if it had struck Raith! Nadine ascertained the sizes required, and the matter was settled.

Rosina left the shop in a much happier frame of mind. Her heart jumped a little when she saw Raith waiting by the open chaise door. But, forestalling criticism, she spoke the instant she reached him, in a low voice meant for his ears alone—for Parton was in the act of letting down the steps of the chaise for her.

'I have no further bandboxes, but you need not scold. Nadine is to have the gowns delivered—together with anything else I may need.'

Raith nodded, and handed her up into the chaise. But once the door was shut upon them, he turned to her.

'I apologise for my treatment of you, Rosina—but truly, it was the outside of enough.'

She looked away, fidgeting with her fingers. Had she not borne enough? What sort of apology was it, that contained its own excuse? From the corner of her eye, she saw his hand reach out. It closed over her own, and the warmth of it sent a charge of violent emotion hurtling into her chest. Her breath stopped.

'Rosy,' he said softly.

A compression seized her heart. She felt him shift beside her, and then his free hand cupped her face, drawing it round to face him. The grey eyes were tender.

'I can't bear this between us,' he told her gently. 'Can we not find a way through it?'

Rosina fought against the riot in her bosom. Her voice did not wish to obey her, coming out in a husky whisper.

'It was not—of my making.'

'I know.' His fingers played absently with hers, and he grimaced. 'You did say you preferred me to rail at you than to retire into my shell.'

The faintest of smiles wavered on her lips. 'I did, my lord.'

Raith warmed, and there was a swelling in his chest. Then she grew serious again, and his heart sank at her words.

'But that was b-before. There were—things said, Raith. I do not know how they are to be got over.'

'Nor I,' he agreed. A heavy sigh left his lips, and he released her fingers.

The loss struck Rosina hard. A bleak look had crept into his eyes, and she saw it with pain. Oh, dear Lord! He must not think that she did not care. With barely realised intent, she reached out her left hand as if she would touch it to his damaged cheek.

Raith saw it, and reflex took over. His hand shot up,

and seized her wrist just before the fingers reached his face. He jerked her hand away, holding her so tightly that his own hand shook with the effort.

Rosina gasped with pain, unable to help crying out. 'You are hurting me!'

His pulse was thundering in his head. He had not meant to stop her. He could not help himself. He heard what she said, but for a moment he did not realise how he was hurting her. Then he saw her hand, the fingers splayed. He glanced at her face. Her lips were parted in a pose of agony, her eyes glued to her imprisoned hand.

Recollecting himself, he loosened his clutch, and let her go. Rosina snatched her hand back, and grasped it just below the point where he had been gripping it, the fingers still spread as they began to curl. She was staring at it, breathing hard, and Raith saw the angry red weal his fingers had made.

He groaned, dropping his forehead into his hand. 'Hell and damnation!' he muttered numbly. After a moment or two, he straightened, and looked round at her. She was nursing her wrist, her lips pinched together. It must be hurting her still. Remorse bit into him.

'There does not seem to be anything I can say, except to beg your pardon.'

'It makes no matter,' Rosina said in a subdued tone. 'It was foolish of me.'

'For God's sake, don't try to take the blame!' he said forcefully.

She was silent. Raith sank back into his corner of the chaise, and closed his eyes. It seemed that no matter how he tried, he was doomed to failure. What in thunder was he to do?

Chapter Six

Rosina was dressing with a good deal of care. She did not wish to provoke another such outburst as had greeted her last night when she had dared to appear for dinner in an old gown. Raith had flown into one of his rages, demanding to know whether she was determined on behaving in this rebellious fashion forever, and adding a rider to the effect that she might hate him as much as she pleased but she was his wife, and she had better dress the part, or it would be the worse for her.

'And don't dare to tell me that the gowns are not yet delivered, for you brought one with you!'

'Yes, but I did not think it mattered quite yet,' Rosina had defended herself.

'Why in thunder do you suppose I troubled to take you?'

'I know, but there is no one here to see me.'

'Except,' her husband had declared bitterly, 'myself. Spare me the insult of telling me that you don't care how you look before me, for that I know already!'

With which, he had stormed off into the dining-room, leaving her to follow how she might. A frosty silence had reigned at the dinner table, and Raith had vanished after she had left him to his port. Rosina had not seen him since—he was undoubtedly off about his estate business, a convenient excuse for his withdrawal from his wife. She had spent the day in a state compound of misery and resentment.

How had she been expected to know that he desired her to change her appearance when they were in private? Was she supposed to be able to read his mind? It was typical of Raith to take an affront into his head. She had not meant anything of the kind—though she might readily have done so had she thought of it. Well might she hate him! Only did he suppose her to have so little regard for her skin deliberately to provoke him? She did not truly believe that he would raise a hand to her, but in his wild moods his tongue was frightening enough. The memory of his face in quite other mood came back to her. Dear Lord, but he was, when softened, all too endearing—and, oh, so difficult to hate! Either side of him could make her pulse race. It was only the lightning changes that she found so unsettling.

It was better not to take any risks. Accordingly, she enlisted Joan's willing assistance with her toilette, bidding her put forth her best efforts. If there was a stirring at the back of her mind of a wish to know how her husband thought she looked in the new fashion, Rosina suppressed it. She was doing this only so that he might not rail at her again.

She was a trifle late, for Joan was as unhandy yet with her hair as she was herself, never having previously attempted to secure it in the topknot advocated by Nadine. At the first attempt it was a degree lopsided, and a vision of Raith's cynical look made Rosina tear out the pins. He would be bound to make some caustic comment!

'But, m'lady, I thought it looked very well,' protested the maid, sighing.

'It was not straight, Joan. I cannot appear before His Lordship looking like a scarecrow! Let us try it again.'

Thus adjured, Joan set to with a will, and Rosina presently arose from her dressing-table with a style that she considered to be at least respectable. She waited while the maid placed the green net cloak about her shoulders, and examined herself in the long pier-glass with a critical eye. The gown was deceptively simple, with a cross-over front cut low to the bosom, from which the skirt fell in soft folds, and with little sleeves ending in ruffled bands, worn over long tight undersleeves of muslin through which the glow of her flesh could be seen. The green net appeared superfluous.

'Not the cloak,' Rosina decided, slipping it off. 'In the daytime, perhaps, but not now. I hope I don't freeze to death!'

But her blood seemed altogether too active to permit of her feeling the cold, pumping rapidly through her veins as she tripped carefully down the stairs, holding up the unaccustomed looseness of her skirts. What if he was still too angry to meet her for dinner? All that effort wasted! Her heart jumping, she entered the saloon.

Raith was standing by the fire, leaning his arm along the mantelshelf. He was himself attired formally, in that dark coat and breeches from their wedding day, with blue silk to his waistcoat. He looked across at her, and straightened abruptly.

Rosina paused on the threshold, watching his reaction, half-hoping for some word of praise. He was staring, but she could not read his expression. Self-conscious, she averted her eyes, and moved into the room.

Raith's gaze remained riveted upon her. He was incapable of words. She took his breath away! If he had before thought of her as delicate, she was now doubly so. The air of fragility was pronounced, for the litheness of her form was accentuated by the strange style. There was elegance, enhanced by the lifting of her hair, which equally emphasised the elfin quality of her countenance. But above all, she exuded so much sensuality that Raith had only one idea in his head. To sweep her up into his arms, and carry her directly to his bed, there to overbear both her resistance and his own scruples, and make her irrevocably his—and his alone.

A disastrous desire! How could he possibly do it? Rosina would fight him with her last breath. Or would she? He had expected continued defiance, and braced himself to face her renewed enmity. Instead she had presented him with a show of obedience. Was it to mock him? If so, she was wonderfully successful, for he could barely contain his yearning.

It was several moments before he was able to command it. By that time, a hint of colour had risen in her cheeks, and he realised belatedly that he had not even had the grace to compliment her.

'You look—' he was obliged to hesitate over his choice of adjective, for everything he wished to say was ineligible '—charmingly,' he finished lamely.

How inadequate a description. He would have preferred to tell her that she was alluring beyond endurance, but he had not the courage. He watched her lips break into a smile, and found his breath unsteady. One moment more, and his control would break!

'Shall we go in?' he said hastily.

He ought to offer his arm, but he could not trust himself to approach her. He watched her hesitate, eye him uncertainly. Abruptly, he snapped.

Rosina felt him pass her as she made for the door. It slammed shut. Her heart jerked. Raith was leaning against it, the wildness of his features heightened by the livid scar, of which he seemed wholly unaware. He radiated dan-

ger—of a kind that made her pulses leap in an erratic
dance. Thought fled. His hot eyes raked her, and a blaze
of heat rose up inside her as the recognition of his intent
drove the blood thrumming into her veins.

Then he reached for her, and she moved as one in a
trance, drawn intimately close by his strong grip. She saw
only the depths of his avid grey eyes, hauntingly near.
Then they closed, and his lips came down on hers. He
mouthed her teasingly, in so tender a minuet that her
bones turned to water.

Raith felt her sag, and caught her close against him,
increasing the pressure of his lips, while the heady delight
of her here in his arms drove from his mind every thought
but one.

'By God, but I want you!' he uttered gutturally against
her mouth. 'From the first I have wanted you—desperately!'

Rosina heard him with a melting at her heart, and
groaned within his kiss. Her limbs trembled uncontrolla-
bly as she became aware of the heat and hardness of the
form against which she was so tightly held. Her breath
shortened as his lips left her mouth to shift down her
cheek, and breathe flame into the hollows of her neck.
She shivered the more, and her hands came up without
intent, grasping at his shoulders, at his face.

Her hand came in contact with an unexpected ridge,
and on the instant that she took in its significance, Raith
froze. For a few hazardous seconds, Rosina held her
breath, as a chill seeped through the fervid heat between
them, like an ill-omened breeze.

Raith fought against the impulse that bade him fling
away her hand, while the driving force within him sought
to speed him to his goal. Slowly he shifted a little away,
bringing his hand up to cover hers against his cheek, holding it there. His eyes found hers.

'You feel it, Rosy?' he said, low-toned and husky. 'The worst of me under your hand. Can you endure to feel it?'

She answered him from instinct, her voice a shaky whisper. 'You d-do not let me f-feel it. Let go my hand.'

It was hard to invite her touch, but it struck him in that instant that to do so would be to invite also her trust. He removed his hand from hers, setting his teeth, unable to help his own stiffening. He watched the movement of her coal-black eyes, willing himself to remain still as her fingers traced along the lengthy ridging line from his eyebrow, down his cheek, and to the corner of his lip. Never had he been so aware of it!

Rosina could feel the resistance that he was holding in check. The wound under her fingertips felt alien, but not as loathsome as it looked. She felt no repugnance, no pity, even, but a kind of morbid satisfaction, as her curiosity, so long aroused, was at last permitted to be indulged. It was a fascinating contour—and so peculiarly Raith! As if the store by which he set his own worth were contained in this unevenly ribbed line.

She would have liked to dwell longer upon it, but she knew his discomfort was too acute. Regretfully, she removed her fingers, and saw, with an inexplicable pain at her heart, the immediate relaxation of his rigidity. Her eyes went to his.

'Well?' he said, and the tight-lipped demand shot her through with distress.

What was she to say? She could hardly reveal to him the obscurely pleasurable sensations of her exploration! She recalled, with a sense of shame, the story he had told of a female who had obtained some sort of sensual satisfaction from the blemish. His disgust had been patent. What would he think of his wife, if she were to confess to such a feeling? Not that she had been moved in *that* way. It had served rather to give her a sense of intimacy, that he had allowed her a share in his deepest agony.

He was waiting. She must find something to say—that would not cause him to retire behind his protective barrier. And fast, for already his eyes were darkening.

'It is not nearly as bad as you think,' she said quickly. She saw that this statement found little favour, and thought fast. 'And—and now that I have once felt it, there can be no shock in my encountering it again—by accident.'

Raith did not know what he had wanted to hear, but these words did not encompass it. His ardour was already damped a trifle, despite the intense allurement of her nearness. It sank still more. He had hoped for better than this, by thunder! What, had he subjected himself to the excruciating disturbance of her touch, to be rewarded with an assurance that she might no longer expect to be shocked? What was she then—a degree less repelled? He was obliged to her for the mitigation!

'Then I may take it that you would have no objection to allow me to take you?' he said, unable to help a sarcastic inflexion creeping into his tone.

A wash of discomfiture flooded her, and she felt her cheeks grow warm. She matched his acrimony. 'Since when have my objections been the subject of your enquiry? You have always assumed them, and conducted yourself accordingly.'

'Because I see nothing other than duty!' he threw at her. 'It appears that I can make you respond to me, but—'

'What more do you want?' she cried despairingly.

'More than you are prepared to give, it seems.'

Frustration sighed out of her. 'Raith, I have never been other than willing. I am at your service, if you wish for it.'

'At my service!' he echoed, hurt beyond endurance.

'Hell and damnation take you, Rosina! Do *you* wish for it?'

She could not answer him. No, she did not—not if he meant to make her a sacrifice to his bitter self-hatred! She bit her lip, mute defiance in her gaze.

'I am answered, I suppose,' he said roughly. 'Would I knew whom it is I have to thank for it. I swear I would throttle him with my bare hands!'

He moved aside, and opened the door, oblivious of the blaze of anger in Rosina's eyes.

'Go in to dinner. I will join you presently.'

She left him without a word, and Raith crossed to the fireplace and rested his hands upon the mantel, staring down into the smouldering logs.

How much more of a fool was he determined to make of himself? He was shocked to realise that, in his need of her, he would have forgone that jealous possession of her maidenhead to which his emotions made him heir. Blood and thunder! Had he not sworn that he would not make himself master of her before he knew the truth? She had been taken—if it was so!—without her consent by this villainous unknown. But he must have taken her roughly, for she responded—and to his cost!—all too readily to gentleness. She had shown herself more than willing— had not she said as much? But, to his chagrin, she would not invite him in! Had she expressed a wish for his caresses, he would have thrown all caution to the winds.

As well that she did not wish for it, for his resolve was just. He owed that much to his name. Yet the blame was his for the close call. Had he not taken her to task last night for refusing to wear the new gown? If he was bowled over by her appearance, it was scarce Rosina's fault. He dared swear he might expect to see her return to her old garments tomorrow. She was unlikely to invite his cursed insanities a second time.

He sighed wearily, as he turned for the dining-room. Their relationship was deteriorating. And he was no nearer to gaining either her trust or her confidence.

Rosina was so choked with upset that she could not eat. She was glad of the excuse afforded by the delay of Raith's appearance, telling Kirkham curtly, as he came to serve her, that she would await His Lordship. His hateful, impossible Lordship! But she did not say it.

How could he be so unkind? Let him wallow in his bitterness, if he chose. Was she supposed to care? If he wanted her, he might have her at any time. It was his right. She had nothing to say to it. He knew as much. And if he hesitated, she was perfectly aware that it was not through any reluctance on her part, but from the dictates of his own masculine pride.

He had confessed, in the heat of the moment, his desire for her. But she had already known it—if not in her head, in the frenzied fire of her blood in response to him. A lump constricted her throat. Such tenderness as he had shown tonight when first he kissed her! It was that she wished for, if he only knew. If he used her thus, he might overcome all the hideous remnant of her guardian's rude betrayal.

Kirkham had poured her wine, and she reached out a quavery hand. A few sips of the red liquid sent a comforting warmth inside her. The slight relaxation released her tight thoughts, and the truth of her distress seeped into her mind.

She felt isolated by Raith's rejection. He was her husband. She would have taken him only for protection, but he wished for more than that. Yet in her darkest hour, she could not look to him for succour. Both his condemnation, and his insistence that she should enter into public acknowledgement of her position—the occasion of her wearing this horrid gown and its wretched sequel!—were alike to blame.

A thought struck her. What if Raith should not be content with showing her to this small public circle? He had already proven that the arrangement she had believed them to have made had not marched with his own understanding. Did she dare to trust him? Might his decision in this not be as changeable as the fiery friction of his moods?

Her fears rose to the surface as Raith entered the room and took his seat. She tried to quiet them for, as things stood between them, the last thing she needed was to let him see her apprehension. If only she could think that she might have overestimated the dangers. She might hope that Herbert Cambois was too drunk to read the journal. And that other? Why should he take time from his gambling to seek her out now? If it were only true that her acquaintance would be confined to the coterie of this small area, she might be less concerned.

'My lord?' she said impulsively.

He glanced at her. 'Ma'am?'

Her heart sank. Were they back to that? 'I wished only to ask—just how public a life you want me to lead?'

What was she at now? Had his unthinking reference brought on a reminder of her fears? Who in thunder was the fellow? But he must not ask that—not before the servants. Let them at least maintain some semblance of rational behaviour!

Yet Raith found himself unable to help an acid note. 'You can hardly call it leading a public life to be toadying to a parcel of neighbours.'

Rosina breathed a little more easily, nodding at the butler who was offering her a serving of artichoke pie to accompany the baked sole nestling on her plate.

'You will not then seek to take me to London?'

'London!' he repeated with loathing. 'You may be sure I shall not.'

But Rosina was not satisfied. 'Raith, do you swear it?'

He found the black eyes upon him in that vulnerable look that had always power to melt him. He fought the sensation, responding with impatience.

'Have a little sense, Rosina! Do you suppose anything would induce me to lay myself open to the sort of vulgar curiosity that I would be obliged to endure there? The very sight of me would set tongues wagging. No, you need not be afraid that I will drag you into London society.'

Rosina doggedly held his eyes, an unyielding compulsion in the black depths of her own. 'But do you swear it?'

Raith could not withstand her. His chest tightened, and he spoke without hesitation. 'I give you my word.'

He watched a measure of relief creep over her features, and saw her draw in a slow but unsteady breath, sighing it out. Then she turned away, and began to address her food. Raith followed suit, a stabbing at his gut for the hideous certainty that attacked him. If she was this much afraid, how could he doubt of his suspicions? She would tell him nothing. Was it because she feared to meet the villain—to her undoing?

Rosina stared at her maid in ill-concealed dismay, and requested her to repeat herself.

'His Lordship's compliments,' said Joan again, her slow delivery showing how careful she was to recall the precise wording that had been relayed to her, 'and please to join him in the antechamber before you retire.'

Rosina had already been halfway out of her clothes when the knock had come on the dressing-room door. She had leaped with shock, but recollected after a moment that

Raith could not yet have come up. Besides, the knock had come from the door that led to the corridor, not to the antechamber.

Joan had already gone to answer it, opening the door a crack and peering out. 'It's Mr Paulersbury, m'lady,' she had announced, and slipped out of the room. By the time Rosina had recalled that this individual was her husband's valet, Joan had come back into the room with this disturbing message.

Rosina was thrown into an agony of apprehension. What now, dear Lord? Was it possible that he had changed his mind? Did he mean this for an assignation? No, it was too absurd. If it were that, he would wait for the servants to leave, and then come himself to her bedchamber. Realising that she was halfway undressed, she began automatically to resume her gown, and then stopped, horrified.

Wear that again? And invite his abortive caresses? No, Lord help her! Hastily, she instructed Joan to help her to change, beset by horrid sensations. They had not talked again at dinner, after she had extracted that promise. Yet Raith had not disappeared, as she had thought he must. Instead, he had come into the saloon where they had taken tea together, and sat in a chair at a distance, looking abstracted. He had not once glanced at her, not even when she said good night. And now this! What did he mean by it?

When she was attired in her nightgown, and covered with a wrapper of blue linen, tied firmly at the waist, Rosina felt several degrees more secure than she had in the new muslin gown. Her hair was already loosened, and she combed it through and placed over it a mobbed nightcap. The ensemble must, at the least, discourage her spouse from any resumption of physical intimacy.

She dismissed her maid, and went to the door of the

antechamber. Her breath caught, and she put her ear to the wood, listening intently for some sound from within. Perhaps he was not yet there. What if she did not appear? Would he let it be, or come to find her? She fought down the flutters in her stomach. What use to defy him? Even if he did not pursue her, she would not escape a raking on the morrow. Better to get it over with, whatever it was he wanted.

She took hold of the door handle, and cautiously pulled it towards her, peeping around it.

'There is no need to be so shy of me—I will not bite!' came Raith's irascible tones.

Rosina stepped gingerly into the room, closing the door, keeping her back against it, and her fingers about the handle.

Raith was standing by the fireplace, where a two-pronged candelabrum threw light on his face from the mantel. It spread over the area immediately before the grate, in which a small fire was throwing up a lick of flame. The chairs had been set facing each other, in evident preparation for a tête-à-tête.

She looked warily at him. He was also clad in his night gear, a green-lined banyan of yellow silk belted loosely over his long nightshirt. His hair was untied, falling raggedly to his shoulders. Light flickered on his scar with the motions of the candlelight. He looked excessively attractive, and warmth flushed in Rosina's depths. His attitude, however, was far from amorous.

'Come here and sit down,' he said in a tone that brooked no argument. 'I want to talk to you.'

Rosina took a single pace towards him. 'Why could you not talk to me in the saloon?'

'Because I don't want to be disturbed. And there is no necessity to keep the servants awake.'

How long did he mean to keep her awake? Her heart

began to thump. Oh, she knew what this betokened! There was no intent of love-making here. He meant instead to question her, she was sure of it. And he had chosen this place so that she was thoroughly at a disadvantage. For to where could she escape? With the servants abed, he might keep her here all night—and none the wiser.

'Rosina, come here, I said!'

Her lip trembled, and tears sprang to her eyes. 'I d-do not w-want to.'

'Oh, good God!' he exclaimed, and moved quickly.

She backed, fumbling again for the door handle, but Raith was quicker. He took her by the shoulders, and she looked up, white-faced, into his shadowed features.

He brought one hand up and cupped her cheek, quite gently. 'Are you crying? Don't be a little fool, Rosy. I mean you no harm, I swear it! Now, come.'

The threat of tears receded. She allowed herself to be drawn to the fire, where Raith obliged her to sit down. She did so, primly, hugging her wrapper about herself.

Raith stood over her for a moment, watching these signs. How ill-at-ease she was! And no wonder. He moved to the other chair, and shifted it so that he sat at an angle, where the candlelight could only fall upon the good side of his face. He had himself well in hand, but the sight of her had given him a jolt. If she had looked enchanting in her new gown, she was unbearably sweet in the blue wrapper and mob-cap. But mercifully less seductive, although the consciousness that she was naked under the thin chemise that peeped below the bed gown had a deleterious effect upon his concentration.

Enough! He must control his thoughts. There was to be none of that. He hastened to come to the point.

'I want to talk to you, Rosy,' he repeated.

Rosina was a little cheered by his persistent use of the

pet name he had recently adopted for her. It augured a benign beginning at least. Yet still she eyed him askance.

'So you said. What about?' As if she did not know!

A faint smile curved his lips. 'You look at me with so much suspicion. The truth is that I am at a loss, dear wife.'

Rosina's gaze became even more suspicious. 'I do not understand you, sir.'

He relaxed into the chair. 'We know so little of one another.' He threw up a hand as she drew back. 'No, I don't mean to pry into your secrets—not yet. I thought I might rather give you some of mine.'

Indeed? He took her for a fool! She eyed him with a touch of scorn in her dark gaze. 'So that you may induce me to open my closet of skeletons in return?'

'At least you admit the existence of skeletons!'

'I admit nothing!'

His features tightened, and her pulse skittered a little. Let him grow angry! She was equally angered by his trickery. He would get nothing from her by this means.

Raith knew not how to proceed. She had found him out. He had arranged this with just that intent. Over dinner, with the persistent allure of his wife's presence at his side—and the goad of that cursedly suggestive promise she had extracted from him—he had begun to chafe at the restrictions of his marriage. How in thunder could he wait until Ottery delivered his findings? It might take weeks to unearth Rosina's history. Even then, how could he know it was the truth? Only Rosina knew that. Impatient, he had instructed Kirkham to have this room prepared, and ordered his wife's attendance. It began to seem as if he was wasting his time and effort.

The thrust of disappointment spurred him. By thunder, he would get what he wanted from her—and tonight!

He leaned forward again. 'Rosina, we cannot continue

in this way. And by God, there is no need for it! If you will only tell me the truth, we can—'

'What truth?' she broke in. 'That which you have built up in your mind? Oh, I know well enough what you think of me!'

He reached out and caught at her unwilling hand. 'If you truly knew it, you would open your mind to me!'

His fingers came in contact with the wrist he had man-handled on the previous day, and Rosina winced, giving an involuntary hiss of pain, trying to pull away.

'Be still, can't you?' Raith said, looking down. He saw a mark, and loosened his clasp, but tried to draw her hand towards him. 'Let me see!'

'It is nothing,' Rosina said quickly, again attempting to withdraw her hand.

He would not let her, and looked up. What he saw there made him respond with less than gentleness. 'Look at me with resentment in your eyes, if you will, but it is of no use to struggle, Rosy. I will not let you go until I have seen it.'

Her breath shortened. He had so much power to control her! Was she to have no will of her own? She let her hand lie in his, but a burning seed of rebellion grew in her breast.

Turning the hand in his fingers, Raith pushed back the wristband of her nightgown. A thin bruise was exposed there, in the soft flesh of the inside of her wrist. The memory flashed in his mind. In the chaise, when she had moved to touch his cheek. This had been her reward!

'I had no notion that I had hurt you so badly,' he uttered remorsefully.

Had he not? And he so apt to hurt! If not her body, then her heart and mind. But yes, her body. What of the sensations he had aroused in her by the intensity of his passion? And then rejected her only because she could not answer him on his terms. Did he ever stop to consider the distress he was inflicting? No—his temper was too ungovernable.

As if he read her thought, Raith sighed. 'I am a brutish husband, am I not?'

Yes, he was! But she did not say it. Yet almost Rosina suffered a reversal of feeling, as he lifted the wrist to his lips and pressed them gently to the wound. Oh, but he could be tender! Then why had he ever to carp at her? She dared swear that in another moment, if she did not do or say as he demanded, he would be railing again.

Raith covered the wrist, keeping her hand imprisoned within his own, and looked at his wife's face. She was eyeing him again with that wary suspicion in her eyes. How could he blame her?

'Why should you trust me?' he uttered, a harsh note in his voice. 'I said I might give you my secrets, did I not? Will you believe then that I know what it is to be in the power of someone who can force you to do what you would not?'

'You know it?' Rosina snatched her hand out of his, and tucked it into the folds of her wrapper. 'And yet you persist in treating me as if I have no power of my own.'

He was startled at her tone, and as of instinct shifted back, away from her. 'That is untrue! Did I force you that night I came to your bedchamber?'

Rosina stood up abruptly, incensed by his obtuseness, by the single track of his thoughts. 'Is that all that is in your mind? What of your insistence upon my staying in this room to be subjected to your questions? What of the manner in which you seized upon me in the saloon when I came down—'

'You need say no more!' he interrupted. He had risen when she did, and the consciousness of the truth of what she said drove him into defence. 'You may reproach me for that if you will, but as for my questions—I am your husband, Rosina. I have a right to know my wife's history.'

'Then why did you not obtain it before you married me?' she demanded, moving away from the chairs towards the window. 'You cared little enough what I might be—or who, if it comes to that. You did not even wish to see me. Why should you have troubled yourself about my past life?'

Raith felt himself to be on acutely assailable ground. How could he tell her that he had seen her, and not deserve the most righteous rebuke? He was obliged to prevaricate.

'What would you, Rosina? I am a peer of the realm, and that has its obligations.'

She turned on him, the black eyes snapping in the gloomy edges of the pool thrown by the candles. 'Obligations, Raith, which you were ready enough to ignore when it suited you.'

Her chest was so constricted that she could barely breathe, but the tide of burgeoning resentment that had so long been held in was overwhelming. She saw him open his mouth to speak, and forestalled him, her voice trembling with the force of her emotions.

'You t-took a wife from ad-advertisement. You c-cared only for the advantage of your f-fortune. Now—because you choose to—to set store by some incautious w-words that I let fall, I am made the—the scapegoat of your jealous fury!'

Raith followed her a step or two, racked by her distress, but hounded by his own need into defending himself further. 'Do you think I want to believe it? Blood and thunder, Rosina! Can you not see how I am tortured by these doubts?'

'Doubts!' she echoed, husky now, the words coming

thick and fast as the dam of anguish burst the barriers of her characteristic diffidence. 'Do you not see how your doubting t-tortures me? If there were any truth in that t-tenderness with which from time to time you move me—with which you touch my heart!—there would be no room in you for doubting. But it is *false*—and I hate you for it, Raith!'

He was aghast, moving to her. 'Rosina—'

'Do not come near me!' she cried, dashing the welling tears from her eyes, and backing away. 'I do not w-want to hear your cozening words—your soft approaches. They can mean nothing—or you would have faith.'

Raith stopped short. 'Blind faith? Is that what you expect?'

'I expect nothing. I have been given nothing!'

'How can you say so?' he demanded, hurt overriding the turmoil of dismay and guilt to which her grief had given rise. 'Is my regard nothing?'

'What regard? You have no regard for me, but only for yourself!' she threw at him. 'And for your arrogant pride.'

'Is it arrogance that a man should wish to assure himself that his wife is chaste?'

'It is arrogance to assume otherwise.'

'I do not assume it!'

'But you suspect it—and that is enough!'

Raith's fingers clutched at his hair. 'Hell and damnation! That you persist in this refusal to enlighten me can only increase my doubts. Why cannot you see that, Rosina?'

She uttered a mewl of equal frustration, throwing her hands to her face. 'Dear Lord, but you are blind! Raith, if you doubt me, you will do so whatever I tell you, unless you have certain proof. Can you deny it?'

Raith seized her right wrist, and pulled her close, a blaze of anger in his eyes. 'I deny it utterly, though I well might have fallen to so base a level. I have been too many times betrayed by the perfidy of women. You play the innocent all too convincingly, but so may the lowest whore!'

The breath was stopped in Rosina's throat. A white heat of rage drove the blood coursing through her veins. There was no thought in her action. Her right hand was imprisoned, but she pulled back a little. Driving with the whole force of her other arm, she dealt her husband a ringing slap, full on his scarred left cheek.

Raith reeled with the blow, releasing her, and throwing an instinctive hand to the stinging sensation on his face. He recovered in a few seconds and, with the realisation of what she had done, he turned astounded eyes upon his wife.

'Why, you vicious little vixen!'

With automatic intent, he advanced upon her. But Rosina threw up both hands, and the violence of menace in her coal-black eyes gave him pause.

'Strike me at your peril!' she uttered, low-voiced and vibrant. 'You have deserved that of me.'

Then she turned from him, and whisked herself through the door into her dressing-room. With shaking fingers, she turned the key in the lock, and then leaned against the door, panting and spent.

Rosina watched the departing coach from the window of the saloon. The local pastor was the third caller that she had received in the last few days. She was relieved to have rubbed through the ordeal of explaining her non-appearance at church, and could not help reflecting that the absence of her spouse had provided an adequate excuse. Besides, had he been here, she would have been so wrought up that she could not have thought of anything intelligent to say.

She dreaded his return, each day expecting that the evil hour could not be any longer delayed. How was she to find the courage to face him? It seemed incredible that here she was in November, almost two weeks a wife, with no idea where her husband was, or how much longer he meant to be away. She knew only that the last she had seen of him had been his face of thunderous astonishment after she had struck at it.

How had she dared? Her heart misgave her whenever she thought of it. Her moment of triumph had been short-lived. Within a very few minutes of that fatal impulse, every ounce of courage had dissipated with the realisation of what she had done. She remembered the sag of her knees, the sudden horrific thought of the pregnable outer doors. Terror had gripped her at the fierce inevitability of Raith's revenge. She had flown to the door that gave on to the corridor from her dressing-room, and locked it with frantic fingers. It had not been enough. *Her bedchamber.*

Her feet had grown wings as she sped through, fleet as the wind, in her mind a startled question. Was there even a key? Her relief, on discovering it in the lock, had been stupendous. She had fallen upon it, like an animal upon its prey—and had such extreme difficulty in making it turn, that she had cried aloud in her frustration and haste.

Once secured within her own apartments, Rosina had backed from the door to sink down upon the bed, her pulse fluttering wildly in her throat, listening intently for the sound of her husband's approach.

But no footsteps disturbed the eerie quiet of the night. There was no rattling at any of the door handles. She had sat for a long while, mumchance, while the teeth chattered in her head, and her whole frame quivered and shook as she cursed and lamented that hideous loss of temper, and wondered at her own foolhardy audacity.

Actually to hit Raith! Had she run mad? What brazen

defiance had driven her to so insane a proceeding? Oh, but he would make her suffer for it!

But when it had appeared that there was to be no immediate reprisal, Rosina had collapsed in a heap on the coverlet, the inevitable tears coursing down her cheeks. Dismayed guilt had warred with dread, buoying her defences.

How could she have done it to him? She had not meant it. No, dear Lord, that was a lie. She had! He should not have driven her so hard. But what had induced her? Never in her life had she lost herself to such an extreme. Only, how could she bear it? Recalling his words, she broke into a fresh storm of weeping. Oh, but it was shameful of him! To equate her so cruelly with a woman of that sort.

But here the deep voice of conscience prodded her. Raith had right on his side. He deserved that his wife be pure. Only if she had not been—if that evil pair had succeeded in their base design!—Rosina would never have given herself in marriage. Not to any man—let alone one whose bruised spirit had commanded the tenderest promptings of her heart. A fresh deluge of tears accompanied this thought. He ought to have trusted her! Oh, cruel—to withstand every impulse that bade him overcome his doubts. She could not but recognise the portent. He could not possibly care enough. Let him not therefore speak of his *regard*. How could he use her so? She was glad she had assaulted him!

But this fierce resurgence of spirit could not long endure. She knew she had been wrong to do it—bitterly wrong. She could not wonder at her spouse's furious intent of retaliation. She had balked him for the moment. But for how long? Unless she were to run away—which was not an option that recommended itself, for where could she go?—she foresaw that she was doomed to run the gauntlet of his just vengeance. The best she could pray for was for the night to cool him, and mitigate the manner of it.

It had been long before she had been able to rouse herself to get into bed. Even longer before she had slept. For whatever hopes she might secretly have cherished, for the resolution of the difficulties of her marriage, were at an end. Whether or not Raith chose to punish her, he would never forgive her. If he could allow the blow—how could he forget the place where it had struck? She had dealt it to him at his most vulnerable point, and he was bound to suppose that she had done so on purpose.

Her dreams had been unhappy, full of ill-omened fragments where Raith and she were ever at outs. Except once, when she had dreamed that he kissed her—and had been awakened by a heavy-handed knocking at her door. She had started up in alarm, the remnants of the dream fading, to be replaced by the cruel memory of last night.

For a dreadful moment, she had imagined that her husband was come at last, to take his revenge. The vision in her head was armed—with a vengeful stick! Her voice had cracked.

'Who is it?'

'It's me, m'lady. Joan.'

Relief had flooded her, and she had struggled out of bed, and staggered across to unlock the door.

'Why, m'lady, are you ill?' the girl had asked, bobbing.

Rosina had seized at the straw, gratefully. 'Yes. At least, I am faint—and have the headache. I will—I will remain in my bed.'

She had accepted with gratitude her maid's assistance to clamber back between her sheets, for she did indeed feel dreadfully weak. She had lain there all day, afraid to get up for fear of encountering Raith. No message or demand had come from him, and she had not dared to ask concerning his whereabouts. She could only hope that he had gone out about the business of the estate, as usual.

By the following morning, however, she'd had time enough to screw up her courage. How she was to face him, she knew not, but the thing had to be done. Better to do it sooner rather than later.

Nevertheless, she had got up late, and dallied over her toilette, dreading the moment of meeting. And then, when she had come down to breakfast, her pulse jumping with fright, she had not known whether to be glad or sorry at the news with which Kirkham had greeted her enquiry.

'His Lordship, m'lady? Why, he has been gone since yesterday.'

A hollow had opened up inside her, and her blood had seemed to stop. 'Gone? Gone where?'

'His Lordship did not say, m'lady. He told me only that he would be from home for he knew not how many days, and that we should not look for him to arrive at any particular moment.'

Rosina had been at first overwhelmed with relief. The evil day had been postponed. But the waiting was proving a good deal worse. Her nerves were beginning to fray, and just three days after that quarrel, with still no sign of Raith, she was fretting herself into a state of unalloyed affliction. Between apprehension that an accident had befallen him, and the fear that he would walk in unannounced at any moment—and belike treat her to a thunderous scold!—Rosina was in constant dread. She was losing flesh, and her wan looks drew comment even from the butler.

As if sent on purpose from the gods to increase her distresses, Saturday had also brought visitors. Fearful of one particular individual, she gave orders that no one was to be admitted without their name having first been brought to her. She was tempted to deny herself, feeling unequal to the task of meeting anyone without her lord's support. But recalling how little support she was likely to feel in his presence after what had passed, she suffered a change of front, deciding that she would do better without him.

As it chanced, the callers were of so much humbler station—expressing their fervent wish not to be backward in paying Lady Raith a visit—that Rosina was not put to any impossible or impertinent questions. Not even the pastor had remained today longer than strict propriety of taste dictated. Rosina saw him go with a sensation of relief, hoping that she would not be obliged to receive many more visitors before Raith's return. Which thought served only to depress her with the remembrance of what must await her when her husband chose to come home.

It was as well for what little peace of mind she was able to command that she did not know how her spouse, in company with Mr Ottery, was scouring the countryside around Brinklow in search of an unknown blind woman and her cottage.

Chapter Seven

'This is ridiculous, Ottery!' said Raith impatiently, setting down the tankard of ale with which he was refreshing himself from the dust of the country roads. 'It may take weeks to cover the ground. Where in thunder are we, by the way?'

'Paylington, my lord,' answered the lawyer, with a slight smile which Raith found distinctly irritating. 'I do not wonder at your finding difficulty in recalling the name of the place. We have covered so much ground.'

'Yes, and much good have we got by it!'

'Patience, my dear sir. We will find the needle, if we take apart the haystack.'

'I'm beginning to believe that we are in the wrong area altogether,' Raith said, sighing as he attacked the vast sandwich with which he had been supplied by the landlord of this particular hostelry. 'And I can't for the life of me remember where we have been.'

'Have no fear, my lord. I have kept a careful account,' said Ottery, taking out a pocketbook and consulting its pages. 'We have so far searched through Conib Abby, Newnham Regis, Fifsenhill, and—'

'Spare me the list!' Raith broke in.

He did not wish to hear it. Suffice it that they had hunted high and low—relentlessly, even through this Lord's day, disturbing simple folk at their well-earned rest. He was sick of jolting over rutty tracks. Parton was loud in disapproval of the wear and tear on his phaeton. But had they found hide or hair of Rosina's blind nurse? No, they had not!

'Well, we have made some progress, my lord,' said Ottery soothingly. 'People have been helpful. We have been regaled with local histories by at least three sightless old women, and as for cottages—'

'If you are seeking to raise my spirits with a pleasantry, Ottery, you may spare your breath. If we have seen one cottage, we have seen fifty. I am full to the brim with cottages!'

He saw, with despair, that his lawyer was regarding him with that knowing look. There was no fooling Ottery. He was well aware of the cause of his client's frustration. How could he not be?

'I am but poor company, by thunder!' he said, laying his hand briefly on the other's arm. 'And you are patience itself, my friend.'

'Why do you not go home, my lord, and leave the business to me?'

Raith looked away, picking up his tankard again. 'You know the answer to that.'

He had been entirely open with the man. After that disastrous night, he had been in need of solid guidance from a well-disposed source. And Ottery was the only person he could trust. He had fled his own home, and driven to Banbury, where he had found his lawyer almost upon the point of setting forth to begin his enquiries on Raith's behalf.

Ottery had ushered him into his private sanctum—that hidden little room behind his office, from where Raith had first secretly seen the disastrous enchantment of his vulnerable waif. Oh, how vulnerable! So destructive had been his treatment of her that she had been driven to lash out.

'She said that I had deserved it of her, Ottery, and by thunder I had!' he had confessed, wrung by his own conscience.

'If you drove her to hitting you, my lord, I must say that I agree with you,' had been the lawyer's uncompromising comment. 'You are not married to a termagant.'

'Far from it.'

He had called her a vixen, in the heat of his shocked response. But he had not meant it. Within two seconds of the door closing behind her, he had been smitten with horror at the remembrance of what he had said to her. She had taken it to herself. He had become confused by the memory. Had he applied that vicious word to her? Surely he had not meant to suggest for one moment that she was herself a whore? How had he put it, that she should take that meaning from his words?

For he could not doubt but that it was what she had thought. His cheek had smarted for some moments, but that was a small affliction. Much worse was the dread consequence of that bitterest of quarrels. Whichever way he looked at it, he could see no possibility of mending.

Rosina had escaped from him, and locked the door. He would not pursue her. To what end? His state of mind was too uncertain to permit him any rational resolution. He knew only too well how uncontrolled was his temper. A family failing. In Piers, it had been vicious. His half-brother had made ro attempt whatsoever to control it. In his father, he had seen it only once, although Ottery had told him that this was due to a steadfast rein that had curbed it through the years.

For himself, he knew it to be a curse, aggravated by the bitter blows to which fate had subjected him. No, he had not been able to unleash himself on Rosina that night. He had slept ill, his mind dwelling upon the undoubted unrest with which he guessed his Rosy was spending the night. And all to be laid to his account.

'I must put an end to it, Ottery. Until this matter is resolved, I cannot trust myself to deal with her as she deserves.'

'And if the matter is resolved to your discontent, my lord?' Ottery had asked, with an accuracy of aim that pierced his defences.

He had sunk his head into his hands. 'Don't. That is the grief under which I hang suspended. It is killing me, Ottery!'

'And Lady Raith no less.'

Raith had jerked up again, his heart twisted by the reproach in his lawyer's voice. 'I know it. You are right to take her part. There are times when I wish fervently that she had not written that accursed letter—and put herself irrevocably into my hands.'

Ottery had leaned across the small desk and placed a hand over those Raith gripped together on its surface. It had afforded him a small degree of comfort—to be understood.

'My lord, if I believed you meant that, I would be advising you this moment to put her aside.'

A wry smile had creased Raith's lips. 'You know me too well.' His hand had turned up and gripped the one above it. 'Help me, my friend. Yet again, I beg of you to help me.'

'You know I will, my lord. What do you wish?'

'I cannot go home,' Raith had said with urgency. 'I cannot face her. At least, I must go back—if only to fetch some toggery and other necessaries. But I need not fear an encounter. If I know Rosina, she will be only too eager to stay out of my way.'

'But where will you go, my lord? You cannot walk away from your own home.'

'Of course not!' he had retorted impatiently. 'For what do you take me? No, no, Ottery. I will go with you to search out this nurse of hers. Until I have the truth, there can be no peace for either of us.'

But the hunt was nearly three days old, and they were no nearer to finding their quarry. His lawyer, however, had been thinking.

'My lord, I wonder if we might do better to go back to the Receiving Office.'

'For what purpose?'

'We have assumed a place within walking distance. I had been holding to the notion that Lady Raith, when she was Miss Charlton, had collected her letters for herself. But figure to yourself this, my lord. Now Her Ladyship is gone to Ratley, how does the nurse receive any letters, if she is blind? Did you not say that Lady Raith had written to her?'

'Blood and thunder! Why did we not think of that before?' exclaimed Raith, half-rising from his seat. 'I franked that letter for Rosina not a week since.'

As they were staying at The Crown at Brinklow while conducting their researches, it was no difficult task to find their way to the Receiving Office upon the morrow, and effect an interview with the individual in charge. This worthy remembered their first visit, when Ottery had asked after 'Miss Charlton.' No one had known from which village she had hailed.

'A blind woman this time, is it?' mused the postmaster, scratching his chin. 'I don't recall no blind woman a-coming here to fetch no letters.'

'But someone might have called on her behalf,' Ottery pressed him. 'A friend, perhaps.'

The postmaster eyed them both dubiously. 'You don't have no name, then?'

'No,' replied Ottery with a patience that Raith could only admire, 'that is why we are asking. We know that the woman concerned lives in a cottage, at no great distance from here. At one time Miss Charlton, about whom we asked previously, was staying with her.'

The postmaster was shaking his head, a frown creasing his brow. There was no recognition here, and Raith's heart sank.

But one of the clerks whose function was to sort the mail had been hovering in the background, apparently waiting on a query. He spoke up suddenly. 'Your pardon, Mr Briggs, but would it be Mrs Hoswick as the gentlemen is after?'

Hope quickened in Raith's breast. 'Who is she, fellow?'

'I don't know no Mrs Hoswick, lad,' objected Briggs.

'I were thinking of Toly Aughton, the apothecary's boy down Hopsford way, sir.'

'Oh, young Toly?' said Briggs, his face clearing. 'Ah, yes, gentlemen, maybe that'll be it.'

Raith was on the point of exploding, but he was checked by Ottery's hand on his arm. As well his lawyer had so ready an understanding of his moods.

'How does this boy Toly come into the picture, Mr Briggs?' Ottery asked gently.

But it was the clerk who answered. 'He come and fetch the letters for Mrs Hoswick, sir, as is blind and lives in a village 'bout a half-mile from his master's shop.'

'That's right,' agreed Briggs. 'Now I think of it, sir, he come in not a few days agone. There was a letter seemingly, wasn't there, lad?'

'Aye, sir,' said the clerk, looking awed. 'Franked by a lord it were!'

Raith exchanged a glance with Ottery. By thunder, they had it! 'What name?' he demanded.

'The lord's name, lad,' Ottery said, clarifying the matter. 'Do you recall?'

'Couldn't hardly read it, sir,' uttered the clerk disparagingly. 'A scrawl it was.'

His Lordship gave a wry smile, as he asked, 'Was it "Raith"?'

'Aye, that would be it.'

Ottery became business-like. 'Right then, my lad. Where may we find this Toly Aughton?'

The cottage was minute. Was it from here that Rosina had written that fateful letter? The woman who opened the door had her eyes, but they moved constantly, in the way of blind people, and it was clear that they saw nothing.

She was a pudgy female, of less than average stature, with a wrinkled face under a large mob-cap, and a slightly grimy apron tied about her middle. She looked, Raith thought, exactly like a nurse.

'Who's this you've brought, Toly?' she said gruffly, just as if she could see them both.

'It's two gennelmen, Mrs H. Come to find you. I didn't rightly know if I ought to have brung 'em. Only I didn't like to refuse, seeing as—'

'I think, ma'am, that we can speak for ourselves,' Ottery interrupted. 'May we come in?'

The nurse raised her chin, moving her head from side to side as though she took in something of the look of her visitors. Almost Raith would swear that she could see. After a moment, she nodded, somewhat grudgingly opening the door.

It led directly into an incommodious kitchen, which must nevertheless, Raith thought, be the biggest room in the place. The two of them, greatcoated as they were, seemed to dwarf the place. The nurse bade them all sit down, herself moving to an open range where she set a copper kettle to the fire. Raith noted how she felt her way about, marvelling at her resilience.

He seated himself on a plain wooden chair at one end of the table, while Ottery took his place next to him. The boy hovered by the door. The elderly dame then turned from the fire, and came to the table. She did not sit.

'You're the one, I think,' she said, turning her face in Raith's direction.

'The one what?' he asked, in quick reaction.

'As wants to see me.'

'Your guesses are uncanny.'

She shook her head. 'It ain't guesswork, sir, not by a long way. When you've lost one sense, you find you can use others a deal better.'

'I have heard it said so,' Ottery put in. 'It is reassuring to discover that it is true.'

'Now you, sir,' said the nurse, turning to him, 'are one as comes along o' the other. It ain't nowise your affair as you've come for.'

'You are perfectly correct,' said Ottery, with a lift of the eyebrow and a smile for his client.

Raith was experiencing the most extraordinary sensation of premonition. This woman knew just who he was.

As if she read his thought, she turned her sightless eyes towards the door. 'I thank you, Toly, and you can leave the gentlemen safe here with me. They ain't nowise harmful.'

'You sure, Mrs H.?'

'Yes, you run along, boy. 'Tis private business as this gentleman has with me.'

She waited only until the young lad who had been their

guide had left the cottage and shut the door. Then she moved back to the range.

'Now, my lord, you'll take tea?'

She did know! Had he not thought it? Raith exchanged a glance with his lawyer, and found his own amazement reflected in the other's face. The nurse was busying herself with a pot and a set of cups and saucers.

'How did you know?' he asked.

'Ah, that would be telling,' said the elderly dame over her shoulder. She spooned tea-leaves into the pot.

Raith grimaced at the lawyer. Ottery grinned. He looked at the woman's back.

'How long have you lived in Withibrooke, Mrs Hoswick?'

'Since just after Mrs Charlton upped and died,' she said, without turning round. 'I'd a deal better have stayed with my dove, but it weren't to be. He wouldn't have me, not as my sight were going.'

Raith mouthed at Ottery, 'Who?' and received a lift of the eyebrows, and a quick shake of the head. Perhaps it was too soon to probe.

She was extraordinarily handy with the teacups for a blind person. Raith jumped up to accept them from her, passing a saucer with a cup containing the steaming brew across to Ottery. It was not a beverage to which he was partial, but it would be politic to drink it. He would not wish to offend this woman's sensibilities. He watched her place her own dish carefully in front of her, some distance from the edge of the table. Then she pulled out a chair and sat down, facing Raith.

'Now, my lord, tell me. How is my Rosy? Fourteen days it's been! Is she well? Is she happy?'

Raith could not speak for a moment, silenced by his consciousness of the distress to which he had reduced the girl for whom this female obviously cared deeply. And she had been counting the days! What in thunder was he to tell her?

He hesitated too long. Mrs Hoswick's head drooped a trifle, and she sighed.

'I knew it. Her letter was all too silent, poor lamb.' She tutted for a moment, sipped her tea, and then looked up, suddenly brisk. 'Well, and what do you want of me, my lord?'

On impulse, Raith reached out to touch one of the work-roughened hands. 'Your help, Mrs Hoswick. I am as anxious as you are for Rosina's happiness.'

She allowed his hand to rest upon hers for a moment without speaking. He removed it, and she stood up.

'Will you allow an old woman a liberty, my lord?'

Raith shot a glance at Ottery, who shrugged expressively. 'Of what nature?'

'Let me feel your face.'

Instinct caused Raith to shrink inwardly. What had Rosina told her in that letter? The thought of those pudgy hands playing over his scarred face was acutely uncomfortable. But if that was what it was going to take! He looked at his lawyer, whose features were creased with concern.

'It is a blind person's way of seeing, my lord,' he murmured, setting down his own cup, and mouthing further on a whisper, 'Will you risk it?'

Raith drew a breath, and mouthed back, 'I have no choice.' Ottery nodded, and Raith turned back to the nurse.

'Very well.'

She moved around the table, obviously so familiar a motion that she did not need to use her hands. Raith shifted his chair, and waited, rigid with tension, as she stood before him.

The fingers that came to rest upon his face were gentle.

He had an immediate vision of Rosina under these hands, stroking comfort. The touch was featherlight, and his rigidity lessened—until it came in contact with his disfigurement, and hesitated. Unlike Rosina, whose finger had traced the line, the nurse's played a rhythmic stroke back and forth across it, at the same time as she did as much on his other cheek.

He sighed out his breath as her examination ended, and saw her nod. 'You'll do,' she said.

Raith was betrayed into a laugh. 'I thank you.'

Ottery intervened. 'Do you feel inclined to help His Lordship, ma'am?'

'I'll tell him only where to find out what he wants to know.'

Raith could take this no longer. 'How in thunder do you know what I want? How did you know it was I?'

The nurse laughed comfortably. 'Ah, you mustn't run away with the idea that I'm a seer, nor nothing like that. Deduction, my lord. You weren't *him*, I'd take my oath. He'd not have come here with no pleasant words for such as I, he wouldn't. Nor he wouldn't bring no one with him—unless it were t'other. Him I'd know, though we ain't met. One whiff of his breath is all it 'ud take, my lord, and that's a fact.'

So that was what she had been doing on the doorstep. Sniffing at them. He glanced to his lawyer and found the same deep appreciation upon his features. But this passage had been all too confusing—besides sending a riffle of that jealous flame burning through him. Two of them, by thunder! Which of these was the man whose throat his itching hands sought to surround and strangle?

'I pray you, Mrs Hoswick, could you sort out one "him" from the other?'

There must have been an indication of his unquiet thoughts in his voice, for she shot her face towards him,

and a frown creased her brow. Raith felt impelled to reassure her.

'Don't be alarmed. I have need of this information—I
will not use it ill, I promise you.'

Mrs Hoswick clasped her hands together on the table.
'The only thing I care for, my lord, is that my Rosy is
safe,' she declared with hostility. 'Now, if you can't make
her so, then you'd best bring her back to me.'

'I want to keep her, Mrs Hoswick,' he uttered raggedly.
'Only I cannot—if I do not…' He faded out, unwilling to
put into words the hideous truth of his intended findings.
He wondered how much she knew. He dared swear she
would not say.

'I can't tell you nothing, my lord,' said the nurse, folding her lips together, and rising. 'You'd best go now.'

Raith leaped up, casting an anguished glance at his lawyer. To his relief, Ottery took over. Rising, too, he moved
to lay a hand on the nurse's shoulder. She must have heard
him approach, but she flinched, throwing it off.

'His Lordship is anxious to find out the truth, ma'am,'
he said gently. 'You cannot wish for Lady Raith—I mean,
for your nurseling, for that is now her name—to find herself back in the hands of the man whom she fears above
all others.'

For the first time, Mrs Hoswick began to look anxious,
kneading her hands in her apron. 'If only I knew what to
do for the best.'

'She is my wife, ma'am,' uttered Raith desperately.
'Neither of us knew, when we wed, that we would find
ourselves with a marriage utterly other than that we had
planned. But it is so. Help me to make it safe for her.'
He hesitated, watching uncertainty ripple across the elderly dame's features.

'I don't know, my lord,' she said, the sightless eyes
shifting with the uneven tenor of her thoughts.

Raith moved to her, and sought her hands, holding them hard. 'Mrs Hoswick, if it turns out otherwise, I promise you faithfully that I will return Rosina to you—intact. And provide you both with means to secure what haven you please.'

'He means it, Mrs Hoswick,' Ottery put in, adding persuasively, 'If you wish, I will write it all out for you, and His Lordship will sign it, that you may be certain of a right in law.'

But the nurse put up her chin, and nodded at last. 'That ain't needful, sir. I couldn't read it nohow, in any event.' She let out a sigh. 'You'd best go and parley with that there Herbert Cambois, as was her guardian.' She turned again to Raith. 'But if you'll take the advice of an old woman, my lord, you'll leave the doing to this 'un, and go your ways. It ain't good for my dove to be left alone, and it's your business to protect her.'

The caller was becoming extraordinarily difficult. The visit had started well enough. A little practice had given Rosina poise, which, blended with her natural air of civil deference, had won for her the amiability of those far less comfortably circumstanced than she now was herself.

But Lady Doddinghurst's baronet husband placed her only marginally lower in the social scale than her hostess, yet Rosina found her quick to demonstrate her superiority of worldly knowledge. Not to say fashion.

Until her arrival, Rosina had been satisfied of the modality of her sprigged muslin gown, with its long sleeves and gathered bodice, a frill adorning the hem. But this matron, fresh from the metropolis, wore a gown of violet crêpe of exquisite cut, enriched by a cloak of purple velvet. A feathered turban completed this formidable toilette, under which a sharp pair of eyes looked down an imposing Roman nose, surveying her hostess from her head to her heels.

'Charming,' she uttered with a spurious smile. 'A trifle countrified, but quite charming.'

Lady Doddinghurst was of an age to claim acquaintance with Raith's own father, and lost no time in putting Rosina in her place. Beginning with this doubtful compliment, she asked who of the surrounding gentry Rosina had already received, and proceeded to a comprehensive lecture upon their strengths and frailties. Rosina listened in amazement, but without any apprehension on her own part, until the visitor switched her attention to Rosina's personal affairs.

'And how did you and Lord Raith become acquainted?' she demanded, with a smile that did not reach her eyes.

Rosina fought down sudden panic. 'In—in the usual way.'

'Is there a usual way?' enquired the dame.

Abruptly Rosina recalled the tale which Mr Ottery had once said should be the preferred report of their union.

'Why, yes. The—the marriage was arranged. Our respective parents had—had planned it. A long time ago.'

A haughty stare was bent upon her from the chair to the window side of the fire. 'Who are your parents?'

'They are both dead,' Rosina stated, hoping that common civility would prevent further questions on this head.

'Ah, how sad,' said the lady, with a pitying smile as she sat back. 'However, it is interesting to hear that Anton's father took pains to ensure his betrothal. Particularly in the light of subsequent events.'

Rosina knew not what to say. Lady Doddinghurst spoke as if she did not believe in the tale Raith had concocted. What did she know that Rosina did not? Everything, since she knew so little! She saw the woman's smile increase— at her discomfiture no doubt—and hurried into speech.

'I believe it was the wish rather of my lord's mother,' she said at random, and hastily borrowed Mr Ottery's amused comment. 'Marriage is thought to be a steadying influence.'

'And yet His Lordship is from home.'

'There is—he is engaged upon business that cannot be laid aside,' Rosina said crisply, beginning to be angry. 'My lord has only just come into the inheritance, you must know, and there is a great deal to be done.'

The other woman laughed with a touch of scorn. 'So I should imagine, after the way Piers treated the place.'

She cast a disparaging glance about as she spoke, and Rosina found herself roused to resentment on her spouse's behalf. She threw out a challenge.

'You seem to know a great deal about the family, Lady Doddinghurst.'

'So much, my dear,' agreed the other, meeting the attack head on, 'that I find it hard to imagine that the second Lady Raith could have thought it necessary to secure the betrothal of a mere boy. After all, he was not yet into adolescence when she was taken off by a fatal illness.'

Raith's mother had died when he was a child? Dear Lord, but he might have primed her on these matters! Now what was she to say? Should she confess her ignorance? No, she would not. This female was altogether too patronising to deserve her confidence. She opted to retire from the lists.

'I am not in a position to comment, ma'am,' she said frostily. 'However it may have been, I was given myself to understand that Lord Raith and I were to be married in due time, and so it proved to be.'

Lady Doddinghurst, looking like a cat who had been at the cream, did not hesitate to harry the retreat. 'How odd that your parents should secure you to a second son with no hope of inheriting, whose sole income derived from the army.'

Rosina was effectively silenced. The best she could do was to eye her visitor with head held high, hoping that nothing of her deep disquiet was visible. For a moment, the elder lady gazed down her nose, as if she dared her to respond. Then she relaxed, sitting back and smiling in a winning way.

'My poor child, I had no intention of putting up your back. If you take my advice, you will persuade your husband to think up a better tale. I am sure he will oblige you. I cannot think that Anton Raith will be eager for yet more scandal to be attached to his name.'

Incensed, Rosina threw aside all caution. 'I am afraid I know nothing of any such stigma. Perhaps Your Ladyship will care to enlighten me as to the meaning of these hints?'

'Oh, my dear Lady Raith, do you mean to say that you do not know? But how foolish of young Anton to have kept you in ignorance. Though I dare say he had hoped that there were few persons old enough to remember the truth about his mother's marriage. And indeed, perhaps the later disgraces, being of a more personal nature, are of closer concern to him.'

An icy voice spoke from the doorway. 'I see, Lady Doddinghurst, that you have not lost your penchant for probing into the private affairs of others.'

Rosina's heart felt as if it sprang almost out of her chest, and she was unable to stop herself leaping from her seat. Dear Lord, Raith was back! He was standing just inside the room, his eyes upon the visitor, his damaged countenance wearing its most cynical look. He had discarded his outer garments, though he was still in travelling dress: a double-breasted frock-coat of rust-coloured fustian with a stand collar, and waistcoat to match, over buckskins and boots.

Rosina was stricken with an abrupt sense of his virility. But it was driven out of her head by the instant remembrance of their last meeting.

'My l-lord!' she uttered faintly, conscious of a tremble starting up in her limbs.

He was coming towards her. What was she to do? She shot a glance at Lady Doddinghurst, and saw that dame's eyes passing from herself to her husband, and back again. She must not let this dreadful female see the true state of their relationship.

'You—you startled me, my lord,' she managed, forcing a smile to her lips as he reached her.

She felt him take her hand, and lift it. It quivered, utterly outside her control, and Rosina met his eyes as he bent his head to kiss the fingers. She read a message of warning in them, and realised—with a flash of resentment in her breast—that he meant to put on a show for the benefit of her visitor.

'A thousand pardons, my love, to be bursting in on you without warning in this way,' he said smoothly, and slightly pressed her fingers.

Rosina withdrew them quickly, and sank back into her seat, conscious of an overwhelming desire to weep. Hateful to have him behave in that familiar fashion, when the truth of their dealing was so very unlike it. *My love,* indeed!

His voice had hardened. 'You have much to forgive, I perceive. I should never have left you to the mercy of your neighbours.'

Glancing swiftly up at him, Rosina thought she detected reassurance in his eyes. Easy to see that this remark had been directed at Lady Doddinghurst. A peal of patently false laughter breaking out behind him confirmed the notion.

Raith turned to confront the most vicious of the local gossips. He was appalled to see her here, and his conscience writhed for Rosina having been obliged to face her alone.

'Very well attempted, my dear Anton,' said the woman, with the smile he detested. 'But you know, it is difficult to be set down by a young man whom one has known since he was in short coats.'

'Difficult, ma'am, but not impossible,' he said, deliberate menace in his tone. 'As you will find, if you persist in troubling my wife with your ill-considered remarks.'

'Oh, pish!' scoffed the matron. 'You do not frighten me, Anton. Recollect that I have brought four sons into the world, and am a grandmother several times over.'

'Then you should have more consideration for the sensibilities of a young lady who has not your worldly knowledge and experience,' he returned.

Rosina saw a flush stain the woman's cheeks, and the smile vanished. She could not but be conscious of satisfaction, and she was cheered by Raith's having championed her. She had dreaded his coming, but this front he had put up to dampen the impertinence of her visitor might give her a respite. He seemed not to have the immediate intention of seeking revenge for her dreadful lapse. Might she dare to hope that the intervening four days had dulled his anger?

But his presence, despite that horrid charade, was sending her heart into high gear. She had feared his return, but she could not withstand the realisation that she had missed him in spite of it. Missed the very sight of him—wrecked features and all. If only circumstances had been different. If she had been able to offer him a history wholly untarnished—if not as tainted as he feared.

'Well, and how are you faring, Anton?' the creature was saying, glossing over the earlier exchange. 'Dodding- hurst had been of the opinion that Piers must have brought the place to the verge of ruin.'

Raith had taken up a pose near the fire, ensuring that Lady Doddinghurst, rather than Rosina, was subjected to the unsightly side of his face. But at this, he turned his mocking grey gaze upon her.

'And hoped to purchase it for a song at the last? I regret, ma'am, that the estate is under entail. It is out of the power of any incumbent to effect a sale.'

He was well aware that since Sir Humphrey Doddinghurst's land marched with his own, the addition of the Raith estate—at a price well under its value— would have been highly desirable. He was glad to see his old enemy redden again under the hit. She rose to retreat, much to his relief.

'I have stayed too long.' She crossed to Rosina and held out her hand as Raith tugged on the bell-pull. 'My dear Lady Raith, I will say farewell for the moment.'

Rosina took the hand as briefly as civility would allow. She was less immediately concerned with the woman's departure, than with the fact that it would leave her alone with her spouse. Her pulse started up the dreadful tattoo that so often attacked her in his presence, and the flutter in her stomach made her feel sick.

The woman turned at the door, and Raith discovered, to his chagrin, that she was not out of venom. 'One last morsel of advice, dear Anton. Don't leave your wife in ignorance, when a little knowledge will prevent her from making a complete fool of herself.'

Raith swore as she swept through the door, which the butler was holding open. He strode into the centre of the room, looking after her.

'That female is the most disagreeable of my acquaintance. Damn her for being so absolutely right!' He turned, his eyes going to Rosina.

At once he forgot Lady Doddinghurst. How white and strained was his waif! She looked thinner. Or was it the effect of the charmingly simple gown? No—for her elfin countenance was drawn. What had he done? He wanted to go to her, draw her up into his arms and hold her comfortingly close. But the consciousness of his own duplicity prevented him.

What would she say, were he to tell her of his activities during his absence? If she were to know that Ottery was even now on his way to Nun Eaton, bent upon bearding the fellow Cambois, who had been her guardian. Raith had hired a chaise for him, and himself driven home in the phaeton with Parton. He had not precisely followed the advice of Rosina's nurse, but rather his lawyer's forceful representations.

'In your present frame of mind, my lord, I must and will conjure you to leave these enquiries to me. I do not wish to be obliged to bring you off from a charge of murder! Besides, you do not know that there is truthfully any occasion for your wrath. Let me handle the business, as Mrs Hoswick suggested.'

It had taken some discussion, but he had at length capitulated, spurred more perhaps by Ottery's further argument. 'You left Lady Raith, as I understand it, in a distinctly perturbed frame of mind. Picture to yourself, my lord, the aggravated distress occasioned by your long absence—with neither explanation, nor opportunity to make up the quarrel.'

And Ottery had been right, by thunder! She looked so much the worse, that he could never sufficiently blame himself. And to crown all, he had left her unsupported to an ordeal which she dreaded, subject to the damned impertinences of Lady Doddinghurst and her like.

'I am sorry that I left you alone like this,' he said rapidly. 'I would not for the world have had you suffer that creature's rudeness.'

Rosina's jumping nerves settled a little at this evidence that he did not mean to upbraid her—at least, not yet. She was tempted to offer her own heartfelt apology for that dreadful blow, which she could never sufficiently regret. But she was too afraid of re-awakening his anger with the memory.

At a loss for anything inoffensive to say, she cast about in her mind, and recalled what he had just said. There was material a-plenty here. Without thought, she plunged in.

'She would not have it that our betrothal had been arranged, as Mr Ottery told me was the planned story. She said that your mother died when you were a boy—and then she spoke of scandal, and…' Her voice died.

What had she been thinking of? That was what came of trying to keep off the subject uppermost in her mind. Now he would retire again behind that impossible barrier of ice.

'I b-beg your pardon,' she uttered in a low tone. 'I d-did not mean to p-pry.'

Raith heard the tremor of her voice with a further twist of the knife in his sorely tried conscience. So strong was the impulse to go to her, that he was obliged to turn away, moving to the window and looking out. But here, at least, was one thing he could remedy.

'You have a right to ask, Rosy,' he began, using the name involuntarily.

Rosina heard it with a melting at her heart. Had his anger then indeed died? When he called her by that nursery name—though it might be in impatience—it seemed always to betoken affection. Was there not a degree of fondness? He had said so—on that fatal night. He had spoken of his regard. And she had rejected it. His gentleness on occasion would indicate it. Only it was not, she reminded herself sadly, strong enough a feeling to withstand what lay between them.

She glanced at him, and found Raith observing her. But the instant he caught her eye, he looked away. Her gaze went to her fingers, unquiet in her lap. Oh, if things could only be other than they were.

'Lady Doddinghurst spoke no less than the truth. I should not keep you in ignorance.'

What was he talking of? Then she remembered. 'Do you mean that there was a scandal?'

'Long ago. It forms, in large part, the basis for my brother's unrelenting enmity.'

Her curiosity aroused, Rosina turned to look at him. 'Was he so much your enemy?'

'Have you not wondered why the lawns are all of ash?' He was staring out at the desolate frontage of the house. His tone was flat. 'Piers had them fired.'

Rosina gasped. 'You cannot mean he caused them to be set alight!'

Raith shifted away from the window, and came to the mantel, looking down into the charring logs below. 'Ottery thinks he had some hope that the flames might spread and burn the house. But since he was in it, he could scarce set the house on fire directly.'

It was stated flatly, but Rosina's shock was intense. 'But how could he—how could anyone do such a thing?'

'A final act of revenge,' said Raith, without moving from where he stood, nor looking round. 'Everything in the house that was worth a groat had been sacrificed to his gambling. The estate was a wreck. I must suppose that he wished for nothing to be left intact.'

To learn that the man had been a gambler was oddly not much of a surprise, although it caused a shiver to run through Rosina's frame. In just such a fashion had her guardian been driven to reduce his own home. But the gambling of Herbert Cambois had been a sickness. This, Raith seemed to suggest, was a deliberate wasting of resources.

'Why should he do that to you?' she asked.

Raith turned, and the bitter look was pronounced. 'Because he chose to believe in the gossip that suggested that I was not my father's son.'

Rosina stared at him blankly. 'Was he blind, sir? Could he not see how you resembled him?'

'He was nine years my senior. The likeness was not readily apparent until I grew to manhood.'

'But why in the world should he think such a thing?' she demanded, caught up in this first hint of the origin of her spouse's deeply felt hurts. This must be the scandal of which Lady Doddinghurst had spoken.

Raith sat down in the chair lately vacated by that dame, and glanced across at her. He was himself so taken up by his memories that he saw his wife's features without taking them in. They were overlaid by the vicious curl of his half-brother's mouth, the taunting voice.

'Spawn of a strumpet! Anton whatever-your-name-is, you are no brother of mine.'

He set his teeth, and his gaze went back to the fire. 'My mother eloped at sixteen, and my grandfather brought her back only on the following day. Papa was a widower, and a close friend of my maternal grandfather. He offered to marry her, to save her name.'

Rosina heard it with mixed feelings. She ached for the pain in his voice. Yet she saw how his history was affecting her own. Small wonder he cared so for the purity of his wife.

'Piers had me almost believing that I was born of that other union, but my father made a point of teaching me that it was not so.' He drew in a breath, and let it out in a sigh of despair. 'I don't know why Piers persisted in the belief. He was the elder son, there was no possible way I could inherit. Perhaps my father petted me too much, or showed me preference because of my mother's youth. I know he was ever kind to her.'

'Some men,' Rosina ventured, out of a yearning to ease his hurt, 'are disposed to evil, I believe. They will use any excuse.'

For a moment or two, Raith came out of the memories. He spoke without thinking, with no intent of upsetting her or probing for a truth that he was in a fair way to find out for himself. 'You speak from experience, no doubt.'

She did not answer, and he relapsed into reverie. He hardly knew that he continued to talk of it aloud.

'Piers was quite inventive. His tortures were inflicted under a cunning guise. The older brother inducting the younger into the sports of boys. He taught me how to shoot and to play at cricket—and other such pursuits. He took me riding, and bird's-nesting. I hated every moment of it!'

'Why did you go with him?' Rosina asked. 'Could no one have stopped him from taking you?'

Raith laughed mirthlessly. 'It was rather encouraged. And one was ever taught that the worst sin was to rat upon one's brethren. Who would have believed me? Piers was impatient of my inability to climb with sufficient speed, or to ride on as fleet a hoof—' the words spitting from him '—and took opportunity to school me for every mistake.'

Rosina shuddered at the horrors she envisaged him suffering. Had he not hinted at this that night? That he knew what it was to be in someone's power. But a child. It was inconceivable that it should have gone undetected.

'But was this your lot for all of your childhood?' she asked, quite aghast.

Raith shook his head. 'Piers was away at school for much of the time. As we grew older, and I was sent to school in my turn, I used to long for the term and loathe the holidays when I must encounter him at home. And it did end at last.'

'How?'

Raith got up from his chair and returned to the fire, supporting his hands on the mantel. 'Ottery caught him at it. Piers was—administering one of his lessons. I suppose he had grown careless. At twenty a man feels invincible, and he'd had me at his mercy for years. He had tied my hands for the purpose, and so there was no possible way that he might persuade Ottery of the legitimacy of his actions.'

'What did Mr Ottery do?' asked Rosina, finding herself unsurprised to discover that gentleman's hand in these events.

Raith's head turned, and there was a wealth of satisfaction in both face and voice. 'He struck Piers to the ground. You cannot conceive with what delight I saw him fall.'

Into Rosina's mind flew an instant vision of her hand slamming into Raith's own cheek. Shame burned into her. Oh, she understood only too well. How she had enjoyed the sensation! Only it was unworthy. There had been no vindictive intent in Raith's treatment of her. If he had earned of her the blow, he had not deserved her rancour.

'What happened?' she asked hastily, to rid herself of the unpalatable memory.

Raith turned fully, and moved restlessly back to the window. 'Ottery haled us both before my father. Piers was loud in denial, and my father, I think, did not wish to believe his son capable of that sort of petty cruelty.' He winced with discomfort at the memory. 'Ottery forcibly stripped me of my shirt to show the evidence.'

He recalled in his mind the lawyer's words, delivered in a voice of leaden fury. '"My lord, how else did the boy acquire these wounds? He could not have inflicted them upon himself."' Ordered by his sire, and encouraged by Ottery, he had been induced to give a halting account of his brother's activities.

Rosina eyed the stiff shoulders, and the set line of his jaw in profile, the white ridging laceration where he had forgotten to turn the other cheek. The certainty gripped her that she had not been told it all. Wherein fitted that blemish, which lay at the root of his bitterness?

'It is the only time I have known my father to lose his temper,' he said evenly. 'It was terrifying to see him extract a confession from Piers. Then he forbade him the house. Had it been within his power, I believe my father would have disinherited him in my favour. I am glad he could not, for the banishment was enough to secure all the justification my brother needed for his enmity.'

There was a silence. Rosina was moved by the story. This last must indeed have caused a deal of talk. Was it that which Lady Doddinghurst had called the 'later disgraces'? That Raith had felt able to share it with her both touched her, and threw her into a fever of anxiety. She was tempted to reciprocate, to give of herself in return. Only she dreaded the inevitable change in his mood—if she were to speak of it. It was his own mother's unchastity that had brought upon him such undeserved punishment. How could she doubt of his being as sickened as she was herself, if he knew the full sum of her own history? She looked down at her fingers, unseeing how one pulled at another.

Was this the truth at last? She had blinded herself to her fears. She had turned her own deep disgust of the event into righteous wrath, and hurled it against Raith. So deep was her shame, that she could not endure the thought of her husband knowing the substance of it. Let alone telling him all. He must turn from her in utter contempt and revulsion. She could not tell him—*she could not.*

'Rosina?'

She leaped with shock, looking up. She had not seen him approach. He was standing near her chair, his hands clasped behind his back, regarding her with a concerned frown.

'My l-lord?'

He reached down and cupped her chin in his hand. 'You are looking haggard. Have you been so distressingly troubled?'

The black orbs darkened. 'How can you ask me?'

Raith's heart twisted. 'I am sorry for it.'

'You are sorry?' On impulse, she reached up and grabbed at his hand, clasping it within both her own. 'Raith, I—'

'Your pardon, my lord.'

Rosina slipped her hands away, and Raith moved swiftly to one side, turning. 'Yes, what is it, Kirkham?'

The butler came into the room, and shut the door carefully behind him. 'I beg your pardon, my lord, but a gentleman has called, and Her Ladyship has requested that no visitor should be admitted before she had been given a name.'

Glancing at Rosina, Raith saw that the interruption had thrown her back into discomposure. Hell and damnation! Must there be a visitor just then? She had been within an ace of offering him something—perhaps her confidence. Now the moment was lost.

But Rosina was almost glad of the butler's unexpected entry. What had possessed her? She had very nearly thrown caution to the winds.

'Who is it, Kirkham?' she asked tightly.

'Lord Forteviot, m'lady.'

Raith cursed. 'Forteviot? That fellow was a friend of my brother's, if I am not mistaken.'

'True, my lord.'

'What in thunder does he want with me?'

He glanced at Rosina as he spoke, and his thoughts stopped dead. She was gazing at Kirkham in dumb horror, her face draining visibly of colour.

Chapter Eight

Rosina was dying inside. He had come! Had she not known that he would? Every moment of her wedded life had been but a prelude to this one. Fate had a hand in it, and the gods were cruel.

'Admit the gentleman, Kirkham.'

Her eyes flew to Raith's face. He had spoken in the hardest voice she had ever heard him use. His eyes were on the door as the butler departed, the wrecked side of his profile hidden from her. The good side was set, the jawline stern, the high cheekbone standing out white against his tan. He did not look in her direction, and Rosina knew that she was lost. She had given herself away—and not a word said.

If she could have fled the room, she would have done it. But her legs were like lead, her heart likewise. Time had no meaning. Numbly, she waited for the entrance of doom.

'Lord Forteviot.'

Into the saloon he strolled. Arrogantly at ease, the thin cruel line of his mouth curled in that well-remembered smile that mocked even as it signalled his intolerable self-satisfaction. He was dressed more conformably and neat than she had been used to see him, presiding over the card table in her guardian's house. There he had sprawled, even in her enforced presence, with cravat untied and waistcoat unbuttoned, eyeing her with that lascivious assurance of ownership.

'My dear Lord Raith,' he uttered, silky-smooth, crossing to her spouse and holding out his hand. 'Or may I call you Anton? It seems excessively strange to be addressing you by your title.'

'No doubt,' said Raith shortly, shaking hands as briefly as he could. 'I was not much more than a youth, when last we met—was I?'

There was an edge to the words that caught Rosina's attention. Raith knew him? Dear Lord, it was worse than she had supposed! They were not of an age, for Forteviot was near forty to her husband's eight and twenty years. What a hideous mischance that he should be acquainted with the man.

'Ah, yes,' Forteviot was saying easily. 'You went into the army, did you not? A worthy career. I am sure you acquitted yourself as heroically as ever.'

Rosina heard his words with a sense of disassociation, as if her mind had become detached from her body. For an icy coldness had so entered her that she was unable to feel anything beyond it. But her thoughts formed clearly, as if she watched a pantomime unfold before her eyes, convinced of its utter falsity.

She looked again at Raith, and saw his own cynical look pronounced. But the next moment, all thought suspended again as Forteviot turned his lizard eyes upon herself. She had ever felt him as reptilian, and the green slits that surveyed her from his invariably half-closed eyelids had borne out the impression. She shuddered inwardly.

'Present me, my dear fellow, I conjure you. This must

be—I feel sure I cannot be mistaken—this must be Lady Raith.'

Without intent, Rosina's glance went to her husband. The chill barricade of his eyes thrust through the protective shell of numbness that had momentarily encased her. Her heart plummeted. She became conscious of faintness, and had to concentrate hard to keep herself from a swoon.

Resistless, she let her lifeless hand be kissed, staring up into that hated face with a complete absence of expression.

'My very dear Lady Raith,' purred softly from his lips, while the contemptuous mockery of his eyes taunted her with an entirely different message. 'I am altogether delighted to make your acquaintance. How fortunate is my dear friend Anton to have secured so elusive a prize.'

Raith's attention caught on the word. It had been so odd a thing to say of her, had he not been already certain of the villain's identity in Rosina's life. This was undoubtedly the man from whom she had sought protection. That tiny clue—or had it been planted deliberately?—confirmed it. *Elusive.* Had she been so to Forteviot? That he had come here seeking her could not be in doubt. Bile rose in Raith's stomach as his imagination painted for him what must be the truth of their previous relationship. Was there to be no end? The fell hand of providence was once more at his throat.

Rosina paced up and down her bedchamber. It was horribly late. Would the creature never go? What was he saying to Raith? Had he betrayed her? Not that it mattered. She had all too clearly betrayed herself!

The nausea in her stomach intensified. Oh, to what torments of horror and despair had she been subjected! Gone was the gentleness that had characterised Raith only moments before Forteviot's arrival. Gone forever, she did not doubt. After the veiled hints that the wretch had thrown out, how could she blame her husband? They were deliberately vague, designed to prey upon the sensitivity of a jealous mind.

'Your features are uncannily familiar, Lady Raith,' he had said at one point, in his silkiest tone. 'Yet I feel sure I would remember meeting you. Is it possible that I am acquainted with one to whom you are related?'

Rosina had not known how to answer him. Had hesitated too long, while Raith's tight-lipped tension grew—to her increasing distress.

'I have few relatives,' she had said, hoping to deflect the man.

Forteviot had smiled upon her in a knowing way, and returned his attention to her husband. How like a snake had been his approaches. He had behaved as if his acquaintance with Raith's half-brother gave him claim upon Raith himself.

'So many years since we met, my dear Anton. And I so fond at one time of your dear brother Piers. How could I fail to take opportunity to renew our acquaintance?'

As if she could be in any doubt as to why he had come here! But to Rosina's consternation, Raith had chosen to accept this, if with a stilted manner of studied civility that had sat uneasily upon him.

'How, indeed? I was not of an age at the time to lend sophistication to your gatherings.'

Then Forteviot had pretended to fall into a mood of reminiscence. His smile had increased, but Rosina had read contempt in his gaze.

'You afforded us a deal of entertainment, I recall. Piers was perhaps less amused by it. But then, there is often that little frisson between brothers where there is a great disparity of age.'

'That *little* frisson, yes,' Raith had responded, so lightly that Rosina was moved to stare at him in perplexity. 'Unhappily, it has proved vain. For there is my poor brother so early in his grave, while I am here in his place.'

'An instance of the strange workings of fate,' had agreed the other man smoothly.

What had they meant by it? She had listened to the give and take of words, breathless with apprehension. An undercurrent of suspicion lay beneath Raith's every utterance, despite the cynical air he had adopted. Forteviot had been all too quick to foster it.

'And here is another instance, my dear Anton,' he had said, turning his mocking eyes upon Rosina again. 'What chance was it, I wonder, that gave into your hands this particular delight? Piers would have wondered at your good fortune.'

Rosina glanced quickly at Raith, and saw the muscle twitch in his jaw, making the scar ripple. But his voice was smooth, as he turned the question back on his opponent.

'Piers would have envied me, I make no doubt. As surely you must, sir, to see me master of this pretty enchantment. Must he not, my sweet life?'

She had shrivelled inside to hear that false endearment on his lips. He had raked her with the cold grey of his eyes, and then turned with a scornful laugh back to that hateful man.

'Modesty forbids my wife to speak.'

His deliberate cruelty had crushed her. And she had vowed to withhold herself from giving him the satisfaction of knowing anything of her story.

But that resolve was fast dying. Forteviot had long outstayed his welcome, yet to her horror, Raith himself had encouraged him to remain.

'We have talked so long, and it is growing dark. You must remain to dine with us, Forteviot.'

Dine with them? So that he might hint and conjecture interminably? No, Lord help her!

'My dear Raith, why not dine with me instead at Kington?' had said Forteviot. 'I am staying at the Cross Keys. We will only bore Lady Raith with our memories. And we might try a hand or two of piquet afterwards, if you should care for it?'

She had felt Raith's glance, and held her breath, un-knowing whether she feared more to be left alone with her husband, or to be relieved of his presence, not know-ing what Forteviot might say to him.

'No, why should we venture into the cold? We can as well play here, sir.'

In that moment, Rosina had wanted desperately to in-tervene. To scream that if Forteviot were to remain in the house, she must leave it. But that would have been fatal. Dinner had been a nightmare, never knowing from mo-ment to moment what Forteviot might not say to undo her utterly.

'Since Forteviot and I are going to play cards, my love,' Raith had said as she had risen, 'you may as well go to bed. I am sure His Lordship will excuse you.'

Excuse her to the freedom of his tongue, no doubt! She had been on tenterhooks ever since. Did Raith truly sup-pose that she could sleep, having no notion what might be said down there in the saloon? Or knowing that her husband had so tight a control on his temper that it could not fail to erupt—doubtless upon his wife's luckless head.

Rosina began to wish that she had swallowed her pride, and found the courage to confess all to Raith. However hideous, it could not have been as bad as this, for what-ever fondness he had begun to cherish for her would un-doubtedly be swept aside.

In a state of mounting tension, she waited to hear the sound of the front door. Her perambulations brought her within sight of the painting of Raith's mother. Pausing, she brought her candle up to the figure on the horse, as if seeking for that vanished gentleness that he must have acquired from this source, for he had it not from the Raiths.

The front door slammed, and she jumped with shock, her heart thudding. She ran to the window, putting the light behind her so that she might see out. A coach was approaching from the stables, and a shadow moved towards it.

Rosina's pulse began to thunder in her head. He was gone, and Raith was done! He would be coming up in a moment. Now that the time was upon her, she wanted to hold it back. She went with lagging steps through to the antechamber door.

Why was she doing this? Raith had told her to go to bed. She was still dressed in the Turkish robe, the most modest of her new gowns, its scalloped folds of the neckline covering the area about her bosom. Would he berate her for having remained up? Why for that, when he had a more cogent reason?

She heard footsteps in the corridor. Her heart fluttered. For a craven moment, she was tempted to withdraw. But her fear of having been betrayed was too strong. She must know!

Drawing a breath for courage, she opened the antechamber door. The room was empty, and in darkness but for the feeble light from her own candle. She moved to Raith's dressing-room door, and hesitated, feeling sick. But it would not do. She lifted her hand to knock—and the door opened.

Rosina stepped back quickly as Raith moved into the doorway. He was stripped to his shirtsleeves and his hair was untied—a *déshabillé* that enhanced his masculinity.

Rosina's throat dried. But the candelabrum in his hand fell upon taut features. Her heart sank.

'Has he gone at last?'

The response was cold. 'He has gone.'

Raith moved to the fireplace, and set the candle holder on the mantel. He was conscious more than anything of fatigue. The effort to contain himself, to beat Forteviot at his own game, had exhausted him. Like that numbness after battle, before reaction set in. Yet he had heard her moving in here as he had begun to undress, and entered on impulse. The questions must be asked, though he dreaded her response. He turned and looked across at her shadowed face by the window.

'Were you afraid that he would tell me everything?'

Rosina's defences went up, overriding the intensity of his attraction. He was unnervingly right. But she was angered to think that he assumed her guilt proven. She refrained from answering.

Raith's voice hardened. 'You had as well tell me as not, ma'am. It makes no difference now. What is this man to you?'

She bit her lip. How could he be anything when Raith was by? Impossible to say that. Yet she must speak, or she would draw his temper.

'Nothing.' It was scarce adequate. She swallowed and added flatly, 'I do not like him.'

'That does not answer me,' he said, an edge to his voice.

Rosina was disinclined to answer him. He had made his own judgements—the more hurtful in light of the sensations his own appearance was invoking. If it made no difference, why should she say anything at all? He would not believe her.

Raith waited a moment. Was she still so stubborn? Why, when she must know how futile a gesture it was to defy him? He turned his eyes away, unable to bear the glinting pallor of her features as they flickered in the light of her candle.

'The man is a gambler. Not as reckless as my brother, but quite as determined. He consorts with men of ill repute, and I know him for a loose-living rake. He is tolerated by the world for his social veneer of charm, I imagine. But men of my father's stamp would not give him the time of day.'

She heard it with resentment, crushing down her awakened senses. Whence this catalogue? To make her feel how low she had sunk in his esteem?

'Why do you tell me this?'

The barb of his bitterness sounded in his voice. 'How do you imagine it makes me feel, to know that you have had dealings with a man of that sort?'

Rosina stiffened in the shadows. 'Dealings? What, pray, is your meaning?'

'You know well enough,' he said roughly. 'You have had some…acquaintance with him.'

Acquaintance! Why did he not say it outright? 'You will have to be more explicit, my lord, if I am to understand you.'

Raith moved swiftly, and Rosina instinctively shrank back. The candle guttered as her hand shook, drawing his attention. He took it from her and set it on the sill of the window, his eyes on her face as it darkened with the removal of the light. His chest felt as though it must burst. He wanted to crush the life out of her!

He hissed in a breath. Had he run mad? He took her throat between his hands, pushing up her chin with his thumbs. He spoke in a guttural whisper.

'Do you know how easily I could break your neck, Rosina?'

She did not flinch, but he could feel the tremble of her

limbs. Her black eyes glittered in the dark. 'If your hatred is so v-vengeful, you had b-better do it.'

A groan escaped him, as his fingers loosened, altering his touch to a caress. 'You think I am driven by hatred? By thunder, I wish it were so!'

Rosina met his eyes, a fierce pulsing war within her, engendered by his proximity. Spasms of need gripped her depths, while a flame of resentment fired her mind, urging her to hit him. Yet as desperately did she yearn for his kiss, the feel of his fingers burning at her flesh.

Raith read the confusion of messages, and his loins flared. His gaze fell to the shiver at her lips, and his mouth came down. But the image of Forteviot's mocking eyes intruded, and he jerked up again.

He took in an unsteady breath, and his hands slid to her shoulders. 'Rosina, I ask you again, what is that man to you?'

His withdrawal shot pain into Rosina's chest, overriding the rest. She pulled back, brushing his hands off. 'Nothing! He is nothing to me.'

'Blood and thunder, *don't lie to me!*'

Her breath caught, and she could not keep her voice from quaking. 'You can m-make me afraid b-by these means, Raith, but you w-will not loosen my t-tongue.'

Raith flung away. His conduct was disgraceful. Hell and damnation, how she aroused him! And he had not wanted to lose his temper. How dangerous in every way it was to be near her!

'Your pardon,' he said, curt and crisp, moving back to the empty fireplace and thus out of range of touching her again. But frustration rapped out of him. 'What is the point of concealment? You know as well as I that you gave yourself away the moment you heard his name. And if you had not, he has said enough to incriminate you.'

Rosina took a hasty step towards him, her voice husky

with dread. 'What did he say to you? What did he tell you?'

'Nothing beyond what you heard,' Raith told her. 'The moment you were out of the room, he was as closed as an oyster.'

Then he had got nothing by his efforts. Rosina sighed with relief. She could not doubt but that Forteviot, had he said anything at all, would have said it in such a way that she was indeed incriminated.

'But that is nothing to the purpose,' Raith pursued. 'You can no longer deny it, Rosina, for God's sake! You are acquainted with this man.'

Rosina's head came up. 'What of it? So also are you, sir.'

A jolt seemed to kick at his chest. 'Then you admit it!'

She threw her hands up to her face, her chest hollowing out. Oh, dear Lord! She had not intended to admit anything. Dared she say that she had meant that her acquaintance with him had begun today? To what purpose? He would never believe it. She sighed, capitulating.

'Yes, I have met him before.'

Raith did not move from where he stood. He could not have done so had he tried. The hurt was too acute. Dully, he repeated his earlier question. 'What was he to you?'

Impatience seethed out of Rosina. 'What do you imagine, Raith? You have seen how I regarded him. Can you then suppose me to have been in love with him?'

'Not—in love.' God, how the word taunted him! 'But I'd stake my oath that he was the man towards whom you exhibited such fear. He was—in despite of your wishes, perhaps—your lover.'

He had said it at last. Had she not known that this was what he believed? But to hear it from him was more wounding than Rosina could ever have imagined. Her heart bled. She had as well have endured her guardian's

lust, and allowed herself to be sold into Forteviot's possession. What had it availed her to escape? She had
snatched at some other life, and been found wanting. In
the process, she'd had a glimpse of tenderness, of what
love might be—and lost it.

She picked up her candle, and showed him an ashen
countenance. 'There is no more to say, Raith. I am going
to my bed.' Then she turned to her door, and quietly left
him.

Raith spent the night in an agony of affliction. When
he remembered back to those moments prior to the fated
arrival of Lord Forteviot, he could not but be struck with
a burning sense of the unfairness of it all. He was ashamed
of his treatment of Rosina. He had come home to make
his peace with her, and had ended in a worse quarrel. A
curse upon the villain! What was his association with
Rosina?

He wished fervently for Ottery's return, knowing he
could not hope for it for another day or two at least. Yet
how might the guardian's testimony help? Only it must,
or Rosina would not have left his house. Had not her nurse
intimated that there were two men involved? Forteviot
must be the other. What was the connection between
them?

He had resolved to curb his impatience, and to treat his
wife with the civility that was her due. He must refrain
from questioning her further, and let her be. Though how
he was to do either of those things when the sight of her
threw his hurt into high relief, he did not know.

He could only be glad that she did not appear at breakfast. He had determined to resume his inspection of the
estate, and had accordingly donned riding dress. It was
Wednesday, and his agent did not yet know he was back.
But he would send to Longridge, and meet him wherever

the man had currently reached in their investigations. He needed occupation, by thunder!

'Your pardon, m'lord.'

He looked up from the coffee he was drinking. 'What is it, Kirkham?'

'Does Your Lordship plan to use Parton this morning?'

'Why?' frowned Raith. 'I was going to send him to my agent, but what do you need?'

The butler coughed. 'You know how short of staff we are, m'lord, and I would be obliged if I might ask Parton to ride to Kington to deliver a letter for Her Ladyship.'

A cold hand seized upon Raith's chest. 'Kington?' He stared at the man, a startled query in his mind. The question rapped from him. 'Where is the letter?'

Kirkham went to the sideboard and picked up a salver. It was of pewter, there being no silver remaining in the house. He brought it to Raith, who snatched up the sealed missive and read the inscription. All thought of inspections went out of his head. He leaped from his chair.

'Have Parton saddle my horse. I will take the letter myself!'

Within ten minutes he was astride his mount, cantering cross-country, making for the bridle path that led over some three miles to Kington. He had taken a snap decision, but as he rode, he had leisure to find justification for it.

If he had felt murderous towards Rosina last night, he was now doubly so—but against Forteviot! He might have broken the seal and read the letter. As her husband, he had the right. What man would not choose to open a letter penned by his wife to another man? And one of whom he entertained the gravest suspicions? He might have confronted her, but that would make her even less inclined to part with her secrets.

No, this was the best solution. It would afford him infinite pleasure to be able to take Forteviot at fault. It would serve him out for at least some of the foul wit he had exercised at Raith's expense.

He had himself played a loathsome part last night. He had acted in much the manner of Piers, and Forteviot had begun, he thought, to believe in it. Why should he not? It was seven years since they had met—for Forteviot had formed one of the party on the fiendish night when he had suffered that final humiliation at his brother's hands. That he had fought back had earned him Forteviot's jeering remark about heroics.

Raith set his teeth, turning the horse onto the bridle path, and letting him have his head. He was no longer a raw youth. Let Forteviot beware him this time.

He covered the ground in some fifteen minutes, cantering easily into Kington, and rode into the yard at the Cross Keys, bidding the ostlers good day. He was already known at this inn, and the landlord greeted him with offers of refreshment.

'I want nothing, I thank you, Tarbert,' he said, divesting himself of hat, gloves and whip. 'I came only to see Lord Forteviot. I trust he is still with you?'

'Oh, yes, my lord. He has just rung for his breakfast. Would you wish me to show you up to his private parlour?'

Forteviot was lounging in a cherry-striped morning gown, a nightcap covering his unwigged head. He was reading a newspaper, but he glanced up as Raith entered the room. A startled look came into his face, but he summoned a smile, and spoke with all his usual urbanity, rising from the chair.

'My dear Anton, what an unexpected pleasure!'

Raith made no attempt to disguise his acute dislike. He stared at the man, and watched with satisfaction as the smile faded. Was that wariness in those slitted eyes? Raith withdrew the letter from his pocket and held it up. He allowed the disgust he felt to sound in his voice.

'This is from my wife. It is addressed to you, Forteviot. Perhaps you would read it, and then be good enough to tell me why my wife is writing to you.'

The other's eyebrows went up. 'Is she, indeed?' He resumed his seat, crossing his legs in an attitude of non-chalance. 'Why don't you read it for yourself, my dear Anton? I feel sure it can contain nothing that cannot be seen by a husband's jealous eye.'

Raith looked him over with contempt. 'Don't attempt to trifle with me, Forteviot! The game is up. I know that you have had dealings with my wife.'

'If you know, my dear Anton—'

'If you once more address me in that supercilious fashion, you lying cur, I shall knock your teeth down your throat!' interrupted Raith with heat.

The other smiled in an infuriating way. 'Yes, I rather thought that your manner of last night was assumed. This is much more like you. My dear—but I must not call you that! Really, how difficult it is to know quite what to—'

'Will you cease this prevarication?' Raith crossed the room, and threw the letter down on the table. 'Read it!'

Forteviot picked up the letter and turned it over, examining the seal. 'You amaze me, Raith. You really have refrained from opening the thing.' He laughed gently, and Raith set his teeth at the sound. 'You know, your chivalry is quite misplaced. Perhaps I would even say, wasted.'

A chill swept through Raith. His eyes narrowed. 'Do you care to explain that remark?'

'Do you know, Raith, I don't care to,' Forteviot said apologetically, breaking the seal on the note. He ran his eyes down the single sheet, and his smile broadened. 'Well, it is what I expected.' He held it out. 'Will you read it now? Or are you still bent upon being noble?'

Raith did not take it. 'I will rather have you tell me the substance.'

Forteviot tutted gently. 'Very foolish, sir. Would you expect me to betray a lady?'

'Spare me your affectations!' Raith twitched it out of his hand, and pocketed it. 'Write a reply, and I will take it to Rosina myself.'

A pitying look was cast upon him. 'Thus forcing her to recognise the unparalleled nature of your forbearance, in the hopes that this will induce her to confide in you. My poor Raith, you must be gravely mistaken in her character.'

Raith felt his temper rising, and reminded himself that the man was bent upon provoking it. That he had doubts himself was one thing. To hear Forteviot impugn Rosina was quite another. He was hard put to it to refrain from striking the villain where he sat. If he did so, he must prepare to be challenged. He had the intention of calling Forteviot to account in due time—but on his own terms.

'You do yourself no good by these hints, sir,' he said instead in a cold tone. 'Unless you can substantiate them, be assured that I will believe no ill of my wife.'

The eyebrows rose again. 'Yet you come here in a righteous fury, demanding to know why she is writing to me. Permit me to tell you that I find you a trifle inconsistent.'

'Call for pen and ink,' said Raith impatiently. 'I have no mind to listen to your smooth-tongued insinuations.'

'As you wish.'

Forteviot rose, and moved across to a small table set in the window embrasure. Upon it rested an inkstand and several leaves of paper. He took up a pen, and dipped it in the ink.

'I did wonder how you had become inveigled—I hesitate to say entrapped—into marriage,' he said, throwing the remarks over his shoulder. 'But I realised how unwitting had been your involvement when I found out about your advertisement.'

Raith heard his words with alarm and puzzlement. He knew about the advertisement? 'How did you find out?'

Forteviot turned slightly to survey him, holding the pen poised. 'I have my sources. An apothecary's boy was extremely helpful.'

Concern for Rosina's nurse attacked Raith. She had half-expected, when he and Ottery called upon her, that her visitors might have been this man or the guardian, he recalled. He did not wish to ask whether Forteviot had seen Mrs Hoswick, for fear of alerting him to her whereabouts if he did not know them. Yet what of the boy Toly, whom he had certainly seen? Had Forteviot bribed him—or used some other method?

'Where did you find this apothecary's boy?' he asked.

'At Hopsford. And by the same method you did, I fancy. Those fellows at Brinklow Receiving Office appeared unsurprised at my enquiries. I suspect, my dear Raith, from the boy's guarded remarks, that my visit followed hard upon your own. What he had to tell me was most interesting.'

'Indeed?' Raith eyed him with growing suspicion. What need had he to make such enquiries, if he had seen—as must be supposed—the announcement of Rosina's marriage in the *Gazette*? And why give her husband this information? What mischief was he brewing? Like a fool, Raith had fallen straight into his trap!

Forteviot was folding his letter. 'I have not a seal with me. No doubt you will carry your nobility so far as to contain your curiosity until you reach home.'

Rosina paced the saloon, in much the same state of tension as she had paced her bedchamber on the previous evening. Had Forteviot yet had her letter? Would he respond instantly? She had known he meant to make trouble! But she was not prepared for the dreadful nature of it.

With her chocolate this morning, Joan had brought the fell tidings, contained in a note from Forteviot that had been brought over from the Cross Keys. She had passed over his sarcastic felicitations upon her marriage, and read quickly to discover what he intended. It had been an unhappy moment.

Since she had deprived him of his prize, he said boldly, it behoved her to repay him what she had been worth to him. Now that she was so advantageously placed, he had no doubt of her being able to do it. She had better find a way, or he would be obliged instead to request it from her husband—and she must know what that would mean.

Blackmail! How could she pay a tithe of such a sum— even had she a mind to do it? It was not her debt, but her guardian's. She had sent Joan for pen and paper, and sat down immediately at her dressing-table to answer him as much. She said nothing of Raith, nor deigned to say that she could not afford to pay him. She recommended him to apply to Herbert Cambois, and let her alone.

Once the letter was despatched, she had become prey to tension, wondering what might be the outcome. Hearing from Joan that Raith had ridden out, she'd had the maid dress her again in the simple sprigged gown and come downstairs to await Forteviot's response.

She dared not suppose that he would accept her refusal to pay him. What would she do if he told Raith everything? Would his version of events march with the truth? She doubted it. It would be better that she tell Raith the whole. What did it matter any longer? Her marriage was all but over.

Raith walked in on her unexpectedly halfway through the morning. He had evidently just ridden in, for he was in his green riding frock and buckskins, his boots a trifle mud-splashed. His aspect was forbidding, and the memory of last night's uncomfortable interview sprang into her mind. She stared at him as he shut the door—and locked it.

'I have no wish to be disturbed,' he said curtly, by way of explanation. He saw alarm enter her eyes, and added, 'I am not locking you in, Rosina. You may leave here at any time that suits you.'

Rosina knew not what to say. Did he mean to renew his questions? 'What is it you want?'

Holding her eyes, he removed both letters from his pocket, and coming forward, held them out to her. 'These are your property. I have not read either.'

Numbly, she took the letters, and knew on the instant what they were. The seal of the one she had written was broken. She spread it open. 'Dear Lord, whence had you this?'

'It came to my hand this morning.' He saw the horror creep into her features, and was conscious of a feeling of guilt. He repressed it. It was time and past that the lies were exposed.

Rosina was opening the other letter. She ran her eyes down the short message it contained. She barely took in the words as the implication sank into her brain. She felt sick.

'You took it to him! My letter—you took it to him yourself. Why did you not read it?'

'Because I wanted him to tell me himself what it contained,' Raith told her flatly. 'When he would not, I told him to write that reply for me to bring back.'

She heard him, but she did not take in much of what he said. Raith had not read the letters—either of them. What should stop him making himself master of their contents? Did he believe that in this extremity she would at last tell him the truth? If so, he was right. What choice had she?

Her breath was ragged. 'I did not s-seek to contact him, Raith.' She dug into the hidden pocket of her gown and produced Forteviot's first letter. 'I wrote in reply to this.'

For a moment she held all three papers within her fingers. Then she thrust them upon him. 'Read them. Read them all!'

Turning, she moved quickly away to the fireplace, and leaning her hands on the mantel, rested her forehead upon them, trying vainly to control the quickened breath that accompanied the palpitations of her bosom.

Raith watched her with a wrenching at his heart. In despite of all, she drew his compassion. His resentment of Forteviot grew, and he unfolded the letters as he moved to the window to read.

So Forteviot attempted blackmail? Hell and damnation! That presupposed that there was some disgrace attached to the matter of this sum of money he demanded, and said Rosina had been worth. In what respect? God send it was not what he was beginning to suspect! What had it to do with the guardian's debt to Forteviot? It began to seem that Rosina had been caught up in a situation which she had no power to control. Had he not suspected as much? Only how far had it gone?

His chest caved in, as he felt the dread certainty of his wife having been obliged to succumb to Forteviot. With unsteady fingers he sifted through the man's last communication. It was a brief statement of his own visit to Forteviot, stating only that Raith had challenged him to account for his correspondence with her, and asking whether she dared to tell her husband the truth. Raith looked up to find Rosina's eyes upon him.

She had turned to watch, finding it more bearable to

see his reaction as he read, than to wait for it in words. He was frowning heavily, and a muscle twitched, shifting the rent of his cheek. But Rosina could not tell what he thought.

He eyed her in silence for a moment. The waif-look was pronounced, and altogether touching. He laid aside the sheaf of letters upon a side table, and came up to her. He reached for one of her hands, and brought it to his lips.

Softly then, he said, 'Can you not trust me, Rosy?'

Tears sprang to her eyes. 'Lord knows I want to, Raith!'

He said nothing, but only enclosed the quivering fingers within his own, holding them tight. Rosina met the tenderness of his gaze, and sighed. She wanted to fall upon his chest, and feel his arms encircle her. She was seized with the urge to touch her fingers to his blemished features, so close, and open to her sight. But to win the right to that—if he could find it in him to forgive the shame of the indignities she had endured—she must open her life to his inspection.

She looked down. 'Very well. Loose me now, if you please. I will tell you it all.'

As Raith released her, the wash of relief that flooded him was tempered by the visible paling of her features. He stood aside, and watched her move to take a chair. She did not look at him, but sat stiffly upright, her fingers pulling at each other in unconscious expression of her inner disquiet.

'You believe,' she began in a tone of forced calm over her tautly held-in tension, 'that it was Forteviot who—who violated my honour. But it was not he, though he is guilty of the intention. It was my guardian who made that attempt.'

'Attempt?' queried Raith quickly. 'Do you mean to imply that he did not succeed?'

Rosina threw up a hand. 'Pray, let me tell the tale in my own way. You will know all—by and by.'

Raith curbed his impatience with difficulty, gripping the mantel with one hand. He set his jaw, and Rosina saw it. She kneaded unconsciously at the muslin folds of her petticoats.

'You are eager to know if he took me,' she said low-toned. 'He did not—' closing her eyes tight shut '—penetrate.'

The word stabbed in his gut. He gripped his underlip between his teeth, his eyes fierce upon her delicate elfin face. What rude invasions had been attempted? How far had been taken this despoiling of her virgin innocence? He saw the black eyes open, and their luminous sheen threw him into acute disorder—and murderous intent. Her guardian was a dead man!

Rosina could not look at him. 'Of what p-purity I may still be p-possessed,' she uttered shakily, 'I must l-leave you to be the judge.'

He flung over to the window, unable to trust himself. Much more, and he would seize her in his arms, and tell her that she need give him no more of this. He had wanted to hear it. But even this little telling was a species of torture. He had wanted to know her to be pure—and she was, it seemed. But at what cost? Behind him, Rosina spoke again.

'I must tell you how it came about. And—and the part played in this by Forteviot.'

Raith set his teeth. This was not helping her. With deliberation, he turned again, and went to sit in the opposite chair. 'I will hear you with patience.'

She cast a look at him, and a tiny smile wavered for an instant on her lips. Then she withdrew her gaze, and clasping her hands tightly together, began her tale, explaining how her pity of her guardian's grief had made him see her as an asset. She twisted her fingers.

'I believed at first that he intended me to marry. He instructed me to be present at his gambling sessions, intimating that I would meet suitable gentlemen. He would not hear of my refusal, though I did refuse. At length he threatened to throw me out if I did not do it. I had nowhere to go. It seemed to me then a lesser evil to comply.'

Raith listened in a steadily increasing state of tension. Guessing what was coming, he ached for the rude shock of awakening that Rosina must have experienced. Too well did he know how unmannerly a thing was the sight of men at play—their behaviour indecorous, their drinking excessive, and using language unfit for feminine ears.

'There were some five or six each night. I was required to refill their glasses, or bring fresh cards. Only Forteviot paid me much heed.' She shifted with discomfort, one hand going up to touch her neck as if she sought to brush away the memory of his lascivious eyes. 'He looked me over in a way that made me feel—unclothed.'

One night, she had gone to the parlour to discover only Forteviot and Herbert Cambois. The mask had been stripped off.

'My guardian told me that a bargain had been struck.'

Raith held his breath. The image of Forteviot's mocking features hovered at the forefront of his mind. He wanted to smash his fist between those slitted eyes!

'I was to be the p-payment for his debts to Forteviot.'

Rosina's voice failed, and she was obliged to put a hand up to her mouth. Raith rose quickly, and took a step towards her. But she threw out a hand, shrinking back.

'I can only say this once, my lord. Pray let me finish!'

But her tears choked her. Raith cursed. He stepped swiftly across to a baize table in one corner of the room, where a decanter and glasses had been forgotten from his

game of piquet with Forteviot. Pouring a measure of
Madeira, he brought it back to Rosina, bidding her drink
it.

'It will calm you.'

She put out a trembling hand, and took the glass, throwing a brief glance up at him as she sipped at the liquid.
She felt the warmth of it spreading through her, and was
presently able to speak again. Raith took the glass from
her and placed it on the mantel, where he remained,
watching her face.

'I cannot describe to you my feelings upon the event.
Forteviot was very frank. I was to be his mistress. When
I failed to—please him, he would cast me off. He thought
I should have no difficulty finding myself another protec-
tor.'

But the worst part of the tale was yet to be told. Rosina
moistened her lips, and her fingers writhed about each
other. Raith watched her with mounting distress, and
black fury in his heart as he learned how, when Forteviot
had gone, Rosina had cast aside all pride, and pleaded
with her guardian to free her from this intolerable future.

'He was adamant. Nothing would serve him but this. I
did not know what to do. If I'd had a way of finding a
post, I would have taken it. But without references, my
situation was impossible. And there was no time.' Her
voice sank. 'I tried to school myself to accept it. But when
I saw how Forteviot eyed my person—I knew I had rather
die by my own hand!'

Raith's fist was clenched so hard that his knuckles
ached. He forced himself to straighten his hand, and
clamped his mouth tight shut on the hot protesting words
that rose to his tongue.

'I resolved to be gone from my guardian's house before
the plan could be put into execution. I had in secret re-

ceived my nurse's direction, and I knew she would give me refuge.'

She had made her plans and enlisted the aid of those two of the servants who were her particular friends. But that night her guardian had stumbled drunk into her bed-chamber.

'He looked just as you did—standing in the doorway with a candelabrum,' she said huskily.

'That is what threw you into the memory, and made you so afraid?'

Rosina nodded, drawing a sobbing breath. 'He meant, he said, to teach me submission. He—he laid down his candle, and—fell upon me. I managed to throw him off, but he pulled at the covers. He caught me, and he is a big man. I thought I was done for.'

She recalled struggling, and the loathsome wetness of his slobbering kiss as she had tried to evade his mouth. He had torn at her nightgown, and she had flailed half-naked in the cold night air. She had felt him thrusting at her thighs, while his hot hands had seized at her flesh.

She had been saved in that moment when he raised himself up in order to effect an entry, for the wine had gone to his head and he had paused, swaying. She had pushed into his chest, driving him off. As he had fallen among the disarranged covers, Rosina had struggled out of the bed, and run as for her life, slamming the door upon his infuriated grunting. She had fled to the attic room of one of the maids, where she had remained for the rest of the night.

'In the early dawn,' she finished, 'we crept out when the other servants had ascertained that he was abed in his own room. He had stumbled about looking for me, we thought, for the place was a wreck. Aggie helped me to pack as much of my belongings as I could carry in a portmanteau, and she promised to send the rest secretly by carrier to Brinklow.'

There was silence for some moments in the saloon. Raith was too harrowed by the tale to speak. The near rape so appalled him that he wished fervently that he had never asked her for this truth. Was not his the cruel demand that had thrown her time and again back into this memory? How hurtful must it have been for Rosina, to be reminded of it each time that he had harried her to tell him.

But Rosina, he saw, was quiescent now. In the telling of it, had she exorcised something of the ghost? Or was it merely that exhaustion now prevented her from feeling anything? It was a sensation he could appreciate.

'How did you get to your nurse?' he asked.

Rosina heaved an unconscious sigh. 'In disguise. A groom stole for me a greatcoat, a slouch hat and a pair of boots from the stables. I looked less like a country wench than a farm boy. I had no money, so I had to make my way by asking lifts from carriers.'

She fell silent again. She felt both exposed and empty. How might Raith be less disgusted than she was herself? She was not impure, nor was it her fault, but she was nevertheless tainted. Had their marriage remained a convenience; he might have been expected to tolerate it. But they were long past that. How could he possibly bear it? If she could only know his present intentions towards her!

'What will you do now?'

Raith straightened abruptly. 'I am going back to Kington.'

Rosina blenched. 'To see Forteviot? To what purpose?'

His jaw was set, danger in his eyes. 'To challenge him with this story—and to dare him to answer me!'

Alarmed, Rosina rose from her seat. 'You will not call him out, Raith?'

'Have no fear! I mean to settle this affair. Do not forget that he has come here with the intention of extorting money.'

He went purposefully to the door, and turned the key in the lock. Rosina followed him, laying one hand upon his arm.

'Raith, wait!'

He turned. 'I must go, Rosina. It is useless to try to stop me.'

'One moment only, I pray you!'

The plea was intense. Raith hesitated, his fingers about the handle of the door. 'What is it?'

Her fingers left his arm, travelling to her bosom as the coal-black eyes searched his face. 'Raith, do you believe what I have told you?'

He frowned in puzzlement. 'Of course I believe it. Why should I not?'

Rosina's lip quivered. 'And when F-Forteviot gives you some twisted v-version of it, to make you think ill of me, will you believe it then?'

Raith's heart contracted. He let go the door handle, and caught her hand. 'How can you suppose otherwise? Do you imagine I would take that fiend's word before yours?'

'Why should you not?' she uttered. 'You know me little better than you know him. How long have we been married?'

'I don't know,' Raith said roughly. 'Two weeks—three? What does it matter? It feels like a lifetime!'

Her fingers clung to his. 'But it is not, Raith. It is little more than two weeks. And that man is persuasive. I have no proof that I am telling the truth. And you have entertained doubts of me from the beginning.'

Raith cupped her cheek, the grey eyes remorseful. 'For which I hope you can learn to forgive me.' Then he drew her to him and dropped a light kiss on her hair. 'But you need have no apprehension. Ottery is even now at the house of Herbert Cambois. I will wager that he will extract the truth. He is no fool.'

But Rosina was pulling away from him, shock in her eyes. Realising what he had said, Raith gave himself a mental kick. It was too late. The murder was out, and his wife's outrage was patent.

Chapter Nine

'Mr Ottery is at Nun Eaton? Dear Lord, you have been spying upon me!' Rosina swung away. 'You have plagued me beyond endurance to tell you these things, and all the time—' Halting in the middle of the room, she turned upon him. 'How could you know where to find my guardian? How did you know his name? Whom did you bully to—' She stopped, checked by a horrifying thought. 'Gatty! You have found my nurse!'

'Yes, we found her,' Raith admitted, torn between guilt and the conviction that his actions had been justified. 'We were searching all the while I was away from here.'

'And you returned to me with soft words and…' She faded out, choked with chagrin. 'How could you use me so?'

'I had no choice, Rosina! You would say nothing. What was I to do? I had to find out the truth in any way I could.'

'But to set your lawyer to spy upon me! And Gatty. What did you do to her to make her betray me to you? She would never have done so without force.'

Anger flared in Raith's breast. 'Is that what you think of me, by thunder? There was nothing of that sort, Rosina.'

The black orbs burned at him. 'What did you do to her?'

'For what do you take me?' he uttered frustratedly. 'I found a poor, blind creature whose sole concern was for your safety. She was only induced to confide the name of Cambois when she understood that I was more fitted to provide your safe keeping than Forteviot himself.'

Rosina's eyes flashed. 'But you did not tell her your suspicions of me. She would have demanded that you return me to her.'

'Which indeed she did,' Raith confirmed flatly. 'I gave her my promise that I would do so, should it turn out...' He paused, realising how infelicitous was this trend.

But Rosina had divined his meaning. The blood drained out of her face, and he saw the waif returning.

'You had as well d-do so at once,' she said huskily. 'There can be no t-trust between us.'

Raith moved to her, and tried to take her hands. She whipped them behind her, stepping back. A weight of anguish hovered above him. He was going to lose her!

'Rosy,' he uttered raggedly, 'don't do this, I pray you!'

She met his eyes full, and the pain within them was echoed in his own breast. 'I d-dare not give in to you, Raith. Your suspicions have wrought h-havoc within me—as they have in you. You think it is over, but I know it is not. Mr Ottery will gain nothing but lies from Herbert Cambois. Between him and Forteviot, they will re-awaken your doubts—I know it!'

'No, Rosina!' he said forcefully. 'Trust me!'

'How can I trust you?' she demanded, anguished. 'You have blown hot and c-cold upon me since the first moment of our union.'

Raith was silenced. He knew it to be true, and knew not how to reassure her. Desperate, he uttered, 'Rosy, we are married, for better or for worse. Nothing can change that.'

Rosina let out a laugh that cracked in the middle, and turned away from him. She found herself unsteady on her feet, and grasped at the mantel of the fireplace for support. She did not look at him. She spoke in the flat calm of despair.

'You speak always from impulse, Raith, and fail to see your own contradictions. But a moment since, you said you had told Gatty that you would return me to her. Now you quote me the marriage vow, and expect me to believe in it.' She took a breath, and looked across at him. 'I must face it, if you will not. We are on the brink of separation.'

A shaft sliced into his chest, and his heart cried out against it. He wanted to seize her in his arms, and over-bear her conviction with the fire of his lips. But she had drifted too far away from him, and a voice at the back of his mind whispered that there was truth in what she said.

'If it should come to that, then know that it will be to my everlasting regret.'

The torment of his heart was in his voice. Rosina heard it with a twisting in her own breast. 'Oh, why did you not meet me before we married?' she cried, distraught. 'Why did you not ask me then?'

He flung it back at her. 'Why did you not tell me at the outset?'

Her lip quivered. 'Would you have m-married me, if you had heard then what I have t-told you today?'

Raith looked at the delicate elfin features, at the lumi-nous appeal of her coal-black eyes, and knew his answer would ever have been the same.

'Yes,' he said simply.

Then he turned on his heel, and left the room, wrench-ing open the door, and slamming it behind him.

Rosina stared at the shut door, frozen as the sound of

his footsteps died out of the hall. Into the numbness of her mind floated the only possible realisation. Raith did care! He would have married her, in spite of all. What could that mean but one thing? She had long suspected it, but had not dared to believe.

Yet how was it possible? He had not known her—not seen her!—until they married. Had his ardour grown so rapidly? Why should it not—when her own had been almost as swift? She could no longer tell at what instant of time her spouse had thus fatally pierced her heart. Might it be that Raith was similarly affected? Oh, he wanted her! But so also did Forteviot, and—

Her thoughts slammed to a halt. Raith was going back to that man! Dear Lord, why could he not see the danger? So small a twist as it needed to turn him against her once more. If it was indeed the case that his heart was touched, then she was lost indeed. For she saw how vital to him must have been the declaration of her chastity. Forteviot would change him. She knew he would. Raith had bade her trust him, but how could she, knowing how subject he was to those lightning fluctuations of temperament? It would take so little!

How was she to bear his renewed hostility, if it was true that he loved her? She could not! Raith—*Raith!*

She did not know whether she cried aloud, as she tore open the door to run from the saloon, crossing the hall on winged feet. Driven by desperate need—some wild half-formed hope of detaining him!—she flung wide the front door, and ran out on to the porch, gulping in the frosty chill of November.

Before her yawned the empty ash-strewn lawns. A sob escaped her, and she ran out on to the drive, forgetting the open front door, the only thought in her mind that she was too late. Raith was already gone!

The certainty of impending loss gripped her. What use

to have confessed it all, when her enemy's cunning could only play on her spouse's jealous heart? If she better understood his anguish, she was doomed to be the poorer for that knowledge.

Only half-aware of what she did, unheeding of the cold that penetrated through the thin muslin of her sprigged gown, Rosina took off along one side of the mansion. As she went, her mind roved without intent, images pricking at her. Visions of Raith's features, the ugly scar slashing his cheek. Ugly? Yes, it was so, and yet she could only regard it with tenderness. Impossible that there had ever been a time when she could see its savagery upon that beloved countenance without a swelling of affection.

Impossible even, that she had fallen in love with him. Had Raith set out to woo her, he could not have done it with more success than he had achieved with his abominable swings from violent rage to tenderness. Why did she care so for him? He had done his best to make her hate him! Only it was the wounded soul within the tiger that had lured her heart. Dear Lord, how was she to bear his loss?

Her breath caught, and tears sprang to her eyes, half-blinding her. She tried to halt them, but the overwrought bursting of her sorrow would not be contained. Choked sobs stifled her throat, and she stumbled on without intent, pushing through stark wood branches that came in her way. She lost all sensation of direction, and had no idea that she had wandered into the woody retreat that abutted the grounds of Raith Manor.

All at once, a violent pain gripped at her womb. She gasped out, grabbing at the nearest tree for support. It came again, and the occasion of it burst into her mind. Oh, no. To be caught unawares with this? Not now. Not here. She must get back to the house.

But the pain intensified, and Rosina felt the first erup-

tion of her flux. She looked wildly round, trying to gather
her bearings. She was in a forest, but she could not be so
far from the mansion. A sensation of cold came upon her,
and she realised belatedly that she had come forth without
so much as a shawl. Another violent wave of agony overcame her. Hanging on to the tree, she waited for it to
pass.

Raith remained by the parlour door, willing himself to
remember the rules of gentlemanly etiquette. He had not
stayed to lay aside his hat and whip, and his right hand
struck a rhythmic beat of the weapon against his boot.
Much as he longed to do it, he could not march across
the room and lift the villain from his seat with an iron
grip about his throat. Nor smash his fist into that compla-
cent countenance! By and by, he would have satisfaction—and enjoy it. But not now.

'Well?'

Forteviot's eyebrows lifted. 'My dear Raith, I do not
deny that there is some substance in the tale.'

'Substance! Do you dare to imply that there is any vestige of a lie?'

'Nothing so blatant, my dear fellow,' tutted the other,
crossing one leg over the other. He had found time to
dress between Raith's two visits, sporting a neat tie-wig
atop a fashionable suit of green broadcloth over a flam-
boyant striped waistcoat. But he lounged still at his ease.

'Enlighten me,' Raith said curtly, moving to throw
down both hat and whip upon a chair. 'What is amiss
with my wife's story?'

A knowing smile curved Forteviot's thin lips. 'Oh, she
warned you, did she? I imagine she might well suppose
that my version of events did not quite mesh with her
own.'

Raith's ire rose the more as he stripped off his gloves.

How poisonous a tongue had this scoundrel! For he could feel the insinuating pull of his own suspicion even from this slight turn. He flung down the gloves and his voice became snappish.

'Be specific—and do not attempt to suborn me with artifice.'

Forteviot spread his hands, his smile broadening. 'I have no wish to do so, Anton.'

'I know what you wish, Forteviot. You think to extract money from me. You will find me an ill subject for extortion.'

The other looked pained. 'So ugly a word, Anton. No, no. If I seek recompense, it is not to be wondered at. Twenty thousand is a goodly sum.'

'Which you won fairly at play. But not from Rosina.'

To Raith's surprise and distrust, Forteviot heaved a sigh tinged with melancholy. 'I thought to win her, you see. You have succeeded—inadvertently, I know—where I could not. I suppose I am too old for her.'

Disgust coursed through Raith. 'Spare me your shams! You are not trying to make me believe that it was marriage you intended? By thunder, but you take me for a fool! You sought to make a harlot of her.'

He all but ground his teeth, and his long riding frock rippled with motion as he jerked across the room.

'You would have taken her innocence, and dropped her without compunction when she no longer suited your purposes.'

Forteviot's eyebrows rose again, and he laughed gently. 'My dear Anton, nothing could have been further from my mind. Naturally I could not marry a girl who came with no dowry or connections. I have a position in society to keep up.'

'Which is as much as to say that I have not.'

'You entirely mistake me, Raith. But you misunderstand. When I say that I failed to win her, I mean that she did not favour me. That did not imply that she was unwilling to take up the role I had outlined. Rosina had no objection to the bargain of itself. It was sealed with her agreement. Indeed, she was very frank with her requirements.'

Raith set his teeth. 'Take care! If you knew how my fingers itch to close about your throat—'

Forteviot threw up a hand. 'Believe me, I appreciate your feelings. But you have come to me with accusations, my friend, and I have my reputation to consider.'

In one violent movement, Raith swung over to the table where the man sat, and slammed his hands down upon it. 'Your reputation is not at stake here, sir. We are discussing the reputation of my wife! I say to you again—*take care.*'

For a brief instant, he saw the flare of retaliation in the other man's eyes. Then they were veiled again, and the habitual urbanity returned.

'I see that you have not lost that hot-headed temperament that was so much your undoing all those years ago.'

Raith did not move from his position. 'No,' he said deliberately, 'I have not lost it. If you value your skin, Forteviot, you will beware of it.'

His tormentor held up one well-manicured hand. 'Consider me warned.'

His jaw tightening, Raith stood upright once more. His tone was biting. 'Very well, then. Tell me this, if you please. If Rosina was willing to become your mistress— I do not mince words, I!—why did she run away?'

Forteviot looked blank. 'Is that what she said?'

Once again, Raith found himself almost caught by the expression of innocent enquiry—as if Rosina had been trapped in a lie. Hell and damnation, but the fellow was

wily! Well, then, let him set his head in a noose. He
clamped his lips upon a sharp retort.

'You have another explanation?' he asked evenly.

'I hesitate to say this, my dear Anton,' said Forteviot
in a rueful fashion, 'for I know how it must wound you.
But the boot was on the other leg. Had I accepted her for
the debt at the last, I should have been obliged to hand
her back. I had not bargained for receiving damaged
goods.'

By extreme effort of will, Raith contained himself. A
muscle twitched in his cheek, and he could barely get out
the words. 'How would you know if they were—damaged?'

Forteviot's lips pursed, and his features became pinched
in an expression of displeasure. 'I am sorry to say that my
partner in the exchange betrayed me.'

An oath left Raith's lips. The wretch knew of that? 'He
told you?'

There was scorn in the other's smile. 'You do not know
Cambois. What would you? He was drunk, as ever he is.
The fellow confessed all to me.'

In spite of himself, Raith could not help the question.
'How do you know that he succeeded—carried out the
attack?'

'Oh, did Rosina say otherwise?' queried Forteviot in-
nocently. 'Dear me.'

He sighed again, and Raith met his eyes, despising himself for the dread rise of uncertainty in his breast.

'Well?' he demanded roughly. 'What is your inference
this time?'

Forteviot spread his hands again in his characteristic
way. 'I hesitate to say it, Anton. You have several times
offered me violence this morning, and—'

'Say it, and be damned to you!' Raith flung at him,
thrusting away to the window.

'Then do not blame me, for I am quoting another.' His voice was matter-of-fact. 'Cambois gave me to understand that someone had been before him. A footman belike. She consorted, he said, a great deal with the servants.' The tone lowered to one of hushed compassion. 'Rosina did not run away, my poor Anton. Cambois was obliged to throw her out.'

For a moment Raith stood just where he was, gazing unseeingly out of the window, struggling with his baser self. How cunning was this history! Marching readily with Rosina's tale, and yet parting from it in just those details that were guaranteed to strike precisely at his questing jealousy. It had to be intended! He strode away, pacing across the little parlour, and back again. Then he faced Forteviot. He spoke in a low tone that was laced with a vibrant chord of hatred.

'You black-hearted devil! I don't believe a word of this!'

A laugh escaped Forteviot. 'How should you?' he said pityingly. 'Who can blame you, my dear Anton? Your affections are deeply engaged.'

'So deeply,' Raith returned, his breath taut, 'that I will trust my own knowledge of her before your trumped-up fictions.'

'In your place, my dear fellow, I should feel precisely the same,' said Forteviot gently. 'You are bound to wish to think the best of her. And she is so very innocent and sweet, is she not? On the surface.'

'*Enough!*' Raith drew several tight breaths before he was able to command himself. 'I know what you would be at, Forteviot! I tell you now that you will not succeed. Neither in this, nor in your vile scheme. If you persist—' with a raking glance that made the other flinch, his voice dropping to a menacing hush '—I will kill you.'

* * *

Raith cantered his sweating mount into the stable yard, and brought him to a standstill. Leaning forward, he caressed the beast's warm neck.

'I have ridden you too hard, old fellow. You will have to forgive your master's blue devils this accursed day.'

He had galloped the animal, in an attempt to rid himself of the seed of doubt planted by the wilful evil of Rosina's enemy. There had been enough of suspicion in his marriage. She had been too much injured already. He would not be cozened into belief.

Dismounting, he looked in concern at the stallion's heaving flanks, the steam rising from his coat. 'We must get you properly looked to, my buck.' Turning, he called into the stable block. 'Parton!'

There was no reply. What in thunder ailed them all? If his groom was not present, one of the two stable lads always came running forth on his approach. He set his hands to either side his mouth.

'Ho, there! What, is no one by?'

He was obliged to call out several more times, before the sound of running feet at last answered him. They came from the side of the mansion, and belonged, he saw in a moment, not to either of the stable boys, but to one of the maids.

'M'lord!' she gasped, as she caught sight of him. 'Oh, m'lord, thank goodness you are come!'

Quick alarm gripped him. Keeping hold of the horse's rein, he moved forward. 'What in thunder is amiss, girl?'

'Her Ladyship!'

Raith's heart stopped. With a claw-like hand, he seized the maid's arm as she came up. 'What has happened to Her Ladyship?'

Wincing, the girl panted out her frantic news. 'Gone— m'lord!'

Hoarsely, his mind blank, he repeated it. 'Gone?'

'Aye, sir. Mr Kirkham—he found the front door open. He asked us all—if we done it. Only no one didn't know nothing about it, m'lord. Then Mrs Fawley—she thought of Her Ladyship. Joan went looking for her, m'lord—and she weren't nowhere to be found. Every one of us has been out this half-hour and more—searching.'

Raith heard her with a mind incapable of any form of action. Only one solid thought drummed insistently in his head. Rosina had left him!

Vaguely he noted the maid's round eyes popping at him. He must seem a very ninny. But her amazement was differently explained. 'You've gone all white, m'lord.'

Raith made an effort to pull himself together. He held out the bridle. 'Take this! Where are they looking?'

The maid accepted the horse's rein from him, and pointed towards the front of the house. 'All the way along the woods, m'lord.'

A sudden distant shout arrested Raith's attention. He strode forward a few steps, and heard answering calls. The maid, he found, had kept pace beside him, leading the horse.

'Likely they've found her, sir!' she said excitedly.

'Keep hold of my horse! I'll send one of the boys directly,' he said. Then he was running.

He was operating on the instinct of command, the long years of campaigning shifting into play. An officer in battle did not think. He took an instant survey and acted. Raith met the oncoming figures of his servants, and took in what they said without stopping to consider what they meant, or to bandy unnecessary words.

He barked orders, handing away his whip, hat and gloves. With effortless remembrance, he sent someone to attend to the needs of his horse back at the stables. And he followed without question the direction indicated towards the apparent whereabouts of his wife.

But unlike a charge in the field, where the same burst of energy was demanded by the exigencies of warfare, he was driven here by an undercurrent of desperate need because Rosina's safety was in question. When at last he came upon the woeful figure, huddled in a heap against the trunk of a tree, he froze for an instant of stopped time, torn between relief and dread.

She was shivering, and her hair had come loose. But she panted as if with heat, and the black eyes were glazed. She was bent forward over herself, her hands hugging her stomach. And then he saw the blood.

'Rosy!' he uttered hoarsely. 'Rosina, what ails you?'

Her head turned at the sound of his voice, and Raith dropped to one knee beside her, reaching to cradle her. She was ice cold. His voice gentled.

'Rosy—sweetheart!'

The endearment penetrated the cloudy haze of Rosina's mind. One hand left off from the vain effort to afford comfort to the wrenching at her womb, and came waveringly up to touch the face that hovered so close to her own.

'You came,' she whispered. 'Help me, Raith!'

'You may be sure I will.' He became aware again of her frozen limbs, and glanced swiftly about at the shock-ridden faces of the servants. 'Someone run to the village for the doctor! Prepare the bed—a hot brick! Something to drink. Anything to keep her warm. *Go!*'

They scattered as Raith stripped off his riding frock, and wrapped it about her.

'Come, Rosy. We must get you into the house.'

The pain had dulled again to an ache, and Rosina had drifted off into the half-swoon that had accompanied each bout of pain, and overtaken her efforts to find her way home.

'Rosina!'

The sharp tone jerked her back into consciousness. She glanced wildly round, and found his face again.

'Raith! Pray don't scold me.'

He drew her close again. 'No, sweetheart, no. Only tell me what has happened to you?'

Rosina groped for his hand, and it closed about hers. 'I scarce know. I came out—I know not why. F-flowers, Raith.'

'Flowers?' he echoed blankly, rendered stupid from fright. Then, with memory of the blood, the meaning of the slang term sank in.

'You mean the monthly flux?'

She clutched his hand. 'I was not expecting…it took me unawares.'

'It is that only?' he gasped out, the frantic tenor of his heart steadying a little. 'Thank God!'

'I could not—find my way. And there was…too much pain.' As she spoke of it, the griping agony took her again, and she cried out, her hand shifting out of his to press at her womb in a hopeless attempt at succour. 'Like this. I cannot move…'

'Hell and damnation!' Raith swore, and without more ado, set his arms under her, and lifted her from the ground.

She groaned as the change of position struck through her a flash of agony and, as of instinct, huddled into his chest, throwing her arms up and clinging with desperately clutching hands about his shoulders. She murmured his name, and he was brought near to weeping by the hint of a knowledge of deliverance that it contained.

'Raith…'

'I will have you safe in no time,' he promised her, and set off for the mansion as speedily as his burden would allow.

* * *

Rosina lay with eyes closed, but she was not asleep. The pain had dulled, due to a judicious dose of laudanum administered by Dr Barcliffe.

This worthy had arrived in haste, having been summoned from his little house in Ratley Grange village, somewhat flustered at being requested to attend Her Ladyship of Raith Manor. He was of too humble a station to be used to giving his services to any but the lesser gentry and the poorer folk hereabouts—most landowners in the area preferring to call upon his more affluent colleague in Kington.

Through the fogging effects of pain, Rosina had vaguely heard him speaking, in a nervous undertone, to Mrs Fawley, who had taken charge of her sickroom.

'I am unacquainted with His present Lordship, ma'am. I know him only by sight. Do you think he will wish to speak with me?'

'Undoubtedly,' had returned the housekeeper quietly. 'But for this present, I pray you be good enough to attend to Her Ladyship.'

'Of course, of course,' had come from the doctor hastily.

Next moment, Rosina had felt a cool hand on her brow, and had thrust her eyes open to find a bewigged and bespectacled face bent over her. It was of indeterminate years, but pleasant enough, if a trifle plump.

'It is not her head, doctor,' had protested Mrs Fawley impatiently.

In a daze, Rosina had heard the housekeeper explaining her predicament, and thought how grateful she had been this once for her new status. She had suffered from a girl, and had been caught out more than once—although never in thus compromising a situation. But not since Mama died had she had the luxury of giving herself over to the ministrations of others. Mrs Fawley and Joan had taken

care of her needs with sympathetic efficiency, and the
stained clothing, which she would have had to deal with
herself in the past, was mysteriously removed.

A hot brick wrapped in flannel had afforded considerable relief, and the application of two additional down
coverlets upon her bed—at, it transpired, Raith's orders—
had rapidly re-warmed her frozen blood.

She had been a trifle put out when Dr Barcliffe had
plagued her with a series of searching questions, which
she had answered with an increasing feeling of impatience.

How long had it been since her last experience? Why,
the usual length of time. Had she always this degree of
pain? Invariably. Was the blood loss any greater than
usual? She could not say. Had there been no warning?
No, none. Had there been any sickness before this? Not
sickness, no. Had she been moody at all? Yes, she must
say that she had.

And on, in much the same vein, until Rosina was ready
to scream. Then he had probed—with admitted gentleness—upon the swollen mound below her belly. Rosina
had endured this with difficulty, for the area was extraordinarily tender. Finally, she had been unable to help a flow
of tears at his intended words of comfort at the conclusion
of his examination.

'I cannot see any reason for Your Ladyship's immediate concern,' he said cheerfully. 'I think you will find that
these trials will end after you have successfully carried
His Lordship's child, and been brought to bed.'

He had coughed, apparently in embarrassment, as
Rosina began to weep. 'Pray do not upset yourself, Lady
Raith! I venture to prophesy that it will not be long before
these discomforts are a thing of the past.'

But the notion of bearing Raith's infant had pierced so
fiercely into the agony of mind that had been pushed aside

by the ills of her body, that Rosina had been unable to stop crying for some little time. He might have secured her safety—and used so tender a name for her that she wondered if it had been a product of her fevered imagination—but that did not mean that she was assured of a future that could include what must be done in order to get her with child.

'Dear, oh, dear!' had fussed the doctor over her head. And Rosina had heard him whisper to Mrs Fawley, 'I think perhaps I had better give Her Ladyship something to induce calm, as well as help the pain.'

Rosina had swallowed the laudanum without protest, and had been glad to find herself alone at length, but for Joan's faithful attendance even to this moment.

She knew, by the whispers exchanged between her maid and Mrs Fawley, that they thought her to have dropped asleep. It was more comfortable to be allowed to lie quiet, for the passing of the greater agonies in her womb had left her thoroughly exhausted. She was past thinking, and wished merely to lie here—forever, if need be. Only as long as she was not expected to take up again the complicated threads of her life.

A change in the quality of the atmosphere penetrated her consciousness. She became aware of added warmth at her cheek, and the near presence of a held-in charge of raw emotion. Her eyelids fluttered open—and she looked straight up into Raith's mutilated face.

She gasped, and found the grey eyes upon her. There was a strength of feeling in their depths that repelled her. She stared up at him, mute, and became aware that the back of his hand was laid against her face.

'I did not mean to wake you,' he said, and she heard effort in his voice.

'I was not asleep.'

He removed his hand, and Rosina discovered that he

was sitting on the edge of the bed. He looked away from her, and the source of the disquieting feel in the room traced down to his other hand, clenched on his knee.

'Oh, what is it?' Rosina asked involuntarily, an instant flittering at her heart.

'What should there be?'

Raith turned his head, and produced a smile. It looked mechanical, she thought. Then she remembered. He had been to see Forteviot. Her heart shrivelled, and she shrank into her pillows. She was not well enough to deal with this. Not at this moment.

'Pray leave me be now,' she uttered faintly.

He rose from the bed at once, and moved across to one of the wide windows. He ought to leave her be. It was shameful of him to be here at all—with these thoughts in his head. She was not fit for it.

But the distress of what had been suggested to him would not permit of his walking out of the bedchamber. His heart was so heavy, he wanted to lay his head upon her breast and weep out the hideous torments of doubt that had taken hold of his mind. But Rosina was ill with the cause of it, and he was no monster to lay his own burden upon her in this weakened state.

His continued presence in the room, however, began to prey upon Rosina's nerves. The dull ache of her womb flashed back into life, and she groaned without awareness.

Raith turned quickly. She had paled, biting her lip. Blood and thunder! 'Have you a resurgence of pain? Do you wish for more laudanum?'

She shook her head feebly, and brought one hand from under the covers to lay across her eyes. She did not want him to see how the intensity of his mood was affecting her. She could read him so well! Another jabbing pain made her gasp. Oh, it was too bad of him! She could not endure it.

'Raith—say what you have to and get it over,' she pleaded, a throb in her voice. 'Or else, go away entirely. You are radiating ill humour, and I am in no condition to deal with it.'

He came quickly across to the bed, and dropped down beside her, taking the hand from her eyes and holding it fast. 'Rosy, don't upset yourself! I don't want to say anything to you now. I will go, if you wish it. Only I am so riven! I can't bear to leave you—and yet I cannot...'

His voice died, as he saw the wetness on her cheeks. The fingers in his were trembling, and he held them to his lips and pressed a kiss upon them.

'Forteviot!' she got out. 'I knew he would do this.'

'No!' Raith said forcefully. 'He tried, but I would not believe him. I promise you, Rosy, I kept faith with you.'

'Then, *why*?' she cried desperately. 'What has occurred?'

'It was the doctor!' he burst out. And instantly regretted it. He gripped her fingers tighter. 'Hell and damnation, I did not mean to say that! The man is ignorant. He knows nothing of—' He checked himself.

Freeing her fingers, he leaped to his feet. 'Forgive me! I should never have begun this. I should not have come in here in this state.'

'It is too late now,' Rosina told him wearily. 'You had as well tell me. I will only lie here in a worse condition for wondering.'

Raith cursed again, and flung over to the window where the dull day had begun to darken. Without turning round, he let it out. Flat, and leaden.

'Dr Barcliffe told me that he believes you may have been pregnant—and have this day miscarried.'

For a long moment, he waited. No sound came from behind him. Not a sob, not a breath, not a word. At length, unable any longer to endure her lack of response, Raith turned to look at her.

Rosina had not moved. She was lying very still, and she was watching him. He went with heavy tread to within a few feet of the bed. The coal-black eyes met his. Never had Raith seen so bleak an expression in them. A pulse started up in his veins, and a horrible sensation of dread enveloped him.

'Rosina?'

She did not answer. Only continued to look at him in the same dead fashion. Panic overcame him.

'Deny it!' he begged. 'Are you not going to deny it?'

For a moment longer, Rosina continued to stare at him. Then she drew the faintest of breaths, and turned her eyes upon the tester above. Her voice was devoid of expression.

'I may be abed for a day or two. I shall be obliged if you will not enter this room again.'

Raith drove his phaeton and pair with a slack rein, so that the vehicle made but dilatory progress along the eight-mile trip to Banbury. He was not keen to arrive at journey's end.

Ottery had arrived back on Saturday, and sent to him immediately. But Rosina had been still abed—or had kept to her room, at least—and Raith had cherished hope. Ottery had written again on Tuesday, yet it was Thursday before Raith reluctantly forced himself to make the journey. Whatever the outcome of his lawyer's enquiries with Herbert Cambois, it would make little difference. He had offended beyond forgiveness. What mattered it whether his wife's story received corroboration?

Had his informant been any other than a medical man, he would never have given credence to the supposition.

The doctor had been apologetic, and diffident to a marked degree.

'My lord, I am most uncomfortable with Her Ladyship's condition.'

'How so?' Raith had demanded, in quick alarm.

'Oh, there is nothing to concern you, sir. She will be well again readily enough.'

Apprehension had made him impatient. 'Then what in thunder do you mean?'

The doctor had coughed, and brought out that damning theory. 'I fear, sir, that Her Ladyship has been so unfortunate as to lose a child.' He had evidently read Raith's reaction in his face, for his own had become suffused with colour. 'It is often so, with the first attempt, my lord. I believe you have been only a short time married.' He had coughed again. 'You need not fear, my lord, that I gave Her Ladyship any intimation of my findings. However, I sense that perhaps she guessed it for herself. She was uncommonly distressed by my attempt to convey a trifle of comfort.'

'What are you talking about?' Raith had asked, confused. The impact of the hideous news had made him stupid.

'I am afraid Her Ladyship wept bitterly, my lord, when I ventured to suggest that her troubles would end with a pregnancy brought to term.'

Raith had stared at the man, unable to comprehend anything more than the bare fact. But Rosina had been in tears! She was in pain. She was overwrought—that must be all. Was he supposed to think that it lent colour to this notion? It could not be true!

'Are you certain of this?' he rapped out.

Dr Barcliffe had shrugged eloquently. 'As certain as one can be, without an examination of the matter expelled.' He had seemed to feel that this answer was un-

welcome, for he had added with a haste that only served
to heighten the likelihood of his earlier assertions, 'But I
may be entirely wrong, my lord. Some females do experience quite shocking disorder upon these occasions.'

He had said enough. Raith had been once again upon
the rack. Almost he had been ready to demand of his
servants the evidence that might already have been removed from her garments, for all he knew. Or lost in the
woodlands. It had been torture to be flung back into that
acute distress of mind of which he had only that morning
been relieved.

The timing of it had been ill, and that was the end of
it. Coming so pat, immediately after the contradictions of
Forteviot's version of events against Rosina's, he had
fallen all too easily into the fatal trap of jealousy.

Truth to tell, Raith no longer knew whether he cared if
his doubts had any foundation. This last week had been
the most melancholy of his life. Rosina had withheld herself utterly. He had perforce obeyed her behest to remain
aloof from her bedchamber, but the days since had been
yet worse.

He could not blame her. The fault, he knew, was his
own—had been so from start to finish. He had made no
attempt to effect a reconciliation, for her withdrawal had
been chilling. He had driven her beyond any hope of pardon.

There was still the matter of Forteviot and this fellow
Cambois to be settled. He had heard nothing from the
former. It surprised him to think that the man had been
sufficiently intimidated by his threats. It might be that he
was biding his time. Or perhaps he had another scheme
afoot. Raith cared little. Nothing seemed to matter beside
the appalling loss of Rosina's esteem and regard.

When she had finally emerged from her room, her wan
looks and haggard eyes, blue-shadowed with strain, had

given fresh impetus to the overriding sensations of guilt and remorse. If, on the instant that he saw her when she entered the saloon before the dinner hour, he could have wiped out the whole of his conduct throughout the short period of their marriage, he would have done it without hesitation.

More poignantly, she was clad in the grey gown she had worn for their wedding. He did not think she had worn it to taunt him. But the message of its resumption—for she had latterly been dressed only in the new-purchased gowns—was clear enough. She wanted no part of her life as Lady Raith. She was once again Rosina Charlton—and beyond his reach.

Through dinner, she had spoken only as necessary, and she had eaten little. Only once had Raith ventured to suggest that even if her appetite was lacking, she ought to try at least to swallow something for the sake of her health. She had turned the black eyes upon him, frowning in that way of narrowing her eyes, as if she had the headache.

'I am not hungry. And my health is my own concern.'

Raith had said not a word more. The consciousness of Ottery's letter in his pocket had irked him. Yet he had delayed his response, beset by a vague hope that Rosina might soften. Ottery had purposely invited him to come to Banbury, so that Raith might hear the tidings he had to tell outside his own home. The implication of this was clear enough. On Wednesday night, Raith felt impelled to inform his wife of his purpose. He hardly knew why, unless it was with a half-formed wish of threshing the matter out.

'I am going into Banbury tomorrow,' he had begun, once they were seated at dinner. He had got no further.

'Your movements have nothing to do with me, my lord,' Rosina had said flatly.

For one seething instant, Raith's hot temper had flared. But he had controlled it, and once again closed his lips upon any further utterance. It was not merely disheartening. It was damning. Rosina had turned into a model of the wife of convenience that he had originally negotiated.

He was entering the outskirts of Banbury, and was obliged to give his attention to his cattle. It did not take him many minutes to make his way to Ottery's offices. He divested himself of his outer garments, and was ushered immediately into his lawyer's inner sanctum. A hearty handshake greeted him, together with his friend's penetrating gaze.

'You look deathly, my lord!' Ottery said frankly.

'I feel it.'

'What in the world has been happening?'

'Don't even ask!' Raith passed a hand through his hair, worn untied and ragged, and sighed. 'I will tell you presently, Ottery—that you may know why I come so late.'

His lawyer eyed him with no little concern, as Raith flung himself into a chair at the small desk, and sank his head into his hands. Ottery closed the little wooden doors to the shelf opening on the wall which gave access to the judas painting within the other room, and crossed to a small table in the window embrasure, on which was placed a tray with a decanter and glasses.

'May I offer you wine, my lord? It is good claret.'

Raith dragged himself up. 'I thank you, no. I must keep a clear head.' He saw the troubled frown in the other's eyes, and attempted a smile. 'You found Cambois?'

'Indeed I did, my lord.' Ottery's features registered distaste. 'An ill specimen, I fear. I did not take to him.'

'That does not altogether surprise me.' Raith set his jaw. 'I am a little better acquainted now with the type of man he is. But let me hear your findings first.'

The lawyer had laid down the decanter, without pouring, and came across to take his own seat opposite. 'Mr Cambois was inebriated for much of the time, which is why it took so long to extract information from him. What I gleaned, I fear, is unlikely to be either to your taste, or your satisfaction.'

Despite all, Raith could not prevent a quickening of interest. And a resurgence of revulsion. He must not forget that this monstrous individual had been guilty of attempting to violate a young girl given expressly into his care. That much even Forteviot's testimony had agreed.

'Go on, Ottery.'

'I will be brief, sir. From what I could understand, Herbert Cambois sought to recoup his losses at the table by a sale of Miss Charlton's person to Lord Forteviot. He further stated that he had discovered Miss Charlton to be…' he hesitated, and Raith held his breath '…I shall say, unvirtuous.' Ottery's voice was entirely without intonation, flat and unemotional, as if he were reading an indictment in court. 'As a result, so he believed, of an illicit association with one of the male servants. The contract was broken, and he turned Miss Charlton out of doors.'

Raith's jaw was set. He could barely get the question out. 'Was she alleged to have been with child?'

Ottery's quick frown of puzzlement threw him into disorder, and he looked away.

'What makes you ask that, my dear sir?'

He clenched his fist. 'Answer, I pray you!'

'It was not even hinted at, my lord. Why—'

Raith threw out a hand. 'A moment!'

He felt choked by his own inward shaking, torn by a measure of relief and fears not wholly allayed. Cambois might not have known that part. He had expected the rest, but that made the hearing no less painful. He had thought that the tearing disquiet was buried under the loss of

Rosina's regard. He had been mistaken. Tortured by uncertainty, it was equally unendurable—to live with her, or without. Which was the more plausible: that Forteviot and Cambois were in a string, and Dr Barcliffe mistaken—or that Rosina had lied to him?

'My lord!'

He became aware that Ottery was calling him. The lawyer was holding out a ruby-filled glass.

'Drink this!'

Raith took it dumbly, and tossed off the wine. As he laid down the glass, his head began to clear. He glanced up.

'Ottery, you must release me from this marriage!'

His lawyer stared at him. 'Have you run mad, Lord Raith?'

Raith buried his head in his hands. 'I have not. But I shall undoubtedly do so if I do not extricate myself from this abominable farce.'

But Ottery was not of a mind to accommodate him. 'My lord, I do most earnestly beg of you to consider well what you are saying!'

Raith leaped from the chair, and paced up and down the restricted space to one side of the desk, reminding his lawyer of a caged animal. 'You do not know the circumstances.'

He gave Ottery a curt account of Rosina's given story, and of his dealings with Forteviot, ending with a brief summary of the diagnosis of Dr Barcliffe.

'I cannot rid myself of the suspicion that she sought the marriage because she saw a means whereby she might hide her condition.'

'And pass off this fictitious infant upon you? Fie, my lord!'

Raith eyed him wearily. 'It is possible, Ottery.'

'And you profess to love her? Think shame to yourself!' uttered the lawyer angrily, rising from his seat. 'Even I would take an oath to know Her Ladyship better than that.'

'Love, Ottery, has a way—for it matters so desperately!—of increasing suspicion and doubt.'

'Then rely on my judgement, my lord, for I have no doubts. If I must place Lady Raith's word against the evidence of two persons whose stories agree in every particular, I prefer to believe in your wife. You look at me with amazement, but think, my lord. Two witnesses—two different pairs of eyes—there must always be variance.'

Raith shook his head painfully. 'I don't understand you.'

'It smacks of collusion, sir.'

'And what of the doctor's evidence?'

'He said himself that he could be wrong,' Ottery pointed out. 'I had far rather trust Lady Raith.'

Raith heaved a sigh, in which desolation sounded. 'So had I, Ottery. Which is exactly why I am unable to do so. I would never be free of the notion that I had deceived myself.'

The lawyer was eyeing him with a trifle of suspicion. 'My lord, I hesitate to say this, but I do not believe this is all your reason.'

'How well you know me.' Despair engulfed Raith, and he sank back against the table. 'She will not even speak to me! What is the use of continuing? She wants to be released as much as I, for she cannot endure the sight of me.'

Ottery laid a hand upon his shoulder, saying in a more moderate tone, 'My lord, you are making assumptions based upon nothing more than your observation of her distress.'

This reminder only served to make Raith writhe the more. 'If you had only seen her! I can never forgive myself—why should she? There is no point in discussing the matter. We must separate!'

'You say so only because you think there is no hope, sir.' His lawyer looked upset. 'You are making a grave error, I am convinced of it.'

Raith shook his head. 'There is more of my brother in me than I knew. Just as his obsession of jealousy ruined my life, so will mine affect Rosina's. I am not fit to be the keeper of so delicate a soul.'

Ottery sighed. 'You do yourself an injustice, my lord. I venture to think that Lady Raith might take a different view.'

'You are mistaken,' Raith said dully.

'Besides which,' pursued the lawyer, ignoring the interjection, 'there is a deal of difficulty about the whole matter. If you were looking to divorce, you must know how problematic is that path. And if you intend only to separate, you will be tied.' He waved a dismissive hand. 'But this is nothing to the purpose.' Abruptly, he seized Raith by the shoulders. 'I cannot approve this course, my lord! Do not, I counsel you, put yourself out of the way of a future which may well prove your salvation.'

Raith took the hands from his shoulders, holding them hard. 'You are a true and loyal friend, Ottery. If I could take your advice, I would do so.'

'But—?' queried the other.

Raith let him go, and smiled, unaware how his features twisted, nor of the husky quality in his voice. 'But Rosina does not want me. I do not blame her for that, but it is beyond my endurance. I had rather live without her.'

Chapter Ten

Rosina stood quiescent while Joan unlaced the bodice of her chintz gown, and dipped her arms back for its removal. As if she had been used all her life to being waited upon, she shifted her limbs as required, almost without thought.

Thought was too painful a luxury. Better this deadness of mind wherein no stray memory was permitted to stir the fringes of that well of sensation that hungered deep within her heart. She had schooled herself to suppress every vestige of feeling. Or she had tried to. Particularly in his presence, when each nuance of expression was a livelier goad than any amount of concentrated imagery.

Memory was an intrusive thing. A dangerous indulgence. But it could be controlled. Reality—in which Raith's charged passion smouldered, reaching out to her despite the shelled protection of her heart—was more potentially explosive. Rosina could only be thankful that her spouse had avoided her as assiduously as she avoided him.

She lifted her arms so that Joan could slip her nightgown over her head, wondering why she was still here, being dressed for her bed. She had expected every day that Mr Ottery would have come to instruct her to pack her belongings in preparation for her journey to Withibrooke. It was not possible that her guardian had not supplied fuel to add to the flame of unappeasable envy that had poisoned her husband's mind against her. Rosina knew her case to be hopeless, and had spent these several days in a mood of dull acceptance of the inevitable.

'Will Your Ladyship sit for me to brush your hair?'

Rosina sat. The feel of the bristles stroking over her head was soothing. She closed her eyes. It was almost like being once again a little girl, with the caress of the brush in Mama's gentle hand, and the crooning voice lulling her closer to sleep. It was how Gatty had comforted her, too, the night she had finally arrived at the cottage—and collapsed into a sobbing heap. Her chest hollowed out. How would Gatty manage this time? There was no comfort that could soothe the void which was opening up before her.

Abruptly, she leaned forward, dropping her face into her hands, catching at her breath as the agonizing sobs fought to be free of her iron restraint.

Two hands grasped at her shoulders. 'M'lady? Oh, m'lady, I do wish as how something might be done for you.'

Rosina pulled upright, thrusting down on the betraying emotion. 'I am quite all right, Joan.'

The maid laid down the brush, and bobbed a curtsy. 'Begging your pardon, m'lady, but I know as you're not. Nor His Lordship ain't neither!'

'Joan, you forget yourself!'

'I know, m'lady, but I'm your personal maid, and if I don't say something, no one won't,' uttered the maid with determination.

Rosina eyed her in the mirror. She should have known that the servants were well informed. Why should they not be, especially with this skeleton staff? But the last thing she wanted was to discuss the intricacies of her marriage with her maid. She had, it appeared, little choice.

'I wouldn't have said nothing, only Mr Kirkham is that troubled over His Lordship, and—'

'Why is Kirkham troubled?' interrupted Rosina, an instant tattoo starting up in her pulse.

Lord knows she was aware of the turmoil of Raith's mind! She had been relieved by his absence from dinner tonight. She had kept her room more than four days, even to the near finish of her troublous monthly time, but she could hardly stay cooped up there. On emergence, the unavoidable encounters at dinner had stretched her nerves to the utmost. She had studiously evaded either Raith's gaze or his conversation. She could not trust herself to look at him, and had to steel herself to withstand the moody emanations of his volatile temperament.

'Mr Kirkham says His Lordship has spent half the night in his library these few days,' disclosed the maid, adding significantly, 'with the brandy decanter. Mr Kirkham is afraid he will drink himself to death, like our late lord!'

Dread rose up in Rosina's breast. 'His Lordship's brother?' But, no—Raith had hated his brother. He would not follow his example.'

'Yes, m'lady,' said Joan, adding darkly, 'and His Lordship come home from Mr Ottery's not a half hour since, looking like a death's head on a mopstick, so Mr Paulersbury says.'

A jolt smote Rosina's chest, and she put up a hand to her mouth. She stared at the maid's apple-cheeked features without seeing her. Ottery was then back! What had her guardian said? What had Raith been told? Despite all her resolution to accept the fate she had assumed to be coming, the prospect of its imminence threw her into instant apprehension. An irregular flutter started up in her pulse, and her mouth went dry.

'M'lady?'

She blinked, and realised that Joan was staring at her. Rosina pulled herself together, and rose from the dressing stool. 'That will be all, I thank you.'

The maid followed her into her bedchamber, and placed a candle by the bed. She waited while Rosina climbed between sheets, and tucked her in.

'Good night, m'lady.' She hesitated, and then dropped a curtsy. 'Mayhap His Lordship is safe in his bed, m'lady. He rung for Mr Paulersbury not a moment before you rung for me.'

This intelligence did nothing to ease the ferment of Rosina's mind. The knowledge that at night Raith was but four doors away had been a species of torture to her. She had lain in her bed, desperately trying not to indulge an idiotic wish that he might come to her. How should he do so—even did he wish to!—when she had withdrawn herself so sternly?

But that he had today seen Ottery, and come home looking—what had Joan said? An expression that gave her a hideous image! It could only mean the worst. This must be the finish. Tomorrow, he would summon her to the saloon, and inform her that their marriage was to be dissolved.

Such an intense shaft of distress shot through her at this thought that she was for several moments incapable of getting her breath. When she did, she blew out the candle, and thrust herself down into the covers, burrowing so that the sound of her bursting sobs might not penetrate through the intervening walls to the ears of the man for whom she grieved.

There was no question of sleep. When her tears abated, she lay in the darkness, listening, against all reason, for the impossible sound of a footstep. She tossed and turned, fighting a growing pressure that urged her to get up and go to him—to know for certain what he intended.

Why question it? She knew what must happen. There could be but one outcome. She had heard nothing from Forteviot, but that did not mean that the evil wretch had not contacted Raith. Now she knew that Ottery was come with information from Herbert Cambois, she could hope for no succour. Had there been a favourable outcome, would Raith not have come to her instantly? He was gently disposed towards her, and would not have kept her unnecessarily in suspense.

At length, Rosina could endure it no longer. She sat up in bed, and groped in the darkness for the tinderbox that was kept on her table. When she tried to strike the flint for a light, she discovered that her hands were shaking. It took some time, but at last she managed to relight her candle.

She got up and shrugged on her wrapper, and in short order had reached the antechamber, where her nerves stayed her from knocking upon Raith's dressing-room door.

For a moment or two, she toyed with the idea of going back to bed. But she would not sleep. And the longer she lay awake, the more her anxiety would grow. It was better to beard Raith now—and find out the worst. After all, if he meant to set her aside, she had a right to know of it.

Screwing up her courage, she returned to the door, and listened for a moment. Suppose he was asleep? She drew a determined breath. If he was, then she must wake him. With the thought, she lifted her hand and rapped smartly on the door. No sound came from within. Rosina bit her lip, and grasped the handle.

It was the first time she had been inside Raith's dressing-room. It resembled her own, and she could see little in the dim light from her candle, but for an apparent overflow of garments. Rosina hurried through to the bedchamber door, and once again halted to listen. She could hear nothing. If he was there, he was certainly asleep.

She did not knock this time, but stealthily opened the door. The curtains were not drawn, and the bed was empty. Rosina swept her candle about, but no movement disturbed the shadows. Rosina did not know whether she was relieved or disappointed. Slowly she advanced towards the door that led to the corridor, recalling what Joan had told her. A frisson went through her at the remembrance of Kirkham's expressed fears.

Moving with a swiftness born of other than her wish to find out her fate, Rosina trod softly down the stairs, and across the hall to a door leading to the rear of the mansion. She had been shown the library but once, by Mrs Fawley, but she remembered the way.

As she approached the door, Rosina could see a glimmer of light beneath it, and knew that her husband was in there. Her heart skittered madly, as the thought of her mission came back to her mind. She hesitated outside the door, fighting an impulse to withdraw again. But it would not do. She gathered her courage, and seized the brass handle.

She did not immediately see him, and for an instant was conscious of disappointment. But a pool of light caught the centre of the room, and Rosina followed it. She saw his arm, hanging slackly over the side of a chair, his fingers just above an overturned glass which must have fallen from his hand.

Rosina came around the chair, and her heart melted. Raith sat slumped, tousled hair ragged about his shoulders, his bed gown open and awry over a long nightshirt. He was asleep, or nearly so, breathing in that stertorous way that Rosina instantly recognised. Her spouse was drunk!

Rosina sought for the bottle. She had seen this often enough at Nun Eaton, and could judge of the level of Raith's inebriation. She found a wine bottle tucked on the floor by one leg of the chair. It was a quarter full. Rosina sniffed the contents. Not brandy, thank the Lord! Then he was probably not more than semi-drunk. She would likely be able to get him to bed.

Any thought of discovering his intentions had gone out of her head. All was forgotten but for his present plight. Her maid's words came back to her. If this was how he had been spending each night—! Small wonder Kirkham was worried.

She placed her candlestick alongside his own on the mantel, and leaned down, taking hold of his shoulder, and shaking him. 'Raith! Raith, wake up!'

She was obliged to call him several more times before any response was forthcoming. But at length he stirred, opening bleary eyes and gazing up at her in apparent recognition.

'Rosy? What are you…?'

He blinked, and Rosina shook him again. 'Raith, you must get up! Come, I will help you to bed.'

The wickedest gleam came into his eyes, and he grinned up at her. 'That, wife, is decidedly inviting.'

A tinge of colour crept into Rosina's cheek. His speech was only slightly slurred, but she was quite aware that it was the wine speaking. He would not otherwise have greeted her in this fashion. Doubtless he thought her a figment of his overheated imagination!

'Come, Raith,' she said again, and pulled at his arm.

'Give me a moment—I will certainly come.'

He sat up with an air of determination, but it was only with Rosina's help that he was able to get to his feet. She snuffed his candle, and then slipped her shoulder under his.

'Lean on me.'

'Too close for comfort,' he muttered. Before she knew what he would be at, he had turned her head to him and planted a quick kiss on her lips.

Rosina's balance gave slightly, and they both staggered. Raith was laughing, and she was obliged to speak sharply to pull him into awareness.

'For the Lord's sake, take care!'

'Don't s-s-scold, wife,' he uttered in an injured tone. 'I am doing my best.'

'No, you are not, Raith. Stand still a moment.'

He obediently halted, swaying a trifle. Rosina shifted her position so that she took a little more of his weight, and then reached to the mantel for her candle.

'A very juggling act, Rosy,' he commented, amused.

'Do you think you can remain on your feet?' she asked anxiously, feeling him sway again.

Raith chuckled. His potations had rendered him pleasantly foxed, but he was not incapacitated. 'I won't fall down.'

'Are you sure? Shall I wake Paulersbury?'

He brought his free hand to the small one that was clutching at his waist, and covered it. 'I had much rather have you. Paulersbury is not nearly s-s-so pretty.'

Rosina was betrayed into a giggle. 'Raith, will you have done?'

'I am yours to command,' he said. 'Lead on.'

It was with difficulty that the two of them negotiated the passage, and at the stairs, Rosina had to withdraw her support.

'I cannot manage with the candle as well. Take the banisters, Raith.'

He grasped them, and she slipped out from under his shoulder. She urged him onward, but Raith did not speak as he dragged himself up the stairs. He was beginning to sober, and the delight of this adventure was slipping away from him. He was not yet capable of working out why Rosina had come to find him. Nor why she should be thus amicable. A hazy idea of the depression of spirit that had driven him to seek solace in wine floated at the back of his mind, but its portent escaped him. He knew only that Rosina's presence was heart-warming. He did not wish to lose that.

Rosina kept close behind him as he climbed the stairs, afraid that he might lose balance and fall. The moment he reached the top, she slipped quickly back into her previous position. She felt his arm come about her, and divined a change. It was rather Raith holding her to him, than she providing support.

Her heart fluttered, and her breath shortened a thread. She could no longer speak, and they entered his bedchamber in silence. Raith dropped to the bed, staring up at her. Rosina avoided his gaze, and laying the candle down, pulled the covers open. Then she came back to him, and her hands reached to push the bed gown over his shoulders.

Raith's fingers came up and caught at hers. Rosina stilled, and her gaze returned to his face, and met the grey eyes full. Her heart missed a beat.

'Stay with me, Rosy!'

Her fingers quivered, and her eyes filled. 'In your bed?'

Raith nodded. 'I am a trifle foxed.'

A smile glimmered on her lips. 'I see that.'

'But I know what I want.' He released her hands, and slipped his arms about her, pulling her to him. 'Stay— this once. Let the devil take tomorrow. I need you to-night.' He laid his scarred cheek against her bosom.

Rosina's heart was in tatters. She could no more have resisted him than she could have flown to the moon. Without a thought, she took hold of his face with both hands, and shifted in his grasp. Raith's head came up, and the next instant he was drawing her down. Their lips met.

It was a blissful dance. His mouth gentled hers, a probing caress that sent heat flittering down her veins. It lasted but a moment, and she felt his indrawn breath. Then her mouth was seized, and she was falling.

Raith brought her to the bed, and rolled so that she lay upon the opened covers. His lips pressured for entry at her mouth, and his hand ran strongly down her waist and hips.

Rosina moaned as the warmth spread through her body. Her lips parted at his insistence, and the velvet touch within threw her into uncontrollable reflex. Her hands clutched about his back, and her mouth answered the demands of his with frenzied need.

He groaned aloud as his lips left hers. 'Oh, Rosy, how I have yearned for this!'

'I, also,' she gasped, and heard his indrawn breath of desire just as his lips closed once more with hers.

His hand slid over her breast, causing a tingling at her loins, and her limbs, seeming as if they had a will of their own, began to twine with his. The kisses intensified, and for several moments, Rosina was lost in the deep well of Raith's passion. But presently, a tugging at her nightgown stirred vaguely at the tortured memory, and she stiffened a touch.

Raith felt it. He came away from her mouth, his breath hoarse, and looked down into the black of her eyes. No! This was not how he had meant to take her. Releasing her, he struggled to his knees, and drew her up also. His fingers caressed her face.

'You are afraid.'

'Yes,' she said, and caught at his hand. 'But I am more afraid of losing you tonight…'

In the glow of the candle, he saw the waif who had

captured his heart, and drew her fingers to his lips. 'Rosy, if you come into my bed, we will both be lost.'

Her breath caught on a sob. 'Then lose me in a memory that I may cherish.'

Raith's heart contracted. He pulled her to him, kissing her with tenderness. Her wrapper slid from her shoulders, and he drew off her nightgown. The candlelight played upon the contours of her slim form, and Raith tugged at his breath.

'You are adorable.'

Rosina blushed. She was acutely self-conscious, and she trembled, not with fear, but with a rise of anticipation that quickened in her veins as she watched Raith remove his own garments and toss them aside. The sight of his unclothed state both shocked and thrilled her. But she saw him only momentarily, for Raith brought her quickly under the covers, and slid down into the bed, bringing her nakedness to rest against his own.

The touch of his skin was warm and dry, but the rough hardness of his limbs made her gasp. Heat engulfed her as his hands pressed her to him, playing over the softness of her buttocks and thighs. She opened her eyes to find his face close to hers upon the pillow. He was lying on his right side, and the ridged cut was hidden from her. But as he raised his head to kiss her, she saw it full and a wave of compassion made her close her body tightly into his—and cling.

Raith groaned, and the demand of his lips increased. Rosina answered him strongly. His hands caressed her limbs, and his fingers rode her inner thigh, seeking her hollows. Rosina gasped, clutching at the tough skin, unknowing where her hands travelled, conscious only of the swelling intensity of her need and the demanding pressure of his mouth on hers.

She was ablaze, breathless as the fever tingled in her

veins. She knew that Raith spoke, but heard him only as a distant murmur, unaware of the meaning of his words.

'Sweetheart, love me! I need you to love me. Give me that at least.'

Even had she understood him, she could answer him only with little moans that escaped her lips. The power of the tempest he was arousing was making her delirious. She gave him her lips, freely, with intent, a vague wisp afloat at the back of her consciousness that this would give him what he wanted.

Raith took the offering, and the wine of her sweetness drove him to mastery—despite that she had not offered him her heart. He covered her, and readied her limbs. Her eyes opened, and he leaned quickly down to kiss her, a resurgence in him of an apprehension of her fears. Then he entered her.

The shock of the invasion made Rosina cry out. It was a small sound, but at once she felt Raith's lips on hers, gentling and murmuring endearments.

'Softly, sweetheart—my lovely rose—hush now.'

He pursued it, and Rosina whimpered. He encountered resistance, but it was not of her making. His heart soared, and he held back, his lips caressing her cheeks, her eyes, her throat. Then he found her mouth and gave a whispered warning against her lips.

'Courage, my sweet, for I may hurt you now.'

He thrust. Rosina uttered a little cry, gripping involuntarily with her thighs, as her fingers clutched at his shoulders. But the piercing was gently made, and his kisses gave her courage to endure it.

Then he lay still for a space and presently the warmth returned, overtaking the ache. It was stronger than before, and her hands slid from his shoulders to caress his back, as her breath hissed. He moved but slightly, and Rosina gasped as the fire intensified. A throbbing at her loins drove her to seek his lips of her own accord, demanding in her turn.

Ardently then, Raith took her, giving her kiss for kiss, until the urgent frenzy of his own need threw him momentarily out of control. Rosina felt the increase of his passion with a soaring flight of ferment, and all thought was gone as she gave herself wholly to his will. There was some sort of explosion in her head, and then she heard only the heave of her husband's breath, and became aware of the spent weight of his body.

Presently he rolled, pulling her with him, but holding her strongly so that they remained entwined.

'*My wife,*' he murmured, in a tone of intense satisfaction, and kissed her.

Rosina hugged as much of him as she could, and wished for this moment never to end.

'Oh, Anton,' she whispered involuntarily.

'Rosy, my sweet,' he breathed, holding her closer.

A few moments later, his clasp about her slackened, and the more even tenor of his breath told her that he slept.

Rosina awoke to find herself tucked into her spouse's body, which followed behind her the contours of her own. One arm was thrown across her and his hand lay slackly over hers, in the place where he had held it as he fell asleep. She recalled that they had woken in the night, and Raith had taken her again, with yet greater passion.

There had been less pain, and she recognised that the ministrations of his hands and lips had been designed to prepare her for his mastery, for she had been awash with desire before ever he covered her body with his own.

Afterwards, he had cuddled her close, and Rosina remembered turning in his arms, half-asleep. She had felt him pull her to him, his lips soft on her shoulder and neck, and his fingers had imprisoned her hand.

Rosina was almost sure that he had said, at a murmured whisper of the night, that he loved her. She did not know whether she had emptied to him the strength of her own feelings. If she had not, it could only be because she could not speak under the violence of passion he had aroused in her to match his own. How ardent had been his lovemaking. If it could but remain so!

She slid carefully from him, and out of the bed, hunting about for her discarded garments. The grey light filtering through the closed drapes at the window showed her the scattered clothing—Raith's and hers—which had fallen to the floor. She found her nightgown, which was cold to the touch, and put it on. She shivered a little as she shrugged into the wrapper, for it was early and no fires had yet been lit.

But she did not wish to be discovered here—especially by Raith himself. He had been drunk last night. Rosina knew how drink had a way of wreathing men's brains with a sort of madness, so that they became no longer masters of their actions. She could not bear it if, upon waking and finding that he had broken his own resolve, Raith's volatile temper would flare. In one of his moods, he was capable of saying the most wounding things. After last night's tender mouthings, it would be altogether agonizing.

She returned to the bed, and watched him sleeping for a moment. Raith's ruined cheek was exposed, his hair falling away from his face. Stealthily, Rosina drew near and reached out. But she dared not touch it, for fear of waking him. Her fingers hovered over it as she traced the line, as if she might imprint the shape of it in her mind's eye, that it would stay with her in memory. It was so much a part of him—of Anton, whom she loved—that she found it endearing. It was odd to think of him as Anton, but it had been easy to call him by his name last night.

'I love you, Anton,' she whispered. And then quickly and quietly crept away to her own apartments.

In her bedchamber, she found the fire already burning. Perhaps it was not so early, after all. A dreadful thought struck her. Had the kitchen wench, whose duty it was to light the fires, come in and found them together in Raith's bed? Fearing to wake them, she must have sneaked away. Lord, the news of their coupling would be all over the house!

On a sudden thought, she went into her dressing-room and felt the jug that stood in the basin. It was warm. Oh, she was undone indeed! Joan had already been into her room and found her missing.

For a moment, Rosina was embarrassed. Then it struck her that she need not go back to bed and dissemble. She returned to her bedchamber and tugged at the bell-pull.

Her maid's demeanour was perfectly respectful. But Rosina caught a knowing glance or two cast her way when Joan thought she was not looking. Yet the maid brought tidings that effectively drove away her consciousness, instead filling her with dismay.

'Begging Your Ladyship's pardon, but there's a gentleman downstairs. Mr Kirkham would have denied him, but he swears as he'll not go until he sees either yourself or His Lordship.'

The pearl of Rosina's happiness shredded away. She had never a hope that it could last. But could she not have been permitted to treasure it for just a little longer? Was it her guardian, come to plague her? Dear Lord, but was there to be no end?

'Who is it, Joan? Did he give his name?'

The maid was apologetic. 'It's Lord Forteviot, m'lady.'

The entirety of her heart's triumph of the night van-

ished at a stroke. The dead weight of inevitability struck
at her once more. Had she dared to imagine that the fact
of Raith having claimed her could change her ill fortune?
She ought to be accustomed to the cruel blows of fate.

'Help me to dress.'

A desperate calm descended upon her as she performed
her ablutions, and allowed Joan to clothe her. She chose
the old gown of blue kerseymere, perhaps with an unconscious wish of appearing before Forteviot in as unattrac-
tive a guise as she could find. She placed one of her close
caps on her head, and then left the bedchamber, unable to
overcome a slight quaking at her breast.

She gripped the banisters hard as she came downstairs,
recalling last night's perilous journey with her husband,
in the opposite direction. But she must not think of Raith!
That were to destroy her composure—and she had need
of it.

Entering the saloon, Rosina stood in the doorway for a
moment, surveying Lord Forteviot. He was standing by
the window, and he looked round at her approach. He was
dressed with his usual flamboyance, sporting a striped
waistcoat under a blue cloth coat and black breeches. He
bowed with a mocking flourish, all his habitual urbanity
in his voice.

'My dear Lady Raith, how do you do?'

Rosina shut the door, and moved into the room. She
wasted no time in pleasantries. 'What do you want?'

He leaned back a little, surveying her. 'You look pale,
my dear Rosina. Have you been unwell?'

She eyed him with resentment. 'I do not wish to discuss
my health with you, sir. Why are you here?'

Forteviot spread his hands. 'But why do you suppose?
I had hoped to see Raith, but I dare say you will do.'

Rosina's pulses stirred, and she walked across to the
fireplace and gripped the mantel. She must not let him

succeed in what she knew to be a deliberate intent to unsettle her. She turned to look at him again.

'Pray, what is it you want, sir?'

The sneer became pronounced. 'My poor innocent, did you imagine, because you have heard nothing from me for a week and more, that I had abandoned my purpose? I regret that I must disappoint you. I have been revisiting the scene of our first meetings, Rosina.'

A shiver shook her. 'You mean that you have been to see Herbert Cambois?'

He nodded. 'It was necessary. The man is unreliable, to say the least. Do you know, the fool had done almost nothing to find you? I rather regretted having left the matter in his hands when I saw the announcement of your marriage.'

Had she not known that it would be her undoing? But a creeping sensation of dismay began to invade her as she recognised the implication of his words. Had he spoken with her guardian before he came here?

'At first I thought he had played me false, perhaps received a higher price for you from Raith—unlikely as that seems, I admit,' he continued. 'Happily, as we discovered, it was but a fortuitous accident.'

'Fortuitous?' She bit her lip, a riot of conjecture in her head. 'How so? How do you know anything of it?'

He smiled in that smug fashion. 'The trail was most interesting. One of the housemaids was able to point the way.'

'Aggie! You fiend, what did you do to her?'

Forteviot laughed. 'Nothing very much. Threats were sufficient, I assure you. The rest was easy. I had primed my good friend before I left. Armed with new knowledge, I came straight on here.'

The whole hideous plot unravelled as if Rosina read it

in a book. They had planned this! Forteviot and her guardian together.

'You will appreciate how important it was that Cambois held to the facts I had outlined—hence the need to visit him. But my anxiety was relieved. He has not failed of his part.'

'You relieve my mind,' Rosina said.

'Oh, bravo, Rosina!' uttered her tormentor. 'Your sarcasm is almost worthy of my own. But I fear it is an empty triumph. You will no doubt know that Cambois has sustained a visit from your husband's lawyer.'

Rosina had known it, and guessed that Ottery had given her spouse an unfavourable account. What else from her erstwhile guardian's lips? But she had not then thought it had been a concerted plan between the two of them.

'You will thus be scarce surprised to hear that your tale is told,' he pursued, in that feline manner that set her teeth on edge. 'Anton was already shaken by my testimony. Though I must say that his efforts to retain his faith in you were quite touching—and of better use than I had supposed.'

A frown creased Rosina's brow. What was he at now? 'I do not understand you.'

The smile grew, and Forteviot moved a little closer, purring. 'How should you? Your naïvety could never appreciate my cunning. There was always the possibility that I might lose the game, for he could choose to set you aside.'

'How do you know he will not?'

'I don't,' he admitted, with no diminution of that smugness that so much disgusted her. 'If he does, I can always use you as I first intended.'

The hot words left her lips without intent, spoken from the heart. 'Over Raith's dead body!'

Forteviot laughed gently, and she instantly regretted her

outburst. 'Precisely. Anton Raith's mawkish sentimentality is likely to induce him to keep you, whether or no he believed me. Which means, my dear, that I shall have my money from him, or raise a scandal about his ears.'

Rosina heard him with a dawning sense of horror. The remembrance of Raith's murmured words rose up painfully in her mind. 'We will both be lost.' Only now did she see what he had meant. That he had given in to his need of her must mean that he would feel himself committed to the marriage, no matter what. And Forteviot would profit by it! Cambois also?

'How did you enlist my guardian's help? Is he to receive a cut of the proceeds for his pains?'

'How clever of you to guess,' sneered the other.

'You vile creature! You intended all along to convince Raith of my guilt,' she accused, her tone vibrant and low. 'You knew he must be hurt by the story becoming known. You knew of his past sufferings at his brother's hands, and now you will play upon his chivalry to undo him. You are despicable!'

Forteviot's thin smile creased his lips, and sarcasm was in his voice. 'Am I? How dreadful! The reflection, I am happy to say, is unlikely to deprive me of sleep.'

She wanted to slap his smug face. But she must deny herself that pleasure. The resolve was forming even as she spoke. Cost what it might, she would not allow this creature to harm Raith.

'Rest assured that my husband will be informed,' she said flatly. 'Now go, if you please.'

Forteviot's smile broadened. 'By all means. I have done what I came to do. Tell Raith that I will come tomorrow— to collect his note of hand.'

The first thing Raith became aware of was the too-bright light. He groaned and closed his eyes again, putting a hand to the dull ache that made itself felt at his brow. He was conscious next of thirst. There was a familiarity about his symptoms, and their meaning crept into awareness.

Hell and damnation! Had he been drinking too deeply again? The sound of drapes being drawn, and a soft footfall indicated the presence of his valet.

'Paulersbury—water!'

'Very good, m'lord.'

Raith cautiously opened his eyes again. The room was a trifle less bright. Paulersbury had evidently divined his condition, for he had half-drawn the drapes once more across the windows. It must have been the opening of them that had woken Raith. He made an effort to raise himself upon the pillows—and made the discovery that he was unclothed.

Blood and thunder! Had he been so far gone that he had been unable to put on his nightgear? No—for Paulersbury had readied him for bed last night as usual. Then—

His thoughts checked on an impossible notion. Rosina! The vague image of tangled limbs and tempestuous kisses erupted into a full-blown remembrance. Raith hissed in a breath on the intense rapture of it. Was it remembrance? Had he dreamed again? His heart twisted. Could he have imagined the sweet abandon of his wife's surrender? An echo of her voice came back to him. *Give me a memory that I may cherish.* Oh, Rosy!

He threw himself up, and was obliged to clutch at his head at the instant protest therein. Through narrowed eyes, he took in the rumple of the bedclothes. She had been with him! An impulse of memory made him throw the covers back. He stared at the spots of red upon the sheets. His eyes pricked.

'Your water, m'lord.'

Instinct made Raith fling the bedclothes over the evidence. A second later he realised that his valet would have discovered it in any event. But nothing, he thought thankfully, need be said. The sheets would be discreetly changed. He took the glass and emptied its contents.

And then he saw the note.

It was lying on the pillow near where her head must have lain. An instant premonition of disaster struck him. No! Rosy, sweetheart, no—*not now.*

He barely had courage to reach out for the folded sheet. A dull thudding started up in his chest. With fingers that shook slightly, he spread it open.

'My lord—' Could she so address him still, after last night? 'My enemy has been here this day.' Forteviot! What in thunder had the villain said to her? A scandal— but he had threatened it before. And it was not news that his hints had been deliberate. Had he not been persuaded of the scoundrel's intent to blacken Rosina's name to him? So it was a plot between Forteviot and her guardian. Ottery had been right.

But as he read the final sentences penned by the waif whom he had hounded, he had no thought of Forteviot or Cambois.

'I tell you this because I would not wish you to be in mystery as to why I am gone. I cannot bear to bring you these distresses. Pray, Anton, let me go. It is better that we part. Mr Ottery will know what to do to make it right. I will remember always—Rosy.'

Remember? Did she imagine that he could forget? Let her go! Rosina, were you mad? Rather than lose her, he would endure ten thousand scandals! But where was she now? How long had she been gone? Perhaps she had not already left.

Urgency threw him out of bed, and he staggered. Leaping to his aid, the valet caught him.

'Take care, m'lord!'

Raith steadied himself, driven by necessity, and shook the man off. 'I am all right. Fetch me a bucket of water so that I may dip my head in it!'

Shifting away, he drew on the robe that Paulersbury was holding out, and made unsteadily for his wife's bed-chamber, throwing open the four doors that lay in his way. The room was empty. But a cursory glance about the dressing-room showed him that a hasty departure had been made. Drawers and closet doors were open, their contents poking forth, a clutter of garments upon the floor.

Raith strode through to the bedchamber and tugged on the bell-pull, his eyes raking the room. The bed was made, and there were no further signs in here. The ache at his head intensified, and he was obliged to hold to one of the bedposts as he attempted to make his way back to the dressing-room.

He was engaged in sifting through her closet, trying to reckon up which gowns Rosina might have taken, when he was disturbed by the maid Joan.

'M'lord!' she gasped, bobbing a curtsy from the door-way to the bedchamber.

'When did Her Ladyship leave?' he demanded without preamble.

Joan looked blank. 'I—I don't rightly know, m'lord.'

'Don't lie to me!' barked Raith.

'But I don't know, m'lord,' pleaded the girl. 'Last I saw she went down to see that there Lord Forteviot, and—'

'You have not seen her since?'

'No, m'lord.'

Raith's heart sank. He moved away from the closet and waved at the maid. 'Are any gowns missing? Quickly, girl!'

Thus adjured, Joan hurried to the closet. Presently she

was able to report that only one had been removed, besides that which Rosina had been wearing. Hope lit in Raith's breast. Perhaps she had not gone with the intention of remaining away for long. But in that case, why had she written as if she meant to leave him? He had supposed at first that she must have gone to her nurse at Withibrooke. But she could not have been safe there. How could Mrs Hoswick protect her?

Blood and thunder, *where was she*?

'Go down and tell Kirkham to come to my bedchamber—immediately!' he ordered tersely, and swept through to his own apartments.

Paulersbury had brought a jug of cold water which he was tipping into the basin. Thankfully, Raith splashed his face. Then he tore off his bed gown and threw the icy liquid over himself in handfuls that wreaked havoc upon the floor of his dressing-room. Ignoring his valet's protests, he performed hasty ablutions, and was in the act of donning his rust-coloured frock-coat and waistcoat, over buckskin breeches, when a discreet knocking heralded the arrival of his butler.

'Kirkham, what an age you have been! For God's sake, where is Her Ladyship? Did you see her leave the house?'

'I did not, m'lord,' admitted the elderly retainer, 'but I have made enquiries, and I understand from Parton that the chaise left not half an hour since.'

'Then Parton knows where she has gone?'

'It appears that Her Ladyship desired Catterline to drive her to Banbury.'

'Banbury?' Of course! Relief swept through Raith, as a line from Rosina's note came back to him. She had gone to consult with Ottery. Consult? Or was it a refuge—from her husband?

Chapter Eleven

Rosina regarded the lawyer seated on the other side of the desk with some anxiety. 'Can you not arrange it, Mr Ottery?'

Under the grey wig, the kindly features creased with concern. 'I can oblige you, ma'am, if you wish for it. But I am loath to do so—without talking to His Lordship. My dear Lady Raith, have you considered the consequences?'

'I need only consider the alternative,' said Rosina desperately, pulling at her fingertips. 'I will not have my husband face the shame and disgrace of hearing my name—no, *his* name, for that is the one I bear—abused.' She looked at the lawyer, all her heart in her eyes. 'You best know how much he has already suffered, Mr Ottery. I will not be the means of bringing to him further cause for bitterness.'

The lawyer rose from his chair, and moved a trifle restlessly about his own office. Rosina watched him, puzzled by his attitude. He seemed deeply troubled. What ailed him? Surely he must see the rightness of her demand?

'What is the matter, Mr Ottery?'

He paused by the desk, looking down at her with an expression hard to interpret. 'Lady Raith, you have put me in a quandary. I saw His Lordship only yesterday, when he came to me here to be given certain information.'

Rosina coloured, looking away. 'I know what it was. Lord Forteviot informed me that my guardian had given you a similar tale to his own.'

'Not similar, Lady Raith. Exactly the same.'

Something in his voice made her look back at him, a wild hope in her breast. 'Can it be…' She swallowed, and tried again. 'Mr Ottery, did you believe him?'

The lawyer shook his head. 'I told His Lordship that I was inclined rather to believe in you, for I felt certain that a collusion had been formed between these two gentlemen.'

Rosina felt a bursting at her heart. Tears welled at her eyes, but she dashed them away. She bit her lip, and turned her eyes away from the intent concern in the lawyer's face.

'But *he* did not accept it, did he?' she uttered huskily.

Ottery did not answer, and Rosina forced herself to look at him. She was right, then. Raith had chosen rather to believe in the falsehood. He had not been drunk last night from elation! Hurt gripped her, and it was some moments before she was able to speak.

'How much do you know, Mr Ottery?' she asked, giving him look for look. 'Why could he not trust me? Was it the doctor's evidence?'

The lawyer compressed his lips, and Rosina found herself burning with resentment. As if impelled, she rose from her chair, leaving in it the cloak that had slipped from her shoulders. She took a hasty turn about the room. His silence was driving her mad!

'Must you be so discreet, Mr Ottery?' she cried, facing him. 'I am sure you know it all. Pray, why must I be left in ignorance? I thought you approved me. I thought—'

'Don't, ma'am!' he interrupted. A sigh left his lips, and

he came up to her. 'Won't you sit down again? Believe me, Lady Raith, I am on your side.'

'As is my husband,' she replied tightly. 'He will not set me aside, no matter what he believes.'

The lawyer's eyes regarded her keenly. 'Are you certain?'

Rosina looked him full in the face. 'He has given me reason enough to be so.' A faint flush stained her cheek. 'That is not to say that he has not thought of separation. But he will not now be willing to part from me. That is why—'

'That is why you are proposing to sacrifice yourself,' put in the lawyer gently.

'I am relying on you, Mr Ottery. Pray help me.'

He took one of her unquiet hands in his. 'Lady Raith, you cannot possibly expect me to aid you to leave him. Especially in the light of what you have said.'

Rosina regarded him with suspicion in her face. 'You would do so, had the request come from him.'

The lawyer looked altogether upset, but before he could respond, they were interrupted by a disturbance outside the office door. There was the sound of a slam, and a raised voice—one all too readily recognisable. Rosina jumped, and her heart began to hammer in her breast. Two other voices answered, and a second later the door flew open, and Raith entered the room.

He stood in the aperture, stripping off his gloves, dangerous under the broad-brimmed hat, the greatcoat emphasising his height. He was pale, and his features were set, the scar standing out white.

His eyes found Rosina. 'I thought so,' he said grimly, and threw aside his gloves on a chair by the door. The hat joined them.

Rosina's pulses were rioting, but she faced him squarely. 'It—it is of no use to t-try to s-stop me, Raith.'

'Rosy, I can't let you do this!' He took a few hasty paces towards her, but checked as Rosina backed away. Hurt entered his eyes. 'What, has nothing changed? Rosina!'

'One moment, my lord,' interrupted the lawyer, moving quickly to the door.

Raith swung round. He had left the door open behind him. He threw a hand to his aching head, and shifted to one of the windows. Rosina had come up against a bookcase, and she stood with her back to it, her hands grasping at its edge.

That Raith had come after her both warmed her heart, and filled her with dismay. That he would fight her going she could not doubt. Lord knew it was difficult enough without that! The very sight of him brought back such a strong recollection of his passion of the previous night that her loins stirred—adding nothing to her comfort, and thoroughly undermining her determination.

Ottery spoke a word of dismissal to the clerks within the other room, and then closed the outer door. He went across to Raith, addressing him with all his habitual calm.

'Allow me to take your coat, my lord.'

With impatience, Raith turned and allowed Ottery to help him out of the enveloping greatcoat, his eyes on Rosina. The lawyer laid aside the garment on a convenient side table, and returned to his desk.

'Lady Raith has asked me to arrange to release her from this marriage, my lord.'

Raith's heart jarred painfully, and he saw the flooding consciousness enter his wife's face. His voice was barely steady. 'So I had guessed. Did you agree?'

'How could I, sir, without knowing your mind?'

A long sigh left Raith's lips. 'You might be pardoned for supposing it to be other than it is.' He looked again at Rosina, and found his waif in residence. Hell and damnation, but this demanded privacy!

He crossed to the inner door, and opened it. 'You will permit us to make use of your room?'

Ottery bowed. 'Lady Raith, will you not go apart with His Lordship?'

Rosina stood her ground, her eyes upon her husband, her voice a trifle shaky. 'No, Mr Ottery, I will n-not. You know so m-much that there can be nothing said between us that you may not hear.'

She saw Raith wince, and was obliged to damp down upon a rise of distress. The lawyer's eyes went from one to the other. He coughed.

'I believe matters ought better to be resolved between you, ma'am, without a witness.'

'No!'

'Rosy!'

With pain, Raith saw his wife fling away to the position he had just vacated by the window. Unable to help himself, he let go the door handle, and came towards her. She threw up her hands, and the dark orbs showed panic.

'No, you must not. Don't come near me!'

He stopped, but his eyes were despairing. 'Not come near you? You cannot be afraid of me, Rosy—not now.'

'It—it is not that.' Rosina looked down at her unquiet fingers. 'You have—too much p-power to affect me. My resolution will f-fail, Raith, if I am alone with you.'

His heart melted, and he moved to her, cupping her cheek. 'I want it to fail, Rosy. I cannot let you go!'

She looked up at him. 'I knew you would say that.'

He released her. 'Yet you took clothes from your closet. You meant to escape me! What, was Ottery to conceal you somewhere? Surely you know that he would not aid you.'

Rosina glanced across at the lawyer. 'No, but he would

do it for you, if I can convince him of the rightness of my request.'

'I beg to differ, ma'am,' came from Ottery himself, bringing Raith's head round. 'His Lordship best knows how much I am against separation.'

Rosina wrenched away from her spouse's hold. 'Then you did mean to set me aside!' She paced away from him, pulling at her fingers. 'Oh, I knew it. Last night—when I came to find you—that is why you had been drinking.'

'Rosina—'

'No, don't say it!' she cried, turning on him. 'You have no need to excuse yourself. I had guessed it, in any event. It was why I had looked for you—to ask you—so that I might know my fate for certain. Only my maid told me that Kirkham had been troubled about you, and in my anxiety I forgot it.'

Raith was very pale. He made no attempt to approach her. His voice was low, but a thread of vibrant passion ran through it. 'You have a right to be wounded, Rosina. But you do not know the whole. There were reasons—'

'I know them,' she interrupted, a break in her voice. 'Why do you suppose I am here? Do not imagine that I blame you, Raith.'

'You may not blame me, but you are wounded none the less.'

Rosina could not deny it, but nor could she say it—and add to Raith's distresses. 'It is immaterial. No one else will believe, any more than you did, that Forteviot and my guardian were lying.'

'Do you think I care any longer?' he uttered. 'Whatever may have been my feelings yesterday—'

'But I care, Raith.'

He was silenced. So wrapped up had he been in his own pride that he had not considered Rosina's emotions. She was right. People would believe what they wished to, and the least hint of the circumstances alone would be enough to damn her. He looked across at Ottery.

'I cannot have her pilloried. We have to stop him!'

'Undoubtedly,' agreed the lawyer, but his glance was on Rosina. Raith looked back at his wife, and found her eyes huge in the white face.

'Raith, I don't care for that.'

'Don't you?'

'I could bear it for myself, but I will not have you condemned for a chivalrous impulse.'

'It has nothing to do with chivalry,' he said hastily. 'If I must care, it can only be on your behalf, Rosina. My concerns were purely selfish, I admit that. I have no interest in what the world may say.'

Rosina eyed him wistfully. 'Could you ignore it—when there is not a soul who will receive your wife? The true facts of our marriage are bad enough, Raith. Lady Doddinghurst was quick to find flaws in Mr Ottery's story.'

'It was poor at best,' admitted the lawyer.

'But it is better than the slightest whisper of what Lord Forteviot proposes to tell the world,' Rosina pointed out. 'Raith, you think you may withstand it, but I know your temperament. I cannot stay with you only to poison your life.'

A constriction lodged in Raith's chest. 'Do you imagine that people will talk any the less for your leaving me?'

Rosina looked away. 'For a while, perhaps. But if I am not there to—'

'If you are not there,' he uttered painfully, 'I had as well cut my own throat now! Rosy, this is pointless.' He crossed to the desk, throwing a wild hand at his lawyer. 'Ottery, for God's sake, help me!'

The lawyer rose up from his desk and came to lay a calming hand upon Raith's shoulder. 'You are too impatient, my lord. Allow Lady Raith at least the opportunity to give rein to the sensations that are driving her.' He gripped the shoulder he held. 'I think you do not understand that her whole design is to spare you, sir. She has no thought of herself.'

Raith let go an uneven breath, and dropped to perch upon the desk. His eyes went to Rosina's. 'Then it makes even less sense that she should wish to end our marriage.'

The bleak look in his face tore at Rosina's heart. 'But I don't *wish* for it!'

'Then—'

'My lord, leave it!' cut in the lawyer sharply.

Raith compressed his lips, and wrenched his eyes away from Rosina's expressive countenance. Blood and thunder, but Ottery was right! Small wonder she would not go apart with him, if he could not let her edge in a word without some forceful interruption. What had she said? That he had too much power over her? He glanced at her again, rueful now.

'Am I ever this overbearing?'

Her tiny smile gleamed on Rosina's lips. 'You are not easy to withstand, my lord.'

'But you have held out against me—several times.'

The smile disappeared, to be replaced by a look of determination. 'I must this time.'

Raith felt the protest welling up, and had to fight to suppress himself from utterance. He looked at his lawyer. 'What am I to do?'

Ottery gave him a grim smile. 'Hold your tongue, sir.' Then he looked across at Rosina. 'I will engage to keep His Lordship in check for the moment, ma'am.'

Raith watched her begin to pace, her fingers busy in that fidgeting way she had when upset or anxiety gripped her. He found himself moved more by her distress than his own selfish need. As the portent of her words began to penetrate, he was affected almost beyond endurance.

'You must not think I blame you, Raith. It is all my fault. I should never have taken this step. If Gatty had not suggested it, I should not have thought of answering that advertisement. I was trying to obtain a post. Any post— though housekeeping was all I knew how to do. I should have done just that. Forteviot could less easily have found me were I occupied as a servant. Even had he done so, it could not have involved anyone else.' She paused, glancing round at her spouse. 'You, Raith. I cheated you from the first. I used you—trying for a security that was impossible to achieve. And this is what has come of it!'

Raith would have spoken then, but Ottery forestalled him. 'My dear Lady Raith, you must not reproach yourself for that. You were as much used.'

'As much cheated!' put in Raith violently.

'Wait, my lord!' Ottery laid a hand on his arm. 'Had you any more to say, ma'am?'

'Any more?' Rosina threw her hands to her face. 'Oh, so much! If I had only known—had I an inkling of who he was.' She wafted vague fingers and looked at her husband. 'I don't mean your identity. But *who* you are. What has been made of you by—by the bludgeoning of fate...' Her voice began to fail, and she had to swallow on the rising tears. 'Had you been any other man—one less affected by... I might have borne to be the means of bringing this trouble upon you.'

The tears escaped, trickling down her cheeks, and Raith's eyes riveted upon them, his heart too full even for thoughts, let alone words or deeds.

'Even could you find a way to stop Forteviot—how can I stay? I could not hope to assuage the torment that lives within you. It is too strong—too deeply set. And for the origin of that wound which you take such pains to shield—'

She stopped, her hand flying to her mouth, as if she would push back the words. But nothing came either from her husband, or the lawyer, and the quivering fingers shifted.

'You see? I cannot even speak of it, for fear of awakening that bitterness with which you scourge yourself—with which you distance me unbearably.'

'Not any more!' burst from Raith abruptly.

'My lord!'

'Ottery, I can be silent no longer!' He was up, moving swiftly across the room towards her. 'Rosina, if you are to leave me because of that—! Don't you know how your presence in my life has changed me?' He took her by the shoulders. 'By thunder, I know how ill I have used you on that account! But only because I was afraid that you could not favour me.'

'You assumed it!' Rosina accused him, wrenching away. 'You would not let me near you.'

'Do not forget your own reluctance!' he returned, stung. 'If common decency led me to refrain from forcing you to endure this repulsive countenance of mine—'

'Raith, it has never been repulsive to me,' Rosina cried despairingly. 'That is what I am trying to make you understand.' She caught sight of the lawyer's face, and shifted towards him. 'Mr Ottery, I appeal to you.'

'I have always believed His Lordship to be over-sensitive,' agreed Ottery, looking at Raith.

Rosina turned. 'There! And you need not imagine that I do not know why it is so. You had not been nearly as aware of it had it not been inflicted by your brother Piers!'

There was a silence. Raith went white, and shot an accusatory look at his lawyer. Ottery shrugged.

'This does not come from my lips, my lord.'

His eyes shifted to Rosina's face. 'How did you know? Unless—was it Kirkham or my housekeeper who told you?'

Rosina sank into the chair before the desk, sighing deeply. 'Release me, Mr Ottery, I beg of you!' Her eyes filled and she looked up at the lawyer, her voice quivering. 'See h-how useless it is? He supposes me to be so g-great a fool that I c-cannot guess at it.'

Raith caught himself up, abruptly recognising how his defences had gone up. 'Oh, God, Rosina! I didn't mean it.'

'No, you never do,' she uttered, clasping her hands tightly together in her lap. 'That is the tragedy.' She saw that Mr Ottery was frowning down at her. 'Pray don't look upon me thus severely, Mr Ottery.'

The lawyer's face cleared. 'Nothing of the sort, ma'am. I was merely trying to decide how best to acquaint you with His Lordship's history.'

'Ottery!'

'My lord, you gain nothing by your silence. Her Ladyship has a right to know. And—if you will be advised by me—the more she knows, the easier it will be for you to communicate upon the subject.'

Raith crossed to the window. It was not a pretty story, and the very mention of it brought to mind the memory of his brother's vicious act. The whistling lash—the distorted witness faces—the shocking violence of the pain— and the welling blood. Behind him, he heard Rosina's voice, the tremble of it a stronger reproach than what she said.

'He n-need not tell me, if he does not w-wish to. Rather let me speak, Mr Ottery. You do not want to hear this, Raith, but I will s-say it now.'

He did not turn, and Rosina continued, husky and low. 'When the first shock had died, I was consumed not with repulsion—but with curiosity. I wanted to touch your face, to know how it felt.' She saw him flinch, and caught the lawyer's eye. Mr Ottery was looking grim, but he said nothing. Rosina was emboldened to pursue her course. 'I was ashamed of myself, and so I did not know how to respond to you, when you spoke of it so bitterly. At last, when you allowed me to touch it, in one of your vile moods—'

'Don't remind me!'

It was a muttered outburst, but Raith remained with his back to the room, staring unseeingly out of the window.

'When you allowed me to touch it,' Rosina resumed, 'the sensation under my finger did not offend me. It was even pleasurable, so that I did not dare to speak of it. For you had told me of that other creature, and—'

'*Enough!*' Raith swung round. His eyes were afire, and Rosina winced. 'Oh, don't look so afraid! If I am angry, it is not with you—but with my brother. He follows me even into my marriage!' A mirthless laugh broke from him. 'Why would he not? It was to prevent me finding a wife that he slashed at my face—with his whip.'

Rosina gasped, her fingers flying to her mouth. 'Dear Lord, but he must have been insane!'

Raith shrugged. 'That—or merely vengeful.'

It was Ottery who took up the tale. 'I must bear part of the blame. I had foolishly told His late Lordship of the inheritance, which, as you know, Lady Raith, was dependent upon matrimony.'

'It was money left to me by my maternal grandfather,' Raith put in.

'But why should the fact of the inheritance affect Piers?' asked Rosina, quite appalled.

Raith looked at Ottery. 'You tell her.'

'Sheer malice, ma'am, for it gave him independence, which prevented the late Lord Raith from giving vent to his lunatic envy. Mr Raith—as your husband was then styled—desired to take up a commission in the army,' explained the lawyer. 'Provision had been left by his father, but his brother refused to honour it. Since it was not in the will, I had no power, even as executor, to force him.'

'I took him up on it, and we quarrelled,' Raith said. 'Piers had guests. Gambling cronies—Forteviot among them.'

'Oh, dear Lord!' uttered Rosina, her countenance paling. 'Then that is why…'

Raith set his teeth. 'Yes, that is why. I imagine it must have been grist to his mill to discover that it was I who had married you.'

'He saw it all?'

'He was witness to my humiliation, yes. We were in the hall, I remember, and the altercation became public.' His jaw tightened, and the scar stood out white. 'Piers snatched up his weapon too suddenly for me to know what he would be at.' His eyes burned at the memory. 'The blow felled me.'

'Oh, Raith!'

'It was viciously done, but I felt more rage than pain. I scrambled up and closed with Piers. I know I managed to get the whip out of his hand, but I was overcome. By the servants, or his friends—I don't know.'

There was fury in Rosina's voice. 'If I had only known this when that vile man came to the house!'

'The next thing I knew, I was sprawling on the ground outside the mansion.' Raith's glance met and held Rosina's. 'That is when Piers chose to jeer at me, bidding me try now to find myself a wife.'

Rosina was harrowed for him. 'What happened to you? How did you manage?'

'He had the sense to come to me,' Ottery cut in.

'Kirkham helped me to a horse, and I rode to Banbury.' He came across the room and placed his arm about his lawyer's shoulder. 'You see now why this fellow can never be sufficiently repaid. Ottery not only took me in, but nursed me until the wound was healed. Finally, he furnished me with the means to obtain a commission—'

'It was, I need hardly say, a loan, which has long since been repaid,' put in Ottery. 'And as for the rest—'

'—and then he packed me off to the Army.'

'—it is only what anyone would have done,' finished the lawyer in the same breath.

'No friend could have done more!' Raith removed his arm, and took a step towards his wife. 'It does not end there, Rosina. He has done more to help me through the exigencies of our marriage than you can ever imagine. If you needs must run away from me, you could not have chosen better.'

Hastily, Rosina rose up from her chair, whisking away. 'I don't know what to do. I wish you had not told me this—no, I don't mean that. I am glad you have told me.' She turned to face both men. 'But I am doubly determined that Forteviot shall not harm you. Pray, Raith, if the only way it can be prevented is for us to part—'

'Here is a change of tune,' he said quickly, coming up to her and seizing her hands. 'Rosy, stay with me, my dearest love! Let us fight him together. Ottery will find a way. And if he cannot, I shall know how to do. That scoundrel will not dishonour your name!'

But Rosina hardly heard him. Her attention had caught on that precious endearment, and her pulse had begun to beat rather rapidly. If only his feeling for her truly went so deep! She did not know how faint was her voice.

'What did you call me?'

The coal-black eyes gazed up at him with so much

wistfulness in them that Raith's heart turned over. 'If you look at me like that, I can't recall anything I said.'

'You said—' She found herself unable to repeat it. She swallowed. 'Never mind it. What can Mr Ottery do?'

'A great deal,' came from the lawyer behind them. 'Better, I feel sure, than what I suspect to be your intended solution, my lord.'

Rosina pulled away, and turned quickly to face him. 'What do you mean, sir?'

But it was Raith who answered—through his teeth. 'He means that, left to myself, I will slaughter the villain!'

'You mean to call him out?' Rosina blenched. 'But he may as readily kill you, Raith—and I should die then!'

Raith's chest hollowed out, and he groped for her hand, his voice pitched low. 'If you care so much, how could you leave me?'

She looked round at him, equally fervid. 'If you care for me, how can you put yourself in danger?'

The lawyer intervened. 'My dear sir, there is no need for any such foolishness. I have the matter well covered.'

Raith released her fingers. 'Then, if it will change her mind, for God's sake, tell her what you may do!'

Ottery retired behind his desk, and sat down. 'The most obvious thing would be to go to Mr Cambois and extract a written statement of the true version of events.'

'You may rely on me for that!' promised Raith threateningly, flexing his fist and moving across to the desk. 'What else?'

'If you will hand into my safekeeping all the pertinent correspondence, I will face Lord Forteviot with the intelligence that I am in possession of sufficient evidence to have him up on a charge of attempted blackmail.'

'Will that suffice?'

'Oh, I think so, my lord. He cannot raise a scandal without involving himself in a public exposure of villainy.

If Her Ladyship is pilloried, we will have enough counter-evidence to support an attack upon his own reputation. I doubt Lord Forteviot will take the risk for a paltry twenty thousand pounds. Men of his stamp drop that much in one night's play.'

'By thunder, you're right, Ottery! There will be no point in it. And I will see to it that Cambois keeps mum.'

Rosina heard it all with a leap of the heart. She had not thought it possible that there might be a solution—other than the one she had sought. Her veins were rioting, and it was with a burgeoning of hope that she saw Raith turn to her again.

'Rosy—what do you say now?'

She glanced at the lawyer. 'May we—can we speak alone?'

Raith's face lit in triumph. 'At last!'

He seized her wrist, and led her hastily to the inner door. 'With your leave, Ottery.'

'You are my guest, my lord,' smiled the lawyer.

A moment later, Rosina found herself in a little chamber behind the lawyer's office, with the door closed, and her husband leaning against it. She moved into the room, pausing by the desk and turning to face him.

'Well?' he demanded.

She bit her lip. 'Raith, after last night—'

'Oh, by thunder, last night!' he breathed.

Rosina flushed, and looked away. 'You—you had not the intention to take me, I know that.'

'Does that rankle?' he asked painfully, coming away from the door. 'Rosy, believe me—though I asked Ottery yesterday to free me, it was not for lack of faith.'

'How can I blame you?' she said, her gaze returning to his. 'After what that doctor said.'

'It is true that I did waver,' he told her frankly. 'I was seduced into the idea that you had married me—'

'To conceal my condition? Oh, Raith.'

'Don't look at me like that, Rosina. I am all too ashamed. If you had heard how Ottery berated me! But he knew it was not truly that which drove me.'

That wistfulness crept into the coal-black eyes. 'How could it be otherwise?'

Raith's heart thrummed unevenly. 'You went away from me—in spirit, I mean. I thought I had lost you altogether, and I swear to you, Rosy, that was more to me than if you had been less than pure.'

Rosina stared at him blankly. 'It is not possible.'

'You may ask Ottery. I thought you hated me, and I could not live with you—knowing that, believing it.'

'I hate you?' Her fingers crept to her bosom. 'Raith, how could you suppose it? You won my heart long since.'

'Rosy!' He came up to her, and caught her wavering fingers to his lips. 'I own I hoped—after last night—that you had some feeling for me.'

'And you for me,' she returned, gripping his hand. 'I thought I heard you say that you loved me, but—'

'Thought!' He dragged her into his arms, and kissed her. 'I am so desperately in love with you that I think I am going mad! I have been so from the very beginning.'

Rosina's heart thumped wildly. 'Raith, that cannot be true.'

'Can it not?' he uttered grimly. Shifting, he turned her to the wall, and went quickly to open the cupboard doors that concealed the aperture through which the dark shadow of Ottery's portrait could be seen. 'Look at this!'

Rosina looked at him in puzzlement, and moved to examine it, but the significance escaped her for the moment.

'Look closely.'

She did so, and gave a cry as she came upon the view, through a slight veil, of Ottery's office. It was obvious that anyone sitting beyond the desk must be visible. The place was empty. Had the lawyer had tact to leave, knowing that he must overhear anything that was said in this room? A surge of emotion rose up in her breast. She turned, unable to find words, merely gazing at her spouse.

He had retreated to the other side of the room, and his look was rueful. 'Yes, I deceived you from the first. I saw and heard all.'

'I felt it,' she said unexpectedly. 'All the while, I felt I was being watched. I thought it had been a trick of those horrid eyes in that portrait. But it was you!'

His hands went up in a gesture of despair. 'What can I say? From the first instant that I saw you—looking quite as you do now, with just such a cap—I was lost. Every moment that you sat in that chair, every word you said, only served to attract me the more. I was too afraid that I would lose you, if you had a sight of my face.' He sighed deeply. 'And then, after we married, and I was so close to you—I was locked in a situation which put me into a state well-nigh akin to madness.'

'Then when you cut at me,' she said slowly, 'and threw your bitterness in my face—'

'I could not tolerate any mention of my disfigurement. Only because I wanted you so badly, and I could not believe that you might begin to reciprocate my affection.'

'But I did so in spite of it—perhaps because of it,' she told him. 'Your very touchiness made me privy to your deepest feelings, Anton.'

'Yet I hated myself for what I was doing to you.'

He dared at last to approach her again, but he did not touch her. Rather his eyes, deeply agonized, searched hers.

'Rosy, I loved you at sight, and time—knowing you, discovering the magical wonder that you are—has only served to strengthen that feeling. If you had left me—had

I tried indeed to put you aside—I could not have endured it! I would not have been able to rest until I had you back.'

At that, her elusive smile played upon Rosina's lips. 'I had every expectation that you might command my return, my dear, imperious lord.'

'Which was why you flew to Ottery for protection,' he said, his features softening.

But Rosina's coal-black eyes looked up at him in some distress. 'But though you might love me enough to waive the matter, I wish I could have a way to prove myself, for how can you ever be sure—'

'Rosy, you little fool!' Her naïvety touched him, and he cupped her face, saying gently, 'My darling, don't you know that last night gave me incontrovertible proof of your innocence?'

Rosina stared. How was it possible? Vaguely she recalled something Mama had said. Only it was so long ago, and the subject had never again been of relevance.

'Do you mean that you knew by—by—'

'By making love to you, yes.'

Her gaze widened. 'Then, if you had done so at the outset, we need never have been through all this agony.'

Raith shook his head. 'I don't think it could have been avoided, sweetheart. In one way or another—and that is my blame.'

'No, it is your brother's,' Rosina said fiercely. On impulse, she reached up and drew his face down to hers, pressing a kiss to the scar. He stiffened, but he made no attempt to draw away. 'There. That is what I think of your countenance, Anton Raith.'

A slow smile crept across his face. 'I own I had rather you kissed it than struck at it.'

Consternation seized Rosina. 'Don't speak of that! I have suffered agonies of remorse. Oh, Raith, forgive me!'

She threw herself into his arms, muffling her face in his shoulder. Raith clutched her to him, pressing her close.

'Don't, Rosy. You have so much more for which to forgive me that I am glad of that morsel of punishment.'

'Don't say so,' she begged, lifting drowned eyes to his. 'I thought you would beat me in revenge.'

'Have you run mad?' He grinned. 'You must have seen that my bark is far worse than my bite. I could never touch you, sweetheart. Except for *this*.'

His lips came down on hers, and his kiss drove away the tears, melting her bones. She sagged into him, and he drew her tighter, crushing her to his chest. His mouth left hers, but only to murmur against her lips.

'Rosy, I adore you.'

'And I love you, Anton.'

He seized her lips again, and the exchange became intense. For quite some time Rosina had no opportunity for speech, but at length, her husband was induced to release her mouth, but only so that he might give out a heated groan.

'God, I cannot wait to get you home again!'

Rosina blushed. 'But it is the middle of the day, Raith. You cannot possibly—I mean, how can we—?'

His arms cradled her, and his lips traced a path about her forehead, cheeks and eyes. 'Very easily.'

'But the servants!'

'There are locks to the doors, are there not?'

'Yes, but—'

Raith raised his head suddenly. 'By thunder, how right you were about the stupid formality of that arrangement of our bedchambers. Shall we choose another—together?'

A shy smile settled upon Rosina's lips. 'But then we could not make assignations in the antechamber. We might choose whether you are to visit me, or I am to come to you.'

Her spouse laughed. 'That, wife, is a most romantic notion.'

'Yes, and only think,' pursued Rosina, becoming momently more enamoured of the idea, 'the servants will never know where to find us in the morning.'

'That will certainly keep them on their toes.'

'Besides which,' she ventured, with a flash cast up at him from those coal-black eyes, 'when you are horrid, which is bound to happen now and then, and lose your temper with me—'

'You may lock the door against me?' enquired Raith politely. 'I dare say you would prefer not to face the consequences of that.'

Rosina giggled. 'Why, would you break the door open?'

'I should not need to. You would have to come out sooner or later. I will bide my time.'

'The day you bide your time, Raith, I will look to see pigs take wing!'

Her spouse grinned. 'Then you will not be surprised at my present impatience for an assignation—and I will not wait until tonight.'

The black eyes flirted up at him. 'I am rather afraid that I may be too exhausted from last night's exertions—'

'Rosy!'

'But if you so command me, my lord,' continued his wife demurely, 'I must obey.'

Raith drew a breath, and sighed it out with intense satisfaction. 'How excellent a thing is the marriage vow.'

And Rosina, as his lips claimed hers in tacit promise of a furtherance of those ecstasies she had enjoyed last night, could not but reciprocate with the deepest approbation of her conjugal duty.

*   *   *   *   *

MILLS & BOON®

Makes any time special™

Mills & Boon publish 29 new titles every month. Select from...

Modern Romance™   Tender Romance™

Sensual Romance™

Medical Romance™   Historical Romance™

MAT2

FREE!

2 Books
and a surprise gift!

We would like to take this opportunity to thank you for reading this Mills & Boon® book by offering you the chance to take TWO more specially selected titles from the Historical Romance™ series absolutely FREE! We're also making this offer to introduce you to the benefits of the Reader Service™ —

- ★ FREE home delivery
- ★ FREE gifts and competitions
- ★ FREE monthly Newsletter
- ★ Books available before they're in the shops
- ★ Exclusive Reader Service discounts

Accepting these FREE books and gift places you under no obligation to buy; you may cancel at any time, even after receiving your free shipment. Simply complete your details below and return the entire page to the address below. *You don't even need a stamp!*

YES! Please send me 2 free Historical Romance books and a surprise gift. I understand that unless you hear from me, I will receive 4 superb new titles every month for just £2.99 each, postage and packing free. I am under no obligation to purchase any books and may cancel my subscription at any time. The free books and gift will be mine to keep in any case.

H1ZEB

Ms/Mrs/Miss/Mr ....Initials....................................
BLOCK CAPITALS PLEASE

Surname...

Address..

....

....Postcode ....

Send this whole page to:
UK: The Reader Service, FREEPOST CN81, Croydon, CR9 3WZ
EIRE: The Reader Service, PO Box 4546, Kilcock, County Kildare (stamp required)